MARIE JOSEPH

Marie Joseph was born in Lancashire and was educated at Blackburn High School for Girls. Before her marriage she was in the Civil Service. She now lives in Middlesex with her husband, a retired chartered Engineer, and they have two married daughters and eight grandchildren.

Marie Joseph began her writing career as a short-story writer and she now uses her Northern background to enrich her bestselling novels. Down-to-earth characters bring a vivid authenticity to her stories, which are written with both humour and poignancy. Her novel *A Better World Than This* won the 1987 Romantic Novelist's Association Major Award.

THE LISTENING SILENCE

Marie Joseph

ARROW

This edition 1993

7 9 10 8 6

Copyright © Marie Joseph 1982

Marie Joseph has asserted her
right under the Copyright, Designs and Patents Act, 1988
to be identified as the author of this work

First published by Hutchinson in 1982

Arrow edition 1984
Random House, 20 Vauxhall Bridge Road, London SW1V 2SA

Random House Australia (Pty) Limited
20 Alfred Street, Milsons Point, Sydney,
New South Wales 2061, Australia

Random House New Zealand Limited
18 Poland Road, Glenfield
Auckland 10, New Zealand

Random House South Africa (Pty) Limited
PO Box 337, Bergvlei, South Africa

Random House UK Limited Reg. No. 954009

A CIP catalogue record for this book
is available from the British Library

ISBN 0 09 934690 7

Printed and bound in Great Britain by
Cox & Wyman Ltd, Reading, Berkshire

For James Stevenson

One

'I think we're moving at last.'

'What did you say, David?'

'I think we're going in now.'

Because she was deaf, Sally Barnes's face had what David Turner always thought of as a listening look about it. It was a bright look, emphasized by the clarity of her blue-grey eyes, and watching her now he wondered why he had never thought of taking her out before. She was certainly attractive, with her dark hair cut into a curly Claudette Colbert fringe, her round face and clear Lancashire complexion. In that spring of 1941, as the German bombers turned their attention to the north-west of England, David found himself wishing Sally lived in a far safer place than the outskirts of Liverpool.

Only the week before, flying over the North Sea bound for Germany, he had found himself thinking about her. Once over the Ruhr, their target for the night, there would be no chance to think about anything but getting through the flak, dropping their bomb load and making for home. But crouched over his instrument table, David's muttered thoughts had taken him by surprise.

'That young Sally Barnes won't be able to hear the blasted sirens if they start up when she's alone. She should have been evacuated along with the kids and pregnant women.'

Then he had raised his head from his calculations to announce unemotionally: 'Skip? Alter course 110.'

'110 okay.'

'Okay.'

Standing now with Sally in the long queue outside the cinema, overcome by the same gut-churning feeling of tenderness, David kissed her cheek, cold as marble from the wind.

'What was that in aid of?' Sally laughed and clung to his arm, startled by the unexpected caress.

'We're going in at last, thanks be to goodness,' she said.

The queue edged its way slowly into the comparative warmth of the foyer, with its hectically patterned carpets and lush-lipped film stars pouting down from framed photographs on the stippled walls. When David stopped at the pay box she ran a finger down the cheek he had kissed, wondering what it would be like to be kissed 'properly' by David Turner. Not that she cared one way or the other . . .

Flying Officer David Turner in his immaculate uniform, with his neat moustache and the observer's wing sewn above his left breast pocket, was still only the polite boy from down the road.

'Care to come to the pictures, Sally?'

He had asked her in a take-it-or-leave-it way, and when Sally had told her mother, Josie Barnes's plucked eyebrows had disappeared into the peroxided fluff of curls on her forehead.

'We *are* honoured! I wonder what his miserable ma has to say about that?'

'Oh, Mum, for heaven's sake! He's lonely, that's all. Flying on operations means he's home quite a lot. Oh, stop looking at me like that!' Sally had tried not to laugh at her mother's expression. 'Going out with David Turner will be like going out with my uncle!'

'Your uncle! Oh, come on now, love! David Turner was born towards the end of the last war, not long after his father was killed in France, so that makes him no more than twenty-three or twenty-four.'

Sally buttoned herself into her dark green coat, frowning at the frayed bit where the buckle had rubbed the stitched belt. Her voice came out louder than she realized.

'He treats me like a *child*. I might be nearly nineteen, but he still sees me as the kid down the road. He's flying on ops, Mum! Night after night, over Germany. He looks so tired he makes me want to cry. He's got lines on his face and his hands tremble. He looks terrible! It's company he needs, that's all.'

Turning away, Sally failed to see the expression on her

mother's face. It was compounded of love and a resigned acceptance of her daughter's naïvety. Josie slowly shook her head from side to side. How was it possible for a girl to be that guileless, with the war in its second year, and Liverpool swarming with servicemen from all over the world?

Sally was, Josie realized, still the happy-go-lucky schoolgirl of two years ago, embarrassed because her breasts bounced beneath her white blouse as she walked into Assembly with other lesser endowed pupils; sitting in the front row in class to facilitate her quite remarkable gift of lip-reading; accepting the teacher's notes at the end of each lesson with a dignified nod of thanks.

By no means an imaginative woman, Josie Barnes could see it all. She could picture the girls Sally worked with in her job as a copy typist, chattering about their conquests, their sexual experiences and near heart-breaks.

And now Sally was getting ready to go out with an airman who looked as if he had left his youth behind him a long, long time ago.

Settling Sally into a seat in the back stalls of the cinema, David Turner watched her unbutton her coat, revealing the round swell of her breasts beneath the pale lemon knitted jumper. Her skin had a sheen on it, and by her ears a fluff of down grew. He wanted to stretch out a hand and trail a finger round and round the endearing softness.

He saw her smile as the white cinema organ rose majestically into view, then clap as the audience realized the organist was home on leave, resplendent in army dress uniform. He saw the way her hands dropped to her lap when the music began, her face stilled into a touching repose.

The soldier organist was working his feet from side to side on the pedals, his back swaying to the rhythm of his frenzied playing. The noise of the chords seemed to vibrate the air – chords which Sally, sitting smiling, could not hear.

David knew that her deafness was almost total, a legacy from measles at the age of eight. But *The Great Dictator* was Chaplin at his best, and if any man could break through the barriers of deafness then surely Chaplin, the little Jew from the East End of London, was that man.

Mesmerized by the changing expressions on her face, David was taken completely by surprise when Sally suddenly turned to stare straight into his eyes.

'Look!' She pointed to the sober-jacketed manager climbing onto the stage. 'That means the sirens have gone.' She squeezed David's arm. 'This is the bit they like best.'

'Ladies and gentlemen!'

The polite opening was drowned in a roar of derision.

'Get on with it! Get your finger out, you soppy 'aporth!'

'Let the poor bugger say his recitation!'

The manager, his bald head gleaming pearl white in a spotlight, held up an arm like a traffic cop.

'A h'air raid warning 'as just been sounded. H'if you wish to leave the cinema, please do so as quietly as possible. Those who wish to remain may do so at their own risk. Thank you!'

To ear-splitting whistles he climbed down. David gently turned Sally towards him. 'Shall we go? What do you usually . . . ?' To his dismay, he could feel his heart beginning to pound. 'Do you want to go?' he whispered again, more urgently.

Sally shook her head. 'No. It's okay. Nobody bothers . . . really.' She gave his hand three little pats before facing the screen again.

Clenching his fists David subsided into his seat. His heart was going like a drum, boom, boom, boom, and any minute now he would have to get his handkerchief out of his pocket and mop his brow. He glanced round. The rows of faces remained forward fixed, like a regiment after the 'eyes front' order, while up on the screen Chaplin's Hitler marched and ranted, the familiar moustache quivering with the passion of his words.

'Tell him he looks a right Charlie!' somebody shouted from the back. There was a ripple of laughter, but David sat rigid, every nerve in his body alive and quivering. When he heard the guns boom out, he imagined the great flashes in the sky outside. When the first crunch of the bombs came, he winced and laced his fingers tightly beneath the greatcoat folded on his knee.

Closing his eyes, he was immediately transported in his mind from the warm darkness of the cinema stalls to the darker interior of a Wellington bomber suspended in space over a German town. It felt as if he were actually there, reminding himself that the survival of his crew depended on the accuracy of his calculations. *Possible* survival, that was all. The odds were no greater than that.

David lowered his head, feeling the perspiration on his forehead cold and clammy. Of the hundred and thirty-odd boys with him on that last raid ninety-three had got back, with a mere handful baling out for the doubtful privilege of spending the rest of the war in a German prison.

He felt very weary, very old, very tired of risking his life over and over again. The euphoria had long since evaporated. As the oldest member of his crew he accepted without conceit that he was considered to be the best observer on the squadron. He often reminded himself wryly that practice could make anyone perfect.

He jerked his head upwards. The last bomb had sounded very close. Some of the audience were moving back to the seats under the overhanging canopy of the circle. He flinched as one of the exit doors down on the right blew open with a great rush of sound.

He felt Sally's hand creeping over the red plush of the armrest dividing their seats. He grasped it firmly in his own, squeezing tight, so that neither knew who was comforting the other.

'If the "all clear" hadn't gone when it did they would have shown the big picture through again.'

Sally was clinging to David's arm as they went out into the street. 'I saw *Pinocchio* twice on the same programme the other week. Once would have been enough for me. It's not all that easy lip-reading a puppet!' She laughed out loud.

It was exactly like the clear easy laughter of a child, David thought. Suddenly he wanted to swing her round to face him, to kiss her cheeks, her nose, and tell her how much he loved hearing her laugh. She was still talking, bending her head close to his shoulder, words bubbling out of her.

'And then, after the second *Pinocchio*, they showed a couple of Food Flashes and a Board of Trade fashion film. Okay for those who fancy cakes made out of carrots, and cami-knickers

11

skimped out of a yard of material.'

'I hope you never go out alone at night.'

David forgot that without seeing him speak, Sally could not hear. He swerved as a lamp post loomed up not six inches away from his face, then drew her to him so that they walked along entwined.

The tram was so crowded that they had to stand together on the boarding platform, bodies touching, moving even closer as people got on or off. Just before the terminus they found seats, but not together. Three-quarters of David's seat was taken up by a heavy-bodied woman with a look on her flat face which said she wasn't going to 'utchup' for anyone, thank you very much.

Sally smiled to herself at the sight of David clinging to the edge, far too polite to do anything about it.

That was it! Sally nodded to herself. That was why she always chattered too much, laughed too much and blushed too readily when David Turner talked to her. It was his old-fashioned courtesy that embarrassed more than it impressed. Like the time he'd worn a brown trilby hat and tipped it at her, sending her into fits of schoolgirl giggles.

All at once, taking her completely by surprise, he turned round. 'All right?' his eyebrows said. Sally nodded, hating the blush staining her cheeks, before she realized that in the near gloom of the darkened tram blushes could come and go unnoticed.

Beyond the terminus the road widened, flanked on either side by dim silhouettes of semi-detached houses set back behind neat front gardens. After walking for ten minutes they came to Sally's house, its gates gone for salvage and its garage doors closed on a car jacked-up for the duration.

The pebble-dashed house looked forlorn and empty, shrouded for the night in its black-out curtains. Sally moved away from David so that his arm dropped from her waist. She stared up into the thin serious face beneath the peaked cap, wishing she wasn't obliged to peer so closely to lip-read whatever he might be saying. He had been holding her so tightly on the way up the road that walking had been difficult, and now he was looking down at her, the fine lines of his face taking on a certain nobility in the darkness.

'Well then?' Sally smiled, then began to feel uncomfortable. Could it be that the polite David Turner from down the road thought she wanted him to kiss her, standing like that with her mouth raised to his? She looked away. 'Thank you for taking me to the pictures. And good luck when you go back in the morning. Take care.'

'Don't go!'

Sally blinked as David swung her round to face him. As he gripped her arms she was shocked to feel a restrained violence shuddering through his fingers. His eyes were suddenly glittering. He looked ill as if he burned with a fever.

'What is it, David?'

The expression on Sally's face, so trustingly turned up to his own, her eyes searching his mouth, snapped the last vestige of David's slipping control.

She gasped as his mouth came down over her own, forcing her lips apart, hurting with the pressure of his teeth. He was holding her round the waist with one arm, pressing the back of her head with his other hand, making it impossible for her to break away. When the long, painful kiss ended he pulled her even harder up against him, burying his face in her neck, whispering words she could not hear.

'Oh, God . . . I'm sorry. Oh God, what's wrong with me? I can't go back tomorrow, yet I know I will go back tomorrow. They'll be there, waiting for me, little Sally. Jock and Tim, Bob and Lofty . . . all the same. Eager bloody beavers, listening to the briefings at six o'clock, so sure it won't happen to them. Oh, God! They're so *young*, Sally. I was flying on ops when they were just rookies doing their square-bashing at Blackpool!'

When she tried to pull away he jerked her closer, sliding his fingers round the back of her neck. 'They actually fight to fly with me. Do you know that? Because they think I'm the tops; because they know I can get them across the Channel with both eyes closed.'

He started to shake so that now it was Sally who was doing the holding. He moaned into her hair. 'But I'm not the tops. And I can't pretend any more.'

'I can't *hear* you, David!'

It was a small, piteous cry, lost in the revers of the heavy Air Force greatcoat.

'I'm scared witless, Sally. When the flak comes at us I keep remembering our last rear-gunner with his face blown clean away. I remember Chris with a piece of shrapnel in his throat, choking with his own blood. And I hear yet another plane screaming down, burning up the crew as it goes.'

'David! Please!' Sally beat at him with bunched fists. 'David? I want to *hear*! I want to listen! Oh, please, lift your head and look at me.'

Her struggles and the sound of her soft voice calling his name inflamed David further. He moved his hands round her throat then slid them down inside her coat. He could feel her breast moving with the agitated beating of her heart. She was all softness. The softness of her meant comfort, and without comfort at that moment he was as bereft as if he were the last man left alive on earth.

When his mouth took hers again it was with a deep hurting hunger. As he ground his body into hers she could feel the heat from his face. When he tore at her coat and she felt the erect hardness of him thrusting and pushing against her skirt her terror exploded into a blinding anger. Fighting like a trapped animal she brought up a foot and kicked him hard on the shin.

'No! Not like this! No!'

Normally in control of the pitch of her voice, Sally shouted her fury and fear aloud. When David, blinded with pain, reached for her she knocked his hand furiously away.

Running headlong up the path she almost stumbled and fell, but the front door was on the latch as usual, and the first thing she saw was the edging of light showing from the living-room.

Tiptoeing through the darkened hall, making for the foot of the stairs, Sally groped her way up, praying she could get to her room unheard.

For a long time David stood there, slumped against the dusty privet hedge. An air-raid warden wearing his tin hat walked briskly past, stopped and turned.

'Are you all right, lad?'

The voice was kindly, but David ignored him to stumble away in the opposite direction. He wasn't ready to face his mother waiting for him in the house further down the road. He wasn't in the mood to face anybody, least of all his mother.

There was a Morrison shelter in the sitting-room, a huge steel table filling half the room, its sides closed in with wire netting. Edna Turner had promised her son to use it when the sirens wailed. She would probably be in it now, half awake and half asleep, peering at him through the mesh, like an animal at the zoo.

Clenching his hands deep down in his pockets, walking with head bent and feet turned inwards, he went on down the road, turning a corner into a rutted lane leading to what had once been a farmstead set in rolling fields.

In the inky darkness his feet slipped and slithered over the rough ground. When he came to a stile at the top of the lane he stopped and leaned against it, pulling his coat collar up and sinking his chin deep. There was a heavy sensation in the lower part of his abdomen, a physical manifestation of his self-disgust. For a long moment he closed his eyes against the memory of Sally's young face lifted with such trust to his own as she struggled to read what he was saying. He smelled again the sweet flower scent of her, saw her eyes searching, watching his mouth, her lips raised in unconscious provocation.

And he had tried to – *needed* to – 'Oh Christ!' The two words were more of a prayer than a blasphemy. He'd got to the state when he no longer knew what he was saying or doing.

Tomorrow he had to go back to Lincolnshire and the planes lined up on the airfield like great black crows with spread wings. But first he had to go home.

'David? Is that you?'

He heard his mother call out as he closed the front door. Her voice was coming from the living-room at the back of the house, so she wasn't in the shelter. At least he was spared that.

'I thought you'd have been in bed by now.' David smoothed back his already smooth hair and smiled stiffly at the little woman sitting in the corner of the sofa drawn up to the fire.

Edna Turner, at the age of fifty, had a face as lined as a woman thirty years older. The wrinkles were accentuated by the surprising blue-black of her hair which she wore in a neat roll tucked over a childish ribbon. She was so thin that her bones seemed to move skeleton-like beneath the folds of her dress, and her eyes had a perpetual red-rimmed look as if she had just finished a long bout of weeping.

She sniffed, a sure sign she was going to say something unpleasant. 'The sirens went, David. I thought you might have come home, knowing I was all alone.'

David fought for control. He looked normal – a quick glance in the mirror over the fireplace had reassured him – yet already the grumbling whine of his mother's voice was sending the blood coursing through his veins. His heart was thudding beneath his ribs. He felt very ill and tired half-way to death.

'I worried about you,' he lied, then looked away from the pathetic cringing creature on the sofa, ashamed because he had needed to lie. 'I hope you went in the shelter,' he said too loudly, then stared into the fire, engrossed in his own private agony.

'I always do go in the shelter.' Edna sighed a deep sigh which raised and lowered an almost non-existent bosom. 'If your father knew what was happening to me, he would turn in his grave.' She gave her son a hard stare. 'Your father died out there in France in the last war, believing he was making a better world for those he left behind. Instead of that, I bring you up only to see you go away like he did. Why you wanted to fly, I don't know. You could have gone to the university on your exam results, or even got a reserved job if you'd tried. How do you think I feel when they give out on the wireless about more of our planes going missing? I'm not like that deaf girl's mother always going out dancing with soldiers. Anyway, Sally Barnes's deafness is a punishment to her mother for leaving her child in bed with the measles and going off to work in that dress shop. Common as muck Josie Barnes is . . .'

For a wild moment David wondered what his mother would do if he slapped her across her mouth to stop its eternal chattering. Or if he blurted out the truth about his desperate loneliness and fear, instead of sitting there calmly pretending to be listening.

'Mother? Help me!' Suppose he said that? He felt hysteria rise up in a hard lump in the front of his throat. He swallowed hard and stared into the fire again.

'Troise and His Mandoliers were on tonight,' Edna sniffed. 'But how could I be expected to listen to *them* when the sirens went? The guns started up so quickly I didn't have time to fill my hot-water bottle. Will you do it for me, David? We'd better

16

be getting to bed with you having an early start in the morning. I might as well be talking to myself, anyway.'

When he came back with the bottle she was going through her normal routine, plumping up cushions, setting the guard round the fire, rolling up her knitting and putting it away in its embroidered bag, her small mouth puckered, the clean parting in her black hair showing like a white painted stripe.

When she left him alone, slipping through the door hugging the hot-water bottle to her flat chest, David pushed the fireguard to one side. He sat down and buried his face in his hands, holding his fingers tightly against his closed eyelids. He had the feeling that if he just sat there quite still, then maybe the fear inside him would dissolve. There would be no more war, no more terrifying flights across the Channel. He could forget the eager faces of his crew, the ones who had died and the ones whose turn would come next. He could forget the face of the girl down the road, eyes and mouth wide with disgust before she ran away from him.

He pressed harder with his fingers. It was soothingly dark behind his closed eyelids, yet he knew that nothing had gone away. Not the war, not his return to base, not the way he had behaved . . . nothing.

Sally knew she would have to go downstairs. She stared at her tripled reflection in her dressing-table mirrors and frowned. There was a tiny blood blister on her lip, and a button hanging loose on her coat where David Turner had thrust a hand inside, squeezing her breast. Her eyes stretched wide as she remembered the terrifying hardness of him when he opened her coat and ground himself against her.

She had been kissed before, at office parties and at Christmas. Sally saw her cheeks turn scarlet. But never, never before like that.

She got up quickly, shrugged herself out of her coat, ran her fingers through her hair, smoothed her skirt down over her hips, tucked the knitted jumper into the waistband, and went downstairs.

In the large, bay-windowed room at the back of the house a small man wearing Home Guard battle-dress crouched on the rug by the fireplace, raking out the ashes for the night.

17

Stanley Barnes stood up as Sally came into the room, pleasure at the sight of her lifting the whippet-thin lines of his face into a boyish smile. She was so bonny, this young lass of his, so loving, so bright, in spite of her deafness. Sometimes he felt he could burst with pride just looking at her.

'Good picture, love?'

'Okay.'

He fancied he heard a slight tremor in her voice as she turned away, but he touched her gently on her wrist, their own private signal that he was going to speak.

'Was there anything interesting on the newsreel?'

He knew that would make her smile, and it did.

'Oh, Dad! You and your news!' Sally wrinkled her nose. 'Let me think. Well, they showed a German raider brought down off the Norfolk coast on its way back from bombing London. There was a lot of cheering and clapping at that. Then there was a bit about the war in the Middle East. Oh, and a scene outside Buckingham Palace after the bomb last week. The King was there in his Air Force uniform walking with the Queen among the rubble. The sirens went right in the middle of . . .'

Her voice tailed off, as, following Stanley's gaze, she saw her mother framed in the doorway laughing at them, unbuttoning her coat and throwing it over the back of a chair before coming over to the fire. As always happened after a long evening spent dancing, Josie looked young and excited, the coral rouge on her cheeks accentuating the vivid blue of her eyes.

'I'll go and make a cup of tea.' Sally walked quickly through into the kitchen, unwilling to meet her mother's eyes. If Josie suspected anything was wrong then she wouldn't mince her words, and an inquisition was the last thing she could cope with at the moment.

'What did you do when the sirens went?' Stanley looked away from the yellow brightness of his wife's hair framing her vivacious face. The thought came to him suddenly that she resembled exactly a china doll in a box. He could feel the excitement emanating from her and for a moment, without knowing why, it sickened him.

Josie held out her hands to the blaze. 'We went in the shelter in Cross Street, Olive and me, though not many bothered.

They were still dancing when we got back.'

Stanley jerked his head in the direction of the door. 'There's something upset her. She went straight upstairs when she came in, and if I'd had to stay on at the Post she would have come in to an empty house.' He frowned. 'I think one of us should be in when the sirens go. I wouldn't like to think of her being alone.'

To his surprise Josie's small face hardened. 'She's not a *child*! We can't watch over her every minute. If she wasn't as she is she'd be joining one of the Services. If you want my opinion that would be the best thing that could happen to her. She's my daughter and I love her, but she's . . . she's *unfinished*. One of these days some boy is going to make a pass at her, because God knows she's pretty enough, and if it was David Turner from down the road then I'd be glad. Because believe you me, she could do a lot worse.'

'Do you know what you're saying?' Stanley's eyes narrowed. 'Sometimes the stuff you come out with appals me.'

'Well, it would, wouldn't it, you with your Methody narrow-mindedness!'

For a moment they glared at each other, then Stanley moved towards the door, limping slightly. 'I'm off to bed,' he said, leaving his wife staring after him, half regretting her last words.

'Enjoy your night out at the pictures, love?'

In the kitchen overlooking the back garden Josie snatched the kettle from the gas stove just in time to prevent it spluttering over.

'Charlie Chaplin. Quite good.'

Sally wished with all her heart that she didn't have to watch her mother's face so carefully. She knew they had been quarrelling again. Without hearing raised voices she knew exactly what had been going on in the room across the hall.

'You should have seen me doing the tango!'

Josie took a few steps across the oilcloth, her body giving off a wave of April Violets scent. She swivelled her head sharply sideways.

'Jealousy. T'was all over my jealousy . . .'

'Oh, Mum . . .' Sally laughed out loud. Two minutes ago she had felt the thickness of tears in her throat, but now the tears were of laughter. Josie looked so funny with her little rounded behind sticking out, her feet in their size three shoes twinkling in the intricate steps. She felt the rhythm tingling in her own toes. 'I think you're enjoying this war, aren't you?'

'What a thing to say!' Josie picked up the two mugs of tea. 'Come on, love. The fire's nearly out, but if I give it a bit of a tiddle with the poker we might be able to toast our bits and pieces round it before we go up to bed.'

She dragged two fireside chairs up close to the hearth, hitching up the skirt of her flowered dress to display small bony knees. 'What a day at the shop! We sold three evening gowns this afternoon, Olive and me. I was up and down the stairs to the fitting-room like a flamin' yo-yo.' She stared at the flames, then turned round. 'Did you go down the road to see David Turner's mother after the pictures? The old sourpuss,' she added without malice.

'No. I came straight in.'

Josie reached out for a box of kirby-grips from the mantel-piece, then started to twist her hair into little snails, anchoring each one firmly to her scalp. 'You *could* dance, you know, love. You don't have to hear the music. It's the rhythm what counts.'

Sally put the mug of tea down on the tiled surround. 'I'm tired, Mum. I think I'll go up to bed.'

Josie shrugged. Being deaf wasn't without the odd advantage. Find the conversation not to your liking and just walk away. Or go to bed. She cupped her hands round her mug of tea and nodded the skull cap of kirby-grips up and down twice.

Walk away . . . that was what *she* should do. Now, before she found it impossible. 'Oh, Bill,' she whispered. 'Why do I have to feel like this? Why, when I thought I would never feel like this again?'

David Turner saw Sally just as the train began to slide out of the station. As he leaned out of the window in the first-class compartment he saw her picking her way through the maze of kitbags, her eyes searching, a woolly scarlet cap on her head a splash of colour against the drabness of khaki uniforms and the wide stretch of grey platform.

Abandoning his natural reserve, he shouted her name.

'Sally!' Then again in desperation. 'Sally! I'm here!'

But with every single window filled with waving arms it was hopeless. He sat down in the corner seat and closed his eyes. The compartment was full, but not as full as at the other end of the train where ordinary ranks had fought with workers for seats. The disappointment had started him trembling again, and opening his eyes David saw the man opposite stare at him before disappearing behind his newspaper. He saw the eyes of a Merchant Navy officer widen in surprise, and he saw a pretty Wren in the far corner half stretch out a hand before she turned in confusion to stare at the grey morning slipping by.

The tears trickling slowly down David's cheeks were of no consequence to him. He just let them fall, making no attempt to lift a hand to wipe them away. The shaking inside him was getting worse, but if he sat quite still it would go.

So he sat quite still, his profile averted, like the head on a coin.

Lee Grant Willis, formerly of the American Volunteer Ambulance Corps before the fall of France, now on a week's leave from an RAF training wing in Cornwall, sauntered down the slope away from the platform to the station forecourt.

With both hands thrust deep into his pockets and his cap pushed to the back of his head he looked a typical Yank in spite of the British uniform. In front of him was a girl in a scarlet cap swinging a brown leather purse. Lee studied her legs, okaying them in spite of the utility stockings washed to a sickly shade of fawn. He quickened his steps.

What happened next happened so swiftly his reaction was purely instinctive. With the girl a step or two in front of him, he came out of the station onto a wide pavement, just as a Post Office van turned at speed out of a side entrance. The van's exhaust was making a hell of a noise, but without even turning her head the girl stepped out into the road.

The horror on the van driver's face registered in Lee's mind in the same split second as he threw himself forward, grabbing the girl, dragging her back and holding her tight up against him.

'You daft bugger!' The driver leaned out shaking a fist. 'Next time you decide to commit suicide try a bloody rope, will you?'

As the van roared away Lee looked into a pair of startled grey eyes. 'You okay, honey?'

Sally stared into a brown face with the skin stretched smooth beneath eyes of a bright periwinkle blue. The eyes were full of compassion, but as she stepped back a pace she saw the compassion change to anger.

'You could hear that goddamned van coming a mile off! What were you doing stepping off the sidewalk like that? Are you deaf or something?'

He was gripping her arm so tightly that she winced. The shock of her narrow escape sharpened her own voice to an anger matching his own.

'Yes, I *am* deaf,' she said clearly. 'I am usually extra careful crossing roads. I have to be, but I was thinking about something. I'm sorry.'

For a moment blue eyes stared into grey, then Lee pursed his lips in a slow whistle. Pushing his cap even further back he scratched his head. 'Well, what d'you know? It's me should be saying I'm sorry, I reckon, bawling you out like that. Here, hold it right there a minute, honey.'

Bending down he gathered the contents of Sally's handbag together, then handed it to her with a flourish. 'There's a place across the street – quick eats by the look of it – I'm going to buy you a cup of tea. Okay?' He grinned. 'You lip-reading me, honey?'

Sally nodded. She wondered if he was a Canadian. One of the girls at the office was dating a Canadian airman, a dark reserved boy totally different from this happy-go-lucky boy now escorting her with old-world gallantry across the street.

'Are you American?' She waited until they were seated opposite to each other across a table still marked with the rings of yesterday's spills. 'You talk like somebody out of a cowboy film.'

Lee laughed out loud. What a sweetie this young English girl was turning out to be. No hiding behind her appalling disability, no rushing away from him; not flirting with him, just sitting there smiling at him with an easy acceptance across that goddamned filthy table.

To tell the truth, Lee Grant Willis was lonely. Since landing in Liverpool the previous October to the sound of anti-aircraft

22

guns chattering, right through his acceptance at Adastral House in London as a candidate for pilot training in the RAF, he had found himself being forced into an unwilling and unnatural role as a loner. One or two highly critical and tactless criticisms of the English way of life had less than endeared him to his English buddies.

'Sure,' he had told them. 'Back home an unskilled workman can and does own a car. Sure, a telephone is an accepted part of the furniture, and okay, so who in his right mind would drink water or beer that wasn't ice-cold?'

He had been merely stating the facts, but what when the facts were construed as offensive showing off?

'Sure I'm an American,' he told Sally. 'And it could just be that I talk like a cowboy on account of most of my ancestors being no-good horse thieves.' He took a sip of the hot tea placed in front of them by a surly middle-aged woman in a green turban. 'I am also unique, honey, coming over here to fight in a war that's none of our business. There were more waiters than passengers on the boat I came over on, originally, that's for sure.'

'Are you reading me okay, honey?' he added with such a worried expression that now it was Sally's turn to laugh out loud.

'Every word,' she assured him. 'It must be the slow way you talk.'

'Plus my big mouth and graveyard teeth.' He bared them in a comical leer that caused the green turban behind the counter to bob up and down in a frenzy of excitement.

'Just like Gary Cooper,' she was to tell her husband untruthfully. 'He had that girl mesmerized, I can tell you. She never took her eyes off his face.'

'I thought Americans drank coffee.' Sally curled her fingers round her cup. 'Not tea.'

Lee shook his head from side to side. 'Just goes to show you don't know nothing. My pa's ancestors were British and we've had a little old teapot in the family for as long as I can remember.' He winked a bright blue eye. 'I can see my ma right this minute putting tea into that old pot then holding it underneath the faucet.' Then because there was something he had to get straight in his mind he failed to see the look of horror on Sally's face.

'But you have to *boil* the water,' she said.

'Were you waving someone off at the station?' he asked quickly.

When she blushed, he reached for a cigarette, cursing his lack of finesse. He sighed as he struck a match. That was what they had, these English. They knew when to ask pointed questions and when to keep silent. Through a spiral of smoke he studied Sally's profile as she turned her head away. To try and hide the blush, he guessed.

'I came down to see someone I've known most of my life back off leave,' she was explaining in that strange soft voice. 'He lives in the same road as me, and he's in the RAF, Bomber Command. I missed him,' she added. 'The tram was crowded and oh, well, I was just too late. He wasn't expecting to see me, anyway.' Her eyes were suddenly bleak. 'He's an observer.'

'I see.' Lee drew smoke deep into his lungs. 'And he's your sweetheart, is he, honey?'

Sally smiled at the old-fashioned word. 'No, nothing like that. Just a friend.' She reached for her bag and looped the strap over her shoulder. 'I have to go now. Thanks for the tea.'

She held out her hand, and solemnly they shook. The watching eyes beneath the green turban widened with a surprised curiosity. As they walked out into the street together, Lee raised a hand and hailed a passing taxi.

'I've plenty of time, honey. I'll see you to where you have to go. Okay?'

'Duckworth Brothers, Shaw Street,' Sally told the driver, then tried to look non-committal as the American climbed in beside her and the driver twisted round in his seat, grey bushy eyebrows expressing his amazement.

'Nay, lass, what do you want a taxi for? It's stopped raining, and besides, you could *spit* that far!'

Less than three minutes later Sally got down from the taxi outside the red-brick building housing the light engineering works of Duckworth Brothers Limited, relieved to find that the blue-eyed American with a mother who made tea from tap water stayed where he was, raising a hand in a farewell salute.

Then she went inside, down the long corridor to the staff cloakroom to stare at herself in the spotted mirror over the row

24

of washbasins, and think about David Turner going back without knowing she was sorry for behaving like a stupid child the night before.

'So that's it, chaps.'

Wing Commander Beaumont, currently in charge of the pre-war RAF station near Lincoln, was a man of few words. When his Squadron Adjutant, a fierce-looking individual with the ends of his handlebar moustache sticking out like Viking's horns, had ushered David's crew into his office, the Wing Commander clasped both hands together on his blotting pad. He gave it to them straight.

'I've been in touch with the AOC at Group Headquarters to ask for replacements of three of my crews. Yours included.' He waved a hand in front of his face as if to prevent any attempt at interruption. 'Some of you . . .' His deep-set eyes flickered in David's direction before he continued. 'Some of you have been on continual operational flying since the start of the war. It's my opinion that you are due for a rest.'

Taking his pipe from its stand he turned it round and round in his big hands. 'Tired aircrew are dangerous, and we can't afford to lose any aircraft through exhaustion.' He pointed the pipe at the six men standing in front of his desk. 'You'll be rested for two or three months, but I'll do my damnedest to keep you together as a crew. You will be notified as soon as possible which Operational Training Unit you're being posted to, but in the meantime . . . well . . . just take it easy, chaps.' He gave his Squadron Adjutant what he considered to be a surreptitious nod, then smiled. 'Thank you . . . that will be all. I'll see you before you leave.'

With that they were dismissed.

There was a party that night in the Mess. It was a party where grown men behaved like schoolboys, where the piano was thumped until its player's finger-tips were sore, and where the words of the songs owed nothing to the original lyricist. When David went to bed at last the sun was beginning to rise in the east over Lincoln Wolds. For the first time in his well-ordered life he was paralytically drunk, so drunk that his own mother would have blinked twice before recognizing him.

Shedding his clothes en route, he took a fire extinguisher

from the wall and tucked it lovingly underneath his arm. Still clasping the extinguisher, he was shoved beneath the covers of his narrow bed by Jock, his gunner.

'Well, at least somebody's happy.'

Grinning from ear to ear, Jock went in search of David's clothes, scattered like drifting flotsam all down the long stretch of corridor. Rolling each garment up with exaggerated care, he made them into an unwieldy parcel and laid them neatly at the foot of David's bed. Then, standing to attention, he solemnly saluted.

'Sleep it off, old man,' he said kindly, then he patted the inert hump beneath the blankets, a sly expression creeping over his flushed face. 'But you'll be the first one of us fretting to get back on the job, old man. I know your sort.'

The sound of his own voice wavered and died away in his ears. With an undignified lunge he dashed for the door, the ten pints of beer in his stomach making their presence felt most uncomfortably.

Two

'David's stationed in Scotland now. He's not flying, at least not on operations. He hasn't written to tell you then? Ah, well . . .'

The glint of triumph in Edna Turner's eyes was unmistakable. Already Sally was beginning to doubt the wisdom of her visit. There were times when the fanciful thought came to her that Mrs Turner was growing out of the sofa with its moquette upholstery and embroidered antimacassar taped into place over the back. They were all there, the trappings of loneliness. Knitting bag, library book, scaled-down war-time copy of *Woman's Weekly*, and the *Radio Times* open at today's date.

A wave of pity swept over her, only to recede when Edna fixed her with a hard stare.

'I don't suppose they would have you in the Forces? With you being deaf?'

The thin lips formed each word in an exaggerated way. Sally guessed she was being shouted at, and tried to hide her irritation.

'No, they won't have me in the Forces, Mrs Turner. I went for an interview and made a mess of it. The sergeant kept writing things down so I couldn't see what she was saying, but the firm I work for makes small parts for guns, so I suppose I am on a kind of war work.' She smiled a smile that was wasted, as Edna seemed to be fascinated by the wallpaper.

'I hope David doesn't have to go back on operations for a long time.' Sally leaned forward. 'Mrs Turner? Are you all right?'

Edna had been feeling ill for a few days. She always felt like this when winter had finally gone and the flop-headed pansies came up once again in the back garden. It was as though everything was coming to life, mocking her because her own life had ended on the day her husband had fallen wounded into a shell-hole and drowned in Flanders mud.

He should have been here now, that other David, the one whose face she could barely remember, keeping her company night after night.

'He never saw his son, you know.'

Her voice was light and conversational, and after she had spoken she went back to staring at the wall behind Sally's head. She couldn't bear to look at the girl if the truth were known. She didn't like her and never had.

'Sally Barnes's mother is common. As common as dirt. She goes with soldiers, you know.' Edna had told David that on the night he had said he was taking Sally to the pictures, and when he had laughed she had wanted to smack his face.

'My husband was an officer in the Coldstream Guards,' she said suddenly.

'Have you any photographs of him, Mrs Turner?'

The girl was saying something, but she wasn't going to take any notice. That girl sitting there, twisting one of her curls round and round her finger, was as bad as her mother. Edna had known that when she had come downstairs for something on that last night of her son's leave and seen him sitting there with his head in his hands, suffering. It was all because of something this girl had said or done, she had known that, but she had crept back upstairs telling herself it was no good trying to find out what was wrong. David might have the same name as his father and look like him, but that was all.

'My husband was a fully fledged chartered accountant when he went to France. With letters behind his name.' Edna almost choked on her bitterness. 'All that studying, and for what? If he'd come back we would have had a better house than this. Up by the park. He'd have had his name in gold letters on one of those office windows in Burscough Terrace.'

Sally chewed on her lip. Mrs Turner was talking to her as if she wasn't there, as if she was using her merely as a sounding-board for her grievances. But she needed to talk, that much was obvious. Surprisingly, it was easy to lip-read the thin mouth stretching and moving round the words. Suddenly the reason came to her . . .

Once, a long time ago, before Edna Turner married David's father and moved a notch or two up the social scale, she had worked as a weaver in a cotton mill. To make themselves heard over the sound of the clattering looms, women had mimed what they wanted to say to each other. When voices were drowned, lips and gestures had taken over, and Mrs Turner had never lost the habit. Like many a Lancashire woman before her, Edna still talked in that clear, well-defined way, the vowels as exaggerated as if she were indeed conversing with the deaf.

'My husband would revolve in his grave,' Edna was saying now, 'if he could see what was going on. You might think this war is terrible, but you should have lived through the last. Day after day with long columns in the newspapers giving the names of officers and men killed or missing. And now they're at it again.'

Her head drooped so that Sally lost the thread of what she was saying. Trying not to fidget, she allowed her gaze to wander round the room. If it had been roped off, she thought, it could easily have been a room in an 'Ideal Home' exhibition, on show to visitors with catalogues in their hands. The silver on the sideboard gleamed, and a bunch of garden flowers in a cut-glass vase had their stems trimmed to a uniform length. Everything that could be stood on a mat did stand on a mat, all exquisitely embroidered in Mrs Turner's satin-stitch and drawn-thread work.

Sally blinked suddenly as Edna leapt up from the sofa, presenting the flat planes of her face to the ceiling, clasping her hands together in supplication.

'Oh, my God! That's the sirens going! I haven't got the thermos flask ready, with you sitting talking your head off.'

Leaving Sally bewildered, not knowing quite what to do, Edna rushed from the room.

'Mrs Turner?' She followed her into the hall, through the breakfast-room and into a scullery at the back of the house. 'Mrs Turner? Won't you come down the road to my house?' Sally winced as an enormous flash of light penetrated a chink in the black-out curtain draped across the window. 'I'll have to go now or my father will be out looking for me, but please, won't you come? I . . . I don't like leaving you here on your own.'

Edna thumped the kettle down on a gas-ring and took a stone hot-water bottle from a shelf, unscrewing the top with quick decisive twists of her sinewy fingers.

'You made my son cry the night you went out with him.'

Her black eyes glittering, the stone bottle clutched to her flat chest, Edna rounded on Sally in a sudden and terrifying fury. 'My David went back upset because of you, and if he'd been shot down it would have been on account of you. He was brave enough to go flying night after night over Germany. Yet *you* made him cry.'

Sally's heart gave a great thud. Switching off the light and pulling back the curtain she saw to her amazement that Mrs Turner's back garden and the stretch of allotments beyond were bathed in a bright light. When Edna Turner immediately switched on the light again she dropped the curtain into place and tried to pull the stiff resisting little figure towards the door.

'Mrs Turner! They've dropped a huge flare! You can see for miles around! Please! Go inside your shelter if you won't come back with me.' She glanced round at the kettle coming to a boil. 'I'll turn the gas and the water off – they're the same as in our house, so I know how. *Please* get into your shelter. Please . . .'

As Edna whipped round, the heavy stone bottle smashed to the floor, missing her feet by a few inches. Sally stared in horror at the white face, the working mouth, the bobbing head. It was like the nightmare she often had where angry mouths opened and closed silently, the distorted faces showing their contempt of her lack of understanding.

Now Mrs Turner was holding out both her arms so that her body formed the shape of a cross. The kitchen seemed to rock and sway, the floor tilting as cups and saucers slid from their places on the dresser.

'Get out of my sight!' she shouted. 'Go! Just go!'

With sharp hurting jabs to Sally's shoulder, she pushed her bodily down the hall to the front door which she opened with a wrench that almost tore it from its hinges.

'Get in the shelter, Mrs Turner!' Sally turned to see the little woman waving an arm eastwards to where the sky glowed red like a blood orange.

'Bloody Germans!' Edna's voice was a clarion call. 'I spit on your faces, the lot of you!' She went inside, slamming the door with such force that the brass knocker did a little dance of protest against the polished oak graining.

Sally ran down the road, her heels clicking like knitting needles on the pavement, dry now after the May shower of heavy rain.

When she opened her own front door, the coats hanging untidily on the hall-stand and the dead flowers on the hall table looked warm and welcoming. She was reaching to hang up her coat when she was suddenly twisted round and held against a khaki uniform.

'John! Oh, John!'

The next minute she was swung up into her brother's arms, her feet clearing the floor. John Barnes grinned, then as suddenly was serious.

'Where the hell have you been, our kid? It's raining bombs out there, you little pillock. No wonder you look scared to death.'

In an instant Mrs Turner and her strange behaviour were forgotten, as brother and sister grinned at each other with genuine affection. John jerked his head towards the living-room. 'Come and see who I've got in there. Okay?'

When he opened the door he pushed Sally in front of him, saying: 'Thank God she's come home. She shouldn't be out on her own.'

'Hello there, Sally.'

The girl sitting on the sofa smiled, her green eyes glinting with amusement, then she turned her head to one side. 'But the "all clear's" going, Johnnie. Besides, they were *miles* away.'

'Hello, Christine.' Sally hoped she wasn't looking as surprised as she felt. John's infatuation for Christine Duckworth, daughter of Amos, Sally's boss, had been a family joke for a long time. Her eyes widened as the beautiful auburn-haired girl put out a hand to draw John down to sit beside her.

Sally backed slowly away as their lips met in a long, searching kiss. They knew she was standing there, yet it was as though she had said a magic word and disappeared in a whiff of blue smoke. Embarrassment held her still, then as John surfaced for a moment Sally backed away.

'Nice to see you, Christine,' she said foolishly, before slip-

31

ping through the door into the hall in time to see Stanley coming in wearing his Home Guard uniform.

'In here, love.' Stanley led the way into the seldom-used front room. 'Still at it in there, are they?' He sat down by the empty grate and took out his pipe and tobacco pouch. 'They came as soon as you'd gone out.' He pressed the tobacco down with a practised thumb. 'John's on embarkation leave, twenty-four hours, that's all, so I suppose he's making up for lost time.'

The room smelled of damp and the possibility of mice. On the hardly ever played piano an empty vase stood next to a photograph of John in his sergeant's uniform. Just before the war a new fireplace had been installed, pale green tiles with a tiny ledge for a mantelpiece. On the wall above, a mirror with scalloped edges hung from a gold chain. Sally saw the frown line in the space between her eyebrows and rubbed it with the cushion of her thumb.

'Where do you think they'll be sending him? The Middle East?'

When Stanley nodded, she sat down on an armchair with an ash-tray taped to its arm on a leather thong. 'I suppose we were a bit silly thinking he'd be kept in this country for much longer.' She sighed. 'I'll be glad when today's over and done with. My mind's been working like an ancient typewriter with the keys coming up and jamming when I try to think straight. I can't take it in about John properly, either about him being serious with Christine Duckworth, or him going overseas. When I was with Mrs Turner I don't think I helped. Well, I *know* I didn't. She's going *potty*, really round the twist, and I left her there.' She smiled ruefully. 'Well, the truth is she shoved me out of the house, then yelled and shook her fist at the sky.'

'We're going now. I'm taking Christine home.'

Sally stopped speaking as she saw Stanley look towards the door. John was grinning, his hair tousled, his face as flushed as if he'd been sitting too long in the sun. 'Tell Mum I'm sorry I missed her but not to wait up. I'll see her in the morning before I go. Ta'ra then. Ta'ra.'

'His mother will give him "ta'ra then" when she comes in and finds she's missed him.' Stanley headed for the living-room and his own chair, but first he turned and touched Sally

32

gently on her wrist. 'Don't worry too much about Mrs Turner, love. She's insulted more folks who were only trying to help her than you've had hot dinners. She's not going to do away with herself, if that's what you're thinking. Your mother reckons that shelter in the front room is more than half full with tins of pilchards!'

Ten minutes later Sally bumped into her mother on the landing. Josie was still wearing her coat and a headscarf and when she turned round, obviously unwillingly, Sally saw that her cheeks were wet with tears. Josie Barnes who never cried – Josie who could lose her temper in a flash, shout and carry on, but who only cried when she was peeling onions.

'You'll see John in the morning, Mum.' Sally put out a hand then drew it back.

'John? Is he home then?' Josie pulled her headscarf off, then with it trailing from her hand walked with dragging feet into the front bedroom.

'I'll go down and put the kettle on.' Equally slowly Sally walked downstairs into the living-room where Stanley sat by the wireless twiddling with the controls.

'Mr Churchill has been speaking to the Poles. I hope some of them manage to listen.' He shook his head sadly. 'What that country suffers doesn't bear thinking about. But we've brought thirty-three bombers down, so the news isn't all bad.'

Forgetting to control the pitch of her voice, Sally shouted: 'That's all you care about, the news. Isn't it, Dad?' She turned to leave the room, with Stanley staring after her in mild surprise.

But the news reader was speaking again, this time about Crete. Stanley pulled at his top lip with a finger and thumb. Now this could be serious. Mr Churchill would take it very hard if we had to leave there. He seemed to have accepted the loss of Greece, but Crete . . . well, that was another matter altogether.

When he turned round again he was alone in the room.

At one o'clock in the morning the sirens wailed and the bombers came back. Now the sky over Liverpool was blood red from a thousand fires. From docks and warehouses, boiling sugar, oil and paint exploded over houses in a terrifying spread of flames.

'God help them,' Stanley said, sitting round the kitchen table sipping his fourth mug of tea. 'It's the women and kids fighting the war at the moment.' He got up and yawned, stretching his arms high above his head. 'I'm off to bed. The worst's over for tonight, and I expect we'll be having John knocking us up soon after the "all clear". I've heard the Duckworths have a shelter in their back garden, complete with all mod. cons.' He pointed a finger in the direction of the door. 'C'mon, Sally. Upstairs! It's all over for tonight.'

They were shuffling into the hall, only half awake, when the floor seemed to erupt beneath them. The windows at the front of the house blew in, and they were lifted bodily, all three of them, to lie in a tangled heap of arms and legs at the foot of the stairs. The house seemed to sway like a tree in the wind, then settled itself as plaster drifted down to cover the carpet like snowflakes.

'Famous last words,' Stanley muttered.

It was dawn before the full extent of the damage to the quiet suburban road could be seen in all its horror. The wide road was littered with broken glass and the jagged edges of broken pipes; four houses had been completely destroyed, and ten or more badly damaged.

Working like Trojans, the men of the rescue parties moved the wreckage of Edna Turner's house brick by brick, working against time, holding up their hands for silence then shaking their heads and starting again.

Stanley wiped the sweat from his face with the edge of his sleeve. 'Mrs Turner would be in her shelter.' His voice felt raw in his dust-parched throat. 'She always went in her shelter.' He stumbled over splintered floorboards and mounds of bricks. 'My daughter was with her last night. She said Mrs Turner was acting strange . . . so there's no telling. She might not have been in the house at all.' He jerked his head towards what had once been a house next door. 'She could have gone in there, and if she did . . .' He sighed heavily, remembering the broken bodies and the firemen slumped on their hoses, standing by, red-eyed and helpless.

'You can forget about Edna Turner being anywhere but in her own house.' A puny little man, his face dirt-streaked, almost unrecognizable as the dapper solicitor's clerk he happened to be, shouted across the rubble. 'Edna Turner wouldn't let any of us help her, and you know it. My wife got tired of asking her to come in with us when the sirens went. Nay, she's under that lot sure as eggs is eggs.' He climbed over to Stanley and lowered his voice. 'Isn't that your lass standing by herself over there? I thought they'd sent the women home hours ago.'

When Stanley turned, he saw Sally at the very perimeter of the rubble, a small hunched figure with arms wrapped round herself to keep out the early morning chill.

'You know you've no right to be here,' he said, climbing over the rubble towards her. 'The warden will see you off if he spots you. What *are* you doing here, anyway?'

'It's Mrs Turner.' Sally shivered suddenly. 'She's somewhere under there, isn't she? David doesn't even know what's happened to her, so *somebody* has to watch for her, Dad.' Her voice shook. 'I keep thinking how she would have hated everything *showing* like this.' She jerked her chin to where a broken wall flew a flag of yellow wallpaper like a strip of pathetic bunting in the breeze.

'When you left her last night, did she say for certain she was going into her shelter?' Stanley's voice gentled. 'It's important, love, because if she is inside then there might be just a chance she's alive.'

'I left her standing on the front doorstep.' Sally bit her lip remembering Edna Turner's lined face twisted with anger as she bellowed her bitterness to the reddened sky. 'No. I remember now. She went back inside. I saw the brass knocker rattling against the door when she slammed it hard. But she was acting so strangely, not frightened or anything, just blazing mad. Partly at Hitler and partly at me.' Sally's voice wavered as she felt her father's touch on her hand.

'Quiet, love. I think they've found her.'

Sally held her breath. It seemed in that moment as if every part of her was holding still. She saw the warden hold up a hand for silence.

'Aye, they've got through.'

A broken window frame was tossed aside. A twisted piece of metal was prized from a deep hollow scooped brick by brick from the mountain of rubble. The silence was as deep as Sally's own private silence as the warden lowered himself down inch by inch into the hole.

She could see instructions shouted through cupped hands as feet scrambled over the high piled bricks and stones. Turning round instinctively she saw a fire engine on its way back from the city, picking its way along the shattered stretch of road. A man appeared in front of her, waving both arms high above his head, and from behind her two stretcher-bearers materialized, almost knocking her over. Sally stared straight in front of her, hearing nothing, but understanding all. All her senses strained into the silence thick as a blanket round her. She prayed that Edna Turner would be found alive, yet even as she prayed she knew the lonely little woman was dead.

When they lifted her out of the black hole, her legs dangled, broken and twisted. She was showing pink knickers, the elasticated legs almost down to the knee. And when they laid her on the stretcher her head fell back so that Sally saw her white parting covered, like the rest of her, with grey plaster.

There was no dignity in the way her shattered body was exposed to neighbours she had shunned and kept away from all her life. In spite of all the feverish activity and the scrabbling helping hands, no one had thought to bring a blanket to cover what was left of Edna Turner.

'And she once told me,' Sally sobbed, 'that if she hung her knickers out at all on the washing line she always hung them close to the house so that the neighbours wouldn't see them. They should have covered her up . . . oh, Mum, they should have covered her up.'

'She's better off dead.'

Josie was sitting in the kitchen exactly as Sally had left her, smoking in fierce little puffs, using a saucer as an ash-tray. Her blue eyes were swollen into slits, and as she stubbed out one cigarette she reached for another. 'Oh, God, there's no need to look at me like that! If you believe what they taught you at Sunday School then Edna Turner's with her husband now, living in a mansion like one of those up Park Road. She always said she should have been in one by rights, anyway.'

Sally didn't appear to be making any attempt to lip-read. 'I've never seen a dead body before,' she said.

'Then you'd better be prepared to see plenty more before this lot's over.' Josie coughed as the smoke caught her throat. 'This flamin' war hasn't lasted for two years yet and look what we've got. Empty shelves in the shops, food rations that have to last a week when they're only enough for a day. Black-out, bombs – and we've seen nothing to what they've been getting in London for months. So it's God rest Edna Turner's miserable soul, I say. I only hope she finds summat to laugh at up there, 'cos nowt ever tickled her fancy down here.'

Josie pushed her chair away from the table. 'And now I'll go upstairs and get meself ready for work. We might have nowt but corrugated paper in our front windows, half our neighbours are dead or had their legs blown off, but there's the Police Ball next week and there's sure to be some silly woman who wants a new dress for it. Oh, and when your dad comes in tell him I put the wireless on and the Nazis are landing by parachute in Crete. I wouldn't like him to miss anything.'

'Mum!' Sally pulled Josie round to face her as she tried to slip past her to the door. 'I can't *hear* you! You've been talking with your head down and I couldn't hear a word.'

'Then *you've* missed nothing neither, have you?' Josie ran upstairs, head down, pulling herself up by the bannister rail. In her room she leaned against the door and held her hands over her face. Oh God, dear God, how was she going to get through the coming days? When Bill had told her last night that he was being posted away, and they had decided, both of them, that this was the time to finish, it had all seemed so right, so much the only thing to do. Yet even now, already, in spite of the raid and in spite of John staying out all night with a girl she hardly knew ... Josie took a deep, shuddering breath ... and in spite of Sally's face stiff with hurt as she struggled to understand ... *nothing*, nothing at all mattered if she never saw Bill again.

'May God forgive me, but I love that man ...' Pushing

herself away from the door Josie went over to her dressing-table and saw that the mirror was broken with an ugly crack running from top to bottom, and all her jars and bottles covered with a powdery layer of grey dust. The face staring back at her was distorted and old, with peroxided hair forming a grotesque halo over pallid cheeks and shadowed eyes.

Downstairs Sally trailed miserably into the hall, picked up a dustpan and brush and swept up the slivers of broken glass revealed more clearly in the morning light. The plate-rack was covered with sparkly dust yet, miraculously, a Blue Willow plate was still in position. She felt vaguely sick, quietly detached, then her face brightened as her brother came in from outside, looking so honestly bewildered that she almost burst out laughing.

'The door's off its hinges!'

John turned to see Stanley standing behind him, his eyes smoke-bleared, his narrow shoulders drooping with exhaustion.

'I didn't know. I'd no idea.' John put up a hand as if taking an oath. 'We knew there'd been a big one over this side, but right till I turned the corner – honest to goodness, Dad, I nearly died!'

'Quite a lot of folks did.'

Josie had worked hard on herself. She had rubbed Crème Simone on her face, patted orange-tinted powder over it, and fluffed her hair out with her fingers. With no more than a cursory glance at her son, she spoke to him over a disappearing shoulder, leaving Sally staring from one to the other in unhappy dismay.

'The "all clear" went at least six hours ago!' Josie whipped round, her blue eyes blazing above the circles of rouge. 'It was more important for you to say goodbye to a girl we hardly know when God only knows how long it will be before you come home again!'

John flushed with a temper that was a match for his mother's, only to close his mouth when Stanley stated baldly in a loud flat voice, 'Your mother's upset, son.'

'We're *all* bloody upset!' Josie shot a baleful glance in her husband's direction. 'And take that flamin' tin hat off! You don't suit it, and never have!'

38

'Mum, for crying out loud, just *listen*!' John followed Josie through into the kitchen. 'How do you think I feel going away, leaving you like this?' He jerked his chin back towards the hall with its drifts of dust and shattered glass. 'I should have come home last night, but hell's bells, if I'm old enough to be sent abroad I'm old enough to stop out all night!'

'So you do admit it, then?' Josie whirled round, the hurt inside her making her lash out. 'You stopped out all night with a toffee-nosed girl who wouldn't give you the time of day if you weren't jazzed up in that uniform! Aw, I know Christine Duckworth, an' I know her mother as well. Tell them they look wonderful in something when they come in the shop, flatter their flamin' egos, and they'll buy owt.' Josie's lips, thickly coated with Tangee lipstick, lifted into a smile that was more of a grimace. 'They'll be laughing t'other side of their faces, those two will, when clothes rationing starts next month. Oh aye . . .' she rounded on Stanley, standing quietly in the doorway, 'that's a bit of news even you missed, isn't it?'

'I'll go up and get my kit together.'

There was no point in staying to hear any more. John knew his mother of old. Let something upset her badly enough and her reaction was to let fly with her tongue. It was up to his dad to stand up to her more, but it wasn't Stanley he was sorry for. It was Sally. The poor kid looked as bewildered as she obviously felt, watching them and only catching a fraction of what was being said. Last night Christine had said Sally was frightened of the boys on the shop floor at the works. Ducked her head and walked away, if they came up to her and tried to speak. On his way upstairs he stopped long enough to ruffle his sister's curly hair.

'I'll ring her up tonight,' he whispered. 'She'll have calmed down a bit by then. Christine's *my* girl, now. I'm going to marry her when this lot's over. Be nice to her, for my sake, our kid.'

He took the stairs two at a time up to his room at the back of the house. There was a long framed photograph of his old school on the wall. His tennis racket in its press leaned against the wardrobe, and on a shelf behind his bed a row of mechanical engineering textbooks stood next to the *Complete Works of Shakespeare* and his Sunday School bible.

It was all so ordinary, so familiar, and in that moment so surprisingly precious. John stood still on the strip of carpet by his bed, taking in every detail, watching the way the sun was beginning to slant across a tiny copper bust of Molière, won in his last term at school in a French-speaking competition.

That day in the office seemed as long for Sally as the lists she typed. They were endless lists to be carbon-copied, tabulated, yellow paper for the firm's files, pink for the Ministry of Supply, green for Mr Duckworth's personal reference, and top white for the recipient of the small gun parts supplied.

She knew the girls were swapping bomb stories, but unable to see their faces all the time she laughed when they laughed, composed her expression into concern when she guessed the stories were harrowing. And all the time she saw in her mind Edna Turner's body flopping on the stretcher as if filleted of all its bones.

In the afternoon a part-time worker was brought into the office, white and shaken, a bare patch glistening on the crown of her head.

'I forgot to put me turban on.' The woman stared round wildly for understanding. 'Me front wave caught in the drill.' She groped for a handkerchief in her overall pocket. 'It was the bombing last night, then coming out of the shelter to hear me sister's boy's gone missing over Germany. I just switched me machine on without thinking. I'm sorry, Mr Duckworth. I'm really sorry.'

'I hear you'd have been scalped but for old Harry's quick thinking.' Sally read Christine Duckworth's father easily. 'We don't need any Veronica Lakes on our shop floor, lass.'

Sally bent her head over her typewriter again, seeing the angry faces mouthing angry words in the kitchen that morning. She saw she had forgotten to indent five spaces before a column of figures, and knew she would have to start all over again.

'Our John telephoned half an hour ago.' Josie Barnes's face was smooth again. 'He didn't say where from, but my guess is they'll be sailing straight away.' She pointed to the dresser.

40

'There's a letter for you. It was behind what's left of the door when I got in from work.'

Sally glanced quickly at the closely written sheet of paper before pushing it back into its envelope. 'It's from David Turner. Written before . . .'

'He'll get compassionate leave.' Josie held a loaf of bread against her chest and began to slice furiously and dangerously towards her left breast. 'Though where he'll stop, I don't know. His mother didn't seem to have any friends. Anyroad, he's not stopping here.'

'Why not?' The idea had never occurred to Sally before that moment, but after a twelve-hour day she was tired. It had seemed the streets were filled with people hurrying home before the sirens went, a lot of them to makeshift meals cooked on makeshift fires. They would be washing in a small bowl of water in some cases – water salvaged from a hot-water bottle from the night before. She lifted her chin. 'If I see David I'll *invite* him to stay with us. It's the least we can do.'

Josie threw the bread-knife down with a clatter. She felt better after talking to John on the telephone, but not that much better. The events of the past twenty-four hours had numbed her mind into a resigned and bitter acceptance of the way things were going to be. Dull grey faces and dull grey clothes, dwindling rations, sleepless nights, when all she had ever asked from life was a bit of laughter, fun, a night out dancing now and again. She felt she didn't care if she never went dancing again. They had drunk what was left of the week's tea ration last night, and Sally was all set to make trouble. She sighed a deep, shuddering sigh.

'We're not starting something. That's what I mean. David Turner stopping here now because of what's happened could mean David Turner coming here for all his leaves. And that could mean you and him getting serious for no other reason than that you've been thrown together.'

'Oh, Mum, that's stupid!'

'*Is* it?' Josie gave a harsh laugh. 'I wasn't born the day before yesterday. There's a war on, remember? He'll be lucky if he comes through it, will David Turner. I'm not having you breaking your heart before you've even begun to live.' Her eyes closed for a moment as she heard the sirens begin their

41

moaning wail. 'You're only a child. Give yourself a chance, love.'

'I'm older than you were when you got married.' Sally blinked as her mother thumped the table hard with a clenched fist.

'That's just what I'm getting at, can't you see? Your father was like David Turner, war weary, with his knee half shot away, an' I saw myself like some flamin' Florence Nightingale eager to cherish him and make him forget.' Suddenly she slumped down onto a chair and buried her face in her hands. 'I went no further in my imagination than that walk down the aisle.'

'I can't hear you, Mum.'

Josie took her hands away from her face. 'And because *my* mother was dead set against it I wanted to get married more than ever.'

'Your *mother*?'

'Yes, my mother.' Josie's blue eyes narrowed. 'Your *grandma*, Sally Barnes. The one who's never mentioned. The grandma who was never quite sure who had fathered her daughter. The grandma who could barely write her name . . . It's a funny thing, you know, but as I grow older I remember her more and more. Why is it you've never once asked me about her, Sally? Why do you and John act as though your mother never had a mother of her own?' She blew a strand of bleached hair out of her eyes. 'I'll tell you why!'

Sally knew her mother was shouting by the way her throat was working. The sky outside was filled with the heavy sound of planes; the guns were thundering, but all Sally knew was that her mother was shouting at her across the width of the kitchen table.

'I married out of my class, Sally, but then you know that, don't you? Oh, aye, you could have heard tongues wagging from here to St Helens about that girl from Foundry Street marrying Stanley Barnes the telephone engineer who was so clever he could build a wireless from bloody scratch. Do you know, your father's sisters never sent as much as a bunch of daisies when my mother died? That was soon after the wedding. They had a right field-day laughing at her that day because they thought her skirt was too short for their narrow

42

Methody eyes. An' when her hat blew off outside the Chapel they sniggered behind their kid gloves. I wanted to kill them. Do you know that?'

Sally patted the letter in her pocket then reached out across the table. 'All that hasn't anything to do with David Turner, has it?' She took a deep breath. 'It hasn't anything to do with the bomb last night, or with John going away.' Biting hard at her lip, she stared at the ceiling for a minute. 'But it has to do with you crying when you came in last night, hasn't it?' She finished on a rush of words. 'It's about the soldier who's been bringing you home from the dancing. Isn't it?'

'What did you say?' Eyes and mouth wide open, Josie stared at her daughter. 'Say that again!'

'The soldier, Mum.' Sally nodded her head up and down twice. 'I've seen you with him. I got on the same tram once, and I saw you laughing with him, then I was looking through my window once when he brought you home.' Her calm little colourless voice never faltered. 'You're worried sick to your stomach, aren't you, Mum? You're not going to have a baby, are you?'

'Oh, my God! Oh, my sainted aunt! You sit there and ask your own mother a thing like that?'

'He's gone away then, hasn't he?' Sally was quietly insistent. 'Was that why you were crying last night?'

'Oh, my God!' Josie said it again before her face crumpled. 'Yes. He's gone away.' Her small chin lifted. 'An' I'll never see him again.'

There was a small silence, then Sally said clearly: 'Just because a person can't hear, it doesn't mean they can't see or notice things. I understand a lot of things.'

'You do?'

'Oh, yes.' Sally nodded again. 'Dad doesn't make you laugh, and he . . . the soldier did. But that doesn't mean . . .'

She flinched as Josie grabbed her wrist, putting a finger to her lips in a warning gesture. 'Your dad's here.'

When Stanley's neat head came round the door his eyes registered immediate relief that the morning's fiasco was obviously over and done with. There they were, the two of them, chatting away as if all hell wasn't being let loose over Liverpool.

Stanley's smile changed to bewilderment as Sally suddenly rushed past him into the hall, bleak and sombre with its cardboard windows. As she ran upstairs she noticed that the last remaining Blue Willow plate had somehow dislodged itself and was lying in smithereens on the tread at the side of the narrow stair carpet.

'What was all that about?' Stanley walked over to the sink and began to wash his hands.

'Search me. She's at a funny age, that's all.' Josie shrugged. 'The poor little devil doesn't even know the sirens have gone.'

They buried Edna Turner on the Wednesday afternoon of the following week, on a day when the trees in the cemetery were heavy with bright green leaves.

David thought how fitting it was that his solitary, lonely mother was being sent to her eternal rest as quietly as she had lived. He only wished he could believe that the father he had never known was waiting for her with outstretched hands. Looking down, he frowned at the shiny toe-caps of his black shoes, then he raised his head to stare at Sally's mother.

Josie had come to the funeral because Wednesday was early closing day, and because she could hardly refuse. She had tied a black chiffon scarf over her hair and coloured her lips the same shade of purple as her fitted coat. There was a letter in her handbag, first sent as arranged to Olive Marsden's address, and the contents were churning her insides with excitement, worrying her to death at the same time.

Stanley was standing to attention, his thin face set in sober lines. He was thinking about the mysterious business of Hess, Hitler's deputy, landing in Scotland. Goebbels was at the bottom of it, Stanley was convinced, but the newspapers were only telling half the truth, he was sure of that. He stole a glance at Sally, then sighed. Just lately her deafness seemed to be worse, if that was possible. Her face was wearing its shut-in look, and in her flowered summer dress with its short sleeves puffed at the top she looked about fourteen years old.

Early that morning David had stood in the road outside the ruins of his home. Already the bulldozers had chewed and vomited the rubble into a dune of gritty dust, and soon there would be daisies, pink campion and purple willow herb. Soon he would be going back on flying duties. Long before the willow herb poked its first green tendrils through the bricks he would be crouched over his instrument table plotting a course so that British bombs could destroy with equal violence.

'Mad,' he had muttered, to the consternation of a man on his way to an early shift. 'We're all mad, the bloody lot of us.'

'Go on then,' his mother had said, as he left for the station that last morning of his leave. 'Go back to the war. You're a man, and men only come into their own when they're fighting each other.'

He had stretched out a hand to her, and she had startled him by covering it suddenly with both her own, holding it fast as if it were a butterfly she was keeping from flying away.

As soon as the short burial service was finished, he walked over to Sally's parents, shook hands with them and thanked them for coming.

'You're sure you won't come back with us? Just for a cup of tea?' Stanley looked as uncomfortable as he felt, wishing his wife had made the invitation.

'I hope it wasn't too difficult getting the time off this afternoon.' David fell into step beside Sally, holding her elbow lightly as they stepped onto the gravel path.

'I'm going straight back now, making the time up this evening.' She was equally polite, equally shy. 'David, I wish I could tell you how sorry I am . . . I wish there was something I could do.'

'It hasn't hit me yet.' He was muttering, holding his head down, forgetting she wouldn't be able to understand what he was saying. 'At the moment I just feel that my mother was so sad, that dying for her could only be what they call a blessed relief.' He felt the blood rush to his face. 'I'm so *angry*, Sally. This morning I picked up a charred stick and poked about in the bricks and the dirt to see if I could salvage anything. My *things*, for Pete's sake! They had dug my mother out of there and all I could think about were my records, my books, and my cricket bat with Ernest Tyldsley's autograph on it. I wasn't thinking about her, Sally. Just my piddling belongings.'

He turned to her, and Sally hoped her expression had been

the right one. It was always the same when anyone confided in her with their head averted. Her grey eyes were steady as she stared into his flushed face.

'You saw my mother that night?' He bit hard at his lip. 'How was she?' He kicked at a loose stone. 'Was she okay?'

'She was fine, David,' Sally lied. 'She had filled her hot-water bottle, and we'd talked, mostly about your father. She mentioned him a lot.'

'She blamed me for leaving her.' David hesitated. 'She thought I should have wangled my way back into civilian life on a reserved occupation. Now she's shown me once and for all that I was somehow in the wrong leaving her all alone.'

'Then *you* would have been killed, David!' The words came out in a rush. 'It was a direct hit. That's a daft way to talk!'

'Sally!' They were nearing the main road now, and Josie and Stanley were waiting for them, standing slightly apart, like two strangers starting a queue. Turning his back on them, his face averted from Sally, forgetting once again in his distress that his words were wasted, David said: 'I . . . that night after the pictures. Do you think we could forget it?'

'Sally! The tram's coming. Come on if you're coming!' Josie was waving an arm, and seeing it Sally hesitated, stepped back a pace, and the moment was lost. Colour flooded her rounded cheeks.

'Thanks for the letter. I'll write.'

'Sally!' Josie was waving frantically now as Stanley, with one foot on the boarding platform, shouted something to the conductor.

When Sally, holding onto the rail, turned her head she saw David standing there, tall, neat and correct in his uniform. The conductor rang the bell and the tram bore her away from him, a lonely figure standing seemingly to attention in the open space where the cemetery gates used to be.

'So you've definitely got a Home Guard "do" on this weekend?'

Stanley twisted round on the tram's slatted seat to stare at his wife. She *never* showed the slightest interest in his Home Guard activities. Right from the beginning when he had rushed to answer Anthony Eden's broadcast the previous May, pleading for volunteers, she had appeared to find the whole concept hilarious.

'A fat lot of use you'd be with your gammy leg.'

He remembered the way her eyes had sparkled with laughter, and the way he had answered her, his face stiff with hurt.

'Military experience is rated more important than physical fitness. The official requirement is that men must be capable of free movement.'

'Free movement? You couldn't cock that leg of yours over a gas-tar bubble in the road! They'll have to be desperate before they take *you* on.'

From that first day Stanley had gone conscientiously to report for duty, walking with his limping glide to drill hall or rifle range, first in a uniform consisting merely of an arm-band with the letters LDV on it, then in battle-dress with his corporal's stripe sewn proudly into position. On the day Josie had found out he had been drafted to the Pigeon Corps, she had shouted with glee.

'Oh, my God! If old Hitler finds out about you he'll throw the bloody sponge in!'

Yet here she was now, her pale face framed in the black chiffon scarf, asking what appeared to be a caring question.

'We have a big show on,' he told her quietly. 'We're getting decent fire-arms now America is coming up trumps. A bit different from the beginning when some of our lot raided Belle Vue Zoo in Manchester for old Synder rifles.'

She nodded, as if with understanding. 'You know Olive at the shop?'

Stanley blinked at the sudden change of subject. 'I should do. You talk about her often enough.'

'Well, she has an auntie at Morecambe, and this weekend Olive's going to stay with her and she wants me to go with her.' Josie lowered her head, biting at the purple lipstick. 'I thought with you being out all weekend I might go.' He saw with surprise that she was clenching her hands so tightly on the clasp of her handbag that the knuckles showed white. 'I know I've been a bit snotty to you lately, with John going away and the bomb the other night.' She shuddered. 'An' just now up the cemetery, when they lowered Edna Turner into her grave, I kept thinking how it could easily have been

47

me – us. Stanley, I'm frightened. I know we're supposed to keep cheerful, but I must be a bloody coward. I thought we were well away from the bombing where we live, but we're not, are we?'

Stanley wanted to put an arm round her. If she would be like this more often, really talking to him instead of putting him down all the time, then things between them might be different. But he couldn't put an arm round her, not on the tram; all he could do was try and comfort her.

'The way I see it, love, is that we're in a sort of no man's land, with the heavy stuff going over our heads. It was like lightning striking the other night. You know it never strikes the same place twice.'

'I'd like to get away for a short while.' Josie pointed to a house, its windows empty of glass, its front door boarded over. 'We're travelling away from the docks and yet there's a lot of houses like that one.'

'But what about Sally?' Stanley's voice was tinged with doubt.

'Good God! She's not a child! I'd been married to you for two years when I was her age.'

'But you weren't . . .'

'Deaf,' Josie finished for him. 'I know that, but can't you see we've got to stop protecting her so much. She's so . . . so innocent it bothers me. She doesn't seem to know how to talk to boys. I was watching David Turner with her just before we got on the tram. She ran off, Stanley. She left him standing there with his mouth open. Just like a girl of fourteen would do.'

Stanley spoke out of the corner of his mouth, facing straight ahead.

'She's sitting right behind us, love. It seems cruel talking about her just because we know she can't hear what we're saying.'

But Josie was no longer listening to him. She would be able to square Olive before Saturday, and write to Bill to say she had managed to get away for the weekend. She closed her eyes against the sudden upsurge of excitement gripping her insides with cramp. For the first time she would lie in a bed with him, in his arms, for a whole night. She resisted the

48

overwhelming temptation to shout her happiness aloud.

'See, it's clouding over. I thought that sunshine was too good to last,' she said.

For something to say.

Three

Christine Duckworth had no qualms about claiming to be on war work. The two full days, plus the Saturday morning stint in her father's office, bored her to distraction. She couldn't make up her mind which was the most tedious – the hours spent at the dark green filing cabinets, or the time spent sitting at the switchboard passing callers through to the right departments.

Her voluntary work at the YMCA was beginning to be deadly monotonous, too. All those hands stretched out for mugs of tea, husbands, sweethearts, most of them newly joined up and homesick, wanting stamps, cigarettes and change for the telephones. Endless trays of sausages to be shoved in and out of the ovens. Rows upon rows, pricked and lined up. When this bloody awful war was over she vowed she would never look a sausage in the face again. When things got back to normal she would go back to her modelling job in Manchester, weaving between the tables in the restaurant of the big store wearing gorgeous clothes, little pill-box hats with eye veils, silk stockings, crêpe-de-Chine underskirts, and French knickers with lace. It was all hush-hush of course, but clothes rationing was bound to come in before long. Daddy had said so.

'There's a glut of machinists,' he had said, 'all better employed on munitions or making parachutes. It's patriotic to look shabby at the moment, anyway. A good idea I reckon if they made Churchill's siren suit the national dress till the war's over.'

'Oh, my God!' Christine had closed her eyes at the thought of her five-foot-tall plump mother in a navy-blue siren suit, flanked by her bean-pole father in a thick khaki ditto. 'Oh, my God!'

Christine was in one of her 'Oh, my God!' moods at the moment. Coming out into the street that wet Saturday lunchtime she looked up at the grey blanket of sky and shuddered. She unfurled her scarlet umbrella, stepped off the pavement and saw the airman leaning nonchalantly against the wall across the road. He was so wet she could see the rain dripping from the neb of his cap, and as she stared a sailor walked past and winked at her, his collar flapping upwards like a sail caught in a sea breeze.

Ignoring him she picked her way carefully over the flagstones. Lifting her head she smiled radiantly.

'Can I help you at all?'

When she spoke to a man Christine's voice automatically changed to a throaty murmur. She had a habit of lowering her green eyes, then raising them quickly. She could recognize even the smallest flicker of interest in a man's eyes before he was aware of it himself, but this time she wasn't too sure.

Lee Willis levered himself slightly away from the wall and grinned at the glossy girl fluttering her eyelashes at him. Her head was swathed in a white turban knotted at the front, showing a glimpse of auburn hair. The collar of her white riding mackintosh was turned up, framing a face of chiselled beauty, in which the sharp boniness of her nose added rather than detracted from the classical perfection. They didn't grow girls shiny as this one in the deep heart of Texas; of that he was certain sure.

'Well now, ma'am. You might just be able to help me at that.'

Christine's eyes stretched wide. Oh, my God, an American! Wearing Air Force uniform, too. A more than presentable one, with eyes as blue as cornflowers. Her voice dropped to an even huskier note.

'You're a long way from home. The Americans haven't come into the war without someone telling me, have they?'

'No, ma'am. I guess I jumped the gun.' Lee's eyes slid away to resume his unblinking scrutiny of the building across the road. 'I'm looking for a girl I met a while back.' He flipped a raindrop from the end of his nose. 'I didn't catch her

51

name, but she's small and kinda pretty with dark curly hair. She works in the place you just came out of, ma'am.'

With difficulty Christine kept the smile pinned to her face. She allowed her head to fall artlessly to one side. 'Oh dear, that's too bad. There's no one in there now.' Her expression changed to one of regret. 'I'm Christine Duckworth.' She pointed to the brass plate at one side of the main door. 'That's my father. If you'd like to . . . what I mean is . . . you'd be welcome . . .'

'There she is! Thanks, ma'am, thanks a lot.'

'Shooting across the street as if he'd been fired from a bloody catapult,' Christine told herself crossly, then watched with narrowed eyes as the American grinned down into Sally Barnes's astonished face.

The deaf girl who sat at her typewriter as if she was growing from it. Sally Barnes with that look about her as if she'd never been exposed, even to the wind.

Johnnie Barnes's sister. Christine suddenly swung the red umbrella down to cover her face. Johnnie, no doubt at that moment on a troopship on his way overseas, leaving her with a disbelieving niggle of worry that at times almost stopped her heart with its implications.

Christine stepped from the kerb straight into a gutter awash with a torrent of water. 'Oh, my God!' she said furiously, before walking away.

'So when we got a forty-eight hour pass before being drafted, I knew I had to get the hell out of the camp.'

Lee stood with Sally at the tram stop, grinning with a boyish delight. 'I've done over fifty flying hours, passed my exams, and now I'm going guess where, to complete my flying training?'

'No?' Sally's delight matched his own. 'Not . . . ?'

'Yep. Back to real coffee, lights that come on when it's dark outside.' He touched her nose with the tip of his finger. 'Not *quite* back home, but to Canada – the right side of the Atlantic for me, anyways up.'

'If you haven't died of pneumonia before you get there.' Sally's rueful glance took in his sodden appearance, from the cap oozing moisture to the trousers clinging black-wet to his legs. Her mouth set in lines of an almost motherly concern. 'We can be at my house in less than half an hour, then you can take those wet things off. My brother's things should fit you.' Gently she pushed him into position in the queue, laughing at him over her shoulder. 'Both my parents are away for the weekend so what I'll find for lunch is anybody's guess. Toasted spam sandwiches most likely.'

Obediently Lee followed her to stand meekly in line. His heart contracted with an emotion he didn't recognize. This girl, this lovely laughing half-child, with the strange inflections in her voice, she was bloody unique. She just had to be. He climbed onto the tram and followed Sally to a seat at the front, rubbing his chin reflectively. Now take that shiny dame, that Christine Duckworth. If she'd made him a proposition like that he would have got the message right off.

'Sure your parents won't mind?'

'Why should they?' Sally's blue-grey eyes brimmed with mischief. 'But it would look better if I knew your name, I suppose.'

So solemnly they exchanged names and as solemnly shook hands.

'Okay. Now we're properly acquainted.' Lee turned to stare out of the window with interest. The English countryside he had found as pretty as a charming water-colour picture. But the cities were another thing altogether.

'Rows and rows of identical houses in sooty brick,' he had written in his letters back home. 'Shabby grimy shops with long queues snaking along grey pavements. Gaps where buildings once stood. It's enough to scare the pants off you.'

'We had a bomb down our road,' Sally told him. 'You remember I told you I'd just missed seeing my friend at the station? Well, his mother was killed, and the whole of his house destroyed.'

'Holy Joe! But that's terrible!' Lee stretched out a big square hand and squeezed Sally's knee. 'That sure was tough luck. What will he do now, your friend? Has he got family to visit with when his furloughs come round?'

Sally's expression was bleak. 'I don't think so. His mother was a kind of recluse, you know? And David . . . well, the Air Force was his career before the war started. He hasn't got any relatives that I know of, and his friends are all in the Air Force. He's very much alone.'

Lee saw the shadows on her face, and to distract her he wiggled his fingers at a small boy sitting in front, kneeling up on the seat and staring with eyes narrowed into suspicious slits.

'Hi there!' he grinned.

'Are you on the films, mister?' The boy's voice was hoarse with excitement.

His mother turned round and smiled an apology. 'He heard you talking in the queue. He thinks you might be Errol Flynn.'

Lee shook his head. 'Nope. I never even got to meet Errol Flynn. He don't have much truck with cowboys like me.'

The boy's eyes stretched wide. 'A *real* cowboy? Shooting Red Indians, mister?'

'Nope. Now how can I shoot Red Indians when my grandma's an old Indian squaw? I can't shoot up my own family. That would be real mean, young guy, wouldn't you say so?'

'Did you mean it when you told the boy on the tram your grandma was an Indian squaw?'

They were in the garden, sitting side by side in deckchairs in the pale afternoon sun. Sally's house had proved a revelation to Lee. The rooms were so small, the neighbours so close, and the garden, which he called a yard, no more than apron-sized. Now that the rain had stopped the air was fresh and clean-smelling. He had talked until his jaw ached, realizing for perhaps the first time how much of a loner he had become back at the camp. He had got used to the way Sally's eyes never once left his face as he talked. She seemed able to read his slow Texan drawl easily, and he marvelled at her expertise.

'Sure,' he told her. 'My momma's momma was a real honest-to-goodness squaw, but I take after my pa. He was raised in Oklahoma. They're a crazy pair. They work that old farm all by themselves now I'm gone, and out of the fifteen acres at least seven are cultivated. We have five black cows, one brown bull, three pigs, chickens, ducks and geese. The yard will be beautiful right now. There's a dark red amaryllis right by the porch, and roses and honeysuckle. And I swear those old beans grow like crazy right before your eyes.'

'It sounds wonderful.' Sally breathed deeply and closed her eyes. She opened them again and caught him staring at her, the bright blue eyes taking in every detail of her face. Acutely embarrassed, she jumped up and began to walk back to the house, moving stiffly in case her bottom wiggled. He was like no man she had ever known. He was *different*, vital, lifting her out of herself, making her feel as if she herself was somehow different, prettier, more vivacious, able to make him laugh at almost everything she said. Just looking at him was exhilarating because he was so . . . so alive, with his big hands and his strong, broad body. And his hair – cut so short, showing a strip of skin above his small ears. Bright gold hair like a baby's, making her want to stretch out a hand and run her fingers through it.

When he came up behind her and touched her shoulder she blushed, and it seemed as if a tide of emotion flowed between them. She moved away, facing him from a safer distance, suddenly unsure of herself.

'Is there anywhere round here we can go dancing, honey?' He snapped his fingers. 'I don't have to leave till late. I sure would like to take you dancing, Sally.'

Her blush deepened so that it seemed her eyes sparkled with tears. 'There's always a dance on at the church hall down the road on Saturday evenings, but it wouldn't be any good. I've never danced.'

Suddenly he leaned towards her, took her face between his hands and kissed her lightly on her mouth. 'Then tonight you dance. With me. Okay?'

When they walked into the hall the trio on the dais were playing a spirited version of 'Roll out the Barrel'. Lee grinned delightedly at the peanut-sized guy on the drums waving his arms about in a frenzy. He was sure he could feel the soles of his feet beginning to itch. He guessed that Sally could feel the floor vibrating, yet when he looked at her there was a frightened stillness about her face that touched some inner core of sensitivity inside him he hadn't known about. With

55

difficulty he suppressed the desire to pull her with him onto the floor to mingle with the dancers.

'There's a coupla seats over there.' He smiled at her, and as she smiled back he saw that her short upper lip was glistening with perspiration.

'Tell me some more about where you live,' she said when they were seated close together on two little hard chairs. 'The weather,' she added feverishly. 'Are the winters cold in Texas?'

The music stopped and two by two the couples left the floor, girls in flowered print dresses, soldiers, airmen, sailors, and the odd ones in civilian suits.

Lee laughed. 'Okay. The weather. Well, the winters back home can be pretty mean. My parents have a big wood-burning stove in their bedroom, and in the winter they go to bed early and stay there till it starts to come light. There's a sort of lake I haven't told you about. It's outside the front of the house and we have a boat. Ouchita she's called. That's the name of an Indian tribe, and most times there's some mighty good fishing.'

Suddenly he got up and jerked Sally to her feet. The band was playing a tortured version of the song on everyone's lips at the end of that second year of the war, a song about a married couple who spent a blissful leave in 'Room Five Hundred and Four'. Feet were moving slowly to the rhythm, cheeks pressed to cheeks, and as Lee pulled Sally into his arms he pressed a hand tightly against her back, guiding her into the steps, willing her to follow. For a moment she seemed to relax against him, then she stumbled, and when he looked into her eyes the blind panic mirrored there made him catch his breath.

'Please! I can't do it! Lee! People are staring at me!'

Her lips were trembling, her grey eyes wide and pleading. She was so devastatingly pretty in her pink dress with its V-neckline edged with white frilling, that Lee gave into temptation, bent his head and kissed her. It was a tender, fleeting caress, meant to calm, but she pushed him from her with a violence that rocked him back on his heels before she rushed away through the black-out curtain over the door into the entrance hall.

He found her outside, leaning against the wall, staring into the pale darkness over the spare land to where a sloping row of terraced houses wound its way down to the canal. Reaching for her hand he felt it balled into a tight fist, the nails digging into her palm. Bewildered, he jiggled it up and down.

'Sally? Honey? I didn't mean no disrespect.' His wide grin showed the gleam of strong white teeth. 'C'mon now. We've been alone in your house for most of the day, so why should I want to . . .' he searched for the right word '. . . ravish you on the dance floor, with Glen Miller in there doing his nut on the saxophone?'

To his relief he felt her fingers uncurl into his hand. 'What's wrong, honey?' He made a move to draw her to him, then stopped as he felt her whole body stiffen in his grasp.

Sally gave a deep sigh. How could she ever explain to this carefree boy with the laughing eyes that back there in the warm darkness, the hand pressing her firmly against him, the mouth suddenly covering her own, had been for a terrifying moment David Turner's hand and mouth, the politeness changed so that he became a stranger with burning face and groping tearing fingers?

'I'm sorry, Lee.' She smiled. 'I was just being stupid. I'm stupid about a lot of things. I'm pretty damn foolish altogether, really.' Then, surprising him, she kissed his face, softly at the side of his mouth. 'Okay. Let's go back inside and try again. Huh?'

And now, back in the hall, as they danced, Sally realized with a sudden upsurge of delight that she was feeling the music in her toes. She was anticipating Lee's movements, matching her steps to his.

'Do you come here often?' he asked, his blue eyes twinkling. 'You dance like Ginger Rogers.'

'I *taught* Ginger Rogers,' she said.

'We must come again.'

'When you come back.'

'When I come back.'

He laid his cheek against hers and they moved as one person. When a small blonde girl stepped up onto the platform and sang in a throaty voice Lee joined in and was delighted when Sally whispered the words softly, following his lips as easily as she followed his steps.

'The girls at work sing it,' she explained, as Lee swung her round before they clapped for an encore.

And this time the fair-haired girl sang about a nightingale in Berkeley Square, but Lee was silent. He was seeing the London square as he had seen it on one of his last leaves, battered and torn by a landmine, with no tiny bird singing its heart out in the leafy splendour of the trees.

There was only a brief moment of panic when a soldier with freckles dotting his face like brown measles excused Sally, but they managed. She managed. With the pride of an indulgent father Lee watched her, and then it was the two of them dancing dreamily through the last waltz, and standing to attention for 'God Save the King' before going out into the blacked-out streets for the short walk home.

'I ought to be going,' Lee said later in the living room of Sally's house. 'But let's sit in the firelight. I don't want to leave you.'

'Then don't.'

'You mean . . . ?' Lee held his breath. Her grey eyes were unbearably young. He pulled her down onto the rug by the fire, trembling as she made no protest.

'You can sleep in John's room, then tomorrow we'll . . . I know what we'll do. We'll go out into the country if it's fine. You can ride a bicycle, can't you? There are two in the shed. I can show you a bluebell wood not far from here.'

'I've never seen a bluebell wood.'

'Well, tomorrow you will. They have long juicy stems and they smell of summer.'

'You smell of summer.'

She smiled, then as he held her face still for his kiss he saw her eyes close and the long dark lashes fan out on her rounded cheeks. When he ran his finger-tips over her breasts she lay still, then when he began to unbutton her dress she sat up suddenly and he saw with surprise that her eyes were wet with tears.

'That was the first time I've ever enjoyed being kissed,' she assured him solemnly. 'I never knew either that happiness could make you cry.'

'I think it's time you went up to bed.' Lee smiled at her,

tucking a wayward strand of curly hair behind her ear. He could feel his heart hammering and the ache of desire like a physical pain.

But a voice somewhere in his head was saying: 'You can't. It's all set up for you, Lee Willis, but you can't. An' you know why? Because her eyes are too *young*, that's goddamned why!'

With his head on John Barnes's pillow and his arms stretched out on John Barnes's dark green taffeta eiderdown, Lee found himself thinking for no good reason he could fathom about the Presbyterian church he attended back home.

No fancy doctrine there, just a plain wood pulpit and the stars and stripes flag in the corner, the preacher in his best Sunday suit, and the hymns set to a swinging rhythm. His momma in her go-to-Chapel hat, and his pa in a checked tuxedo, the love of a munificent God, and His wrath for the wrongdoers.

'You'd have been mighty proud of your wandering boy tonight, momma.' He whispered the words aloud, then his thoughts switched off abruptly as he heard the sirens wail, followed almost at once by the ponderous drone of planes.

Jumping out of bed he went over to the window and drew back the lined curtains, opened the casement window and leaned far out, his eyes searching the night sky. It was the roar, it seemed, of hundreds trundling over the rooftops like massive steamrollers, filling the air with a continuous pulsating thunder. He imagined the German aircrews hours back being briefed, saw the hurry and bustle on that far-off airfield with a gasoline lorry chugging around filling tanks. He imagined the men struggling into flying suits, strapping on their parachutes. He thought about the incongruity of it all.

Then he went across the landing into Sally's room.

There was no air-raid warning at Morecambe. The Lancashire holiday resort slept beneath a peaceful sky. Bill Green, Glasgow born, bull-necked and ruddy of complexion, with two small sons built on the same sturdy lines and a wife he loved in his own fashion, woke from a deep sleep and turned his head to stare at the platinum-blonde head on his pillow.

The extent of Josie's passion had delighted him at first, then dismayed him.

'I love you, love you,' she had moaned, nipping his flesh with her teeth, kissing him all over in a way his wife would have thought disgusting and abandoned. 'Bill, oh Bill, my own sweet love,' she had groaned, twisting her sweat-drenched head from side to side on the pillow. 'Oh no, no, no, not yet! Please, oh please . . .'

Now she was sleeping, her face small and pinched beneath the pale halo of her candy-floss hair, her lips slightly open and a purr of a snore irritating and preventing him from going back to sleep again.

Pushing himself up on his elbows, Bill reached out and took a cigarette from the packet on the bedside table, lit it and blew a cloud of smoke straight up to the rather dirty ceiling of the little guesthouse.

Okay, okay, so he'd wangled a weekend together for them. Okay, so his wife need never find out. Okay, so Josie's old man thought she was spending her time with Olive Marsden from the shop. It was merely what his mates would have called a dirty weekend. In his book too. Bill dragged deeply on the cigarette, drawing the smoke into his lungs, then coughed.

Immediately, as he had feared she would, Josie woke up and within seconds her arms were round his waist, holding him tightly. Her voice, soft with sleep, had a dreamlike, childish quality in it.

'Bill . . . Oh, Bill, did you ever dream it could be like that?' she purred, snuggling against him like a kitten. 'I ought to feel guilty, but I don't. I feel happier than I've ever felt in my life. Bill? Loving somebody like I love you can't be wicked, can it?'

She tried to pull him down beside her in the bed, but he held her off, deliberately puffing hard at the dwindling cigarette. 'Men wouldn't even think of it as being wicked,' he told her, holding her wandering hand in a firm grasp. 'But then, men are different, and that's a fact.'

'I *know* they're different.' Josie's hand freed itself, making him cry out before he leaned across to stub out the cigarette.

'Only one more day,' she whispered, when it was over. 'I

can't go back, Bill. You've no idea what it's like.'

With trembling hands he reached out for another cigarette. 'A fine PT instructor I'll make next week. I doubt if I could blow a fly off a rice pudding at the moment! What've you been doing, lass? Saving all that up till you met me?'

Too late he realized his mistake.

'Yes.' Josie sat up and asked for a cigarette. 'I should never have married him, Bill.' As he flicked his lighter he saw how her eyes were ringed with smudged mascara and the sight somehow sickened him. All the times they'd spent dancing together, even from his new posting to Lancaster Barracks, he had thought how marvellous it would be to take this crazy bottle-blonde away for a passionate weekend. Their own Room 504. Just a bit of the old that there, a lot of fun and no harm done. Now she was playing it all wrong. He narrowed his eyes against the up-curl of smoke.

'Look, lassie.' He balanced a round glass ash-tray on the sheet between them. 'I'm a married man with two kids. You've always known that. I may not be God's gift as a husband, but I'm not exactly a Casanova either. I don't make a habit of this. It's the war. It splits families up and makes us do things we wouldn't dream of doing normally. When it's all over we'll just go back to the way we were before. I'd almost finished my stint in the army anyway, and once we've got old Hitler licked I'll be mowing the lawn of a Sunday and taking the kids fishing. This is just a dream, a ruddy marvellous dream, but a dream just the same.'

'Not for me it isn't!' Josie's voice was choked with sobs. 'We love each other, Bill. You said I was like your other half, but that's not true. I'm more than that. I *am* you, and without you I have nothing.' She began to cry, ugly tearing sobs that wrenched her face out of shape. 'If the war ending means I'm going to lose you then I hope it goes on for ever! I'll get away to see you again – nothing can stop me! The only time I'm really alive is when I'm with you. You're my sort. You don't mind hurting people if hurting them gets you what you want. You haven't told me much about your wife, but I know her. Oh, yes, I know her, Bill, because I've got a partner like her at home. Too bloody good to live. An' I won't spend the rest of my life pretending that everything's okay. I can't!'

61

To his dismay her voice rose hysterically. 'Do you know what I call him? "Once a fortnight", that's my private name for my husband. And when the day comes round he *asks* me! We can be sitting round the fire and he'll look at me and say: "All right tonight, love?" Then when it happens it's over, quick as a flash, an' he thinks he's . . .'

'Stop it!' Almost without volition Bill shot out a tattooed right arm, snatched the cigarette from her and ground it out along with his own in the glass ash-tray. 'You know what you're doing, you stupid woman? You're making me feel *sorry* for him, not sorry for *you*! That sort of talk makes me sick to my stomach. So put a bloody sock in it, will you?'

Then, because he couldn't bear the sound of her sobbing, he put his arms round her, staring blindly over her shoulder, feeling disturbed, disgruntled and illogically betrayed.

The next afternoon Sally and Lee rode their bicycles out into the country, and just as she had promised when they came to the woods by the sides of the river they could smell the heady crushed scent of the first bluebells. A rather reluctant sun was warm on their faces, and when they propped the bicycles against a hedge and sat side by side on a fallen log Lee decided that this part of England was the part he would always want to remember. In his mind he was already composing his next letter back home describing the fields like parklands where sheep grazed, the stone cottages set behind neat gardens, and the winding lanes where hedgerows grew greenly on either side.

The long vigil he had kept in Sally's room the night before had left him with a strange floating tiredness, so that when they sat down on a low stile and he lifted his eyes to where the trees made a jig-saw pattern against the blue sky he experienced a sensation of dizziness. Amazingly, because he hadn't known her long enough to realize the extent of her deafness, the noise of the bombers had failed to penetrate the layers of her deep sleeping. So he had let her sleep. He had sat bolt upright in the chair by her bed, watching her face on the pillow, hearing the guns with their staccato bark, and the crunch of bombs not quite far enough away to be reassuring.

'You look tired,' she said, and he turned and smiled at her.

'I suppose it was sleeping in a strange bed,' she said wisely. 'It's always the same the first time. Mum's always saying she'll get a new mattress for John's bed, but he won't let her. He says it fits his body after all these years.' Her eyes clouded. 'I wonder how long it will be before we hear from him? Dad says Crete will be the next to go. He's sure John is out there somewhere.'

'This war . . .' Lee took her hand in his and ran his thumb slowly over and round the pulse at her wrist. In her green jumper and thin skirt her figure was as rounded and firm as an apple. He wanted to take her in his arms, hold her tight against him, keep her safe, and promise to cherish her for ever. Instead he said: 'I shouldn't be away all that long. Will you write to me and be here when I come back? Will you be my girl, Sally, honey?'

'You can kiss me,' she said. 'Like you did last night, then I might consider it. It was lovely . . . And so was that,' she added, when the long, tender kiss was over.

Her beautiful eyes were sparkling with happiness, not slumberous with desire. When they mounted their bicycles again she began to freewheel down the hill, her skirt riding up, showing for a tantalizing moment a strip of flesh between the top of her stocking and the lace frill of her knickers. 'Try and catch me!' Her voice floated back as the road dipped then wound its way upwards again. 'Yes, I will!' she called. 'I'll be your girl if you want me.'

If he wanted her! Holy Joe! She was teasing him, and the goddamned thing was she didn't know it. She was as naïve as a child, as soft and sweet-smelling as the bluebells. This was England, fighting for its life, and somehow he had found himself an English girl as untouched and innocent as a new-born babe. Where the hell had she *been* all her life? Lee pedalled after her, letting her win, his heart swelling with an emotion he wasn't ready to place. Not yet.

'Have you never been away from home?' They sat outside a tiny eighteenth-century inn, their drinks on a rough-hewn oak table in front of them. 'Never been to college?'

Sally wrinkled her nose at him above the glass tankard. 'No. You know something? I've never even had a holiday away from my parents.' She looked away from him. 'They worry about me being . . . about not hearing. A doctor wanted me to go to a special school once, but they wouldn't let me go. The only extra thing I had was lip-reading lessons, then my father fought to have me accepted at the local grammar school.' Her chin lifted. 'I passed my scholarship when I was ten, Lee Willis, that's a year early, and I was half-way through the oral examination at the Education Office before the three examiners realized.' Suddenly her eyes flashed. 'I'm deaf, not daft!'

'Oh, Sally . . .' He put an arm round her, drawing her close. 'Why do I have to go away, right now?'

His throat tightened with an almost unbearable sadness. At twenty-three, and surely worldly-wise, Lee was experiencing the acute pain of his first real love, painfully serious and tenderly solemn. 'If anyone ever tries to hurt you, I'll kill them,' he whispered. When she raised her head and asked him to repeat what he'd just said, he shook his head and said it didn't matter.

It wasn't until they were on their way home that Sally remembered the bluebells.

'We forgot to pick them,' she said. 'I wanted us to ride back with huge bunches tied to our handlebars, with the long stalks all pale and juicy and the flowers as blue . . .' she hesitated '. . . as blue as your eyes. Is that a soppy thing to say to a man?'

'Not the way you say it.'

'It's been a lovely day, hasn't it?'

'Wizard.'

She laughed out loud. 'You sound like an Englishman when you say that. David talks like that sometimes. Wizard. Good show. Bloody good show.'

'David? The guy from down the street?' Lee felt a dark fear run over him. 'Will you be seeing him while I'm away?'

'I don't expect so.' Sally shrugged her shoulders. 'When will you be back? Can you say?'

'About four months, I guess.'

'When the leaves turn brown.'

'When the leaves turn brown, in the fall, honey lamb.'

He allowed her to walk with him down to the tram stop when the time came to go, but shook his head firmly when she wanted to go all the way to the station. He had the strangest feeling as he kissed her goodbye and swung himself onto the boarding platform. It was a feeling compounded of the surety of joy. He knew that he would return to find her waiting for him. He would have his wings, and a commission, God willing. He would come back to this little blacked-out island and she would be there. It was as simple and inevitable as that.

Sometimes the trams came with long waiting distances in between, with queue-conditioned Britishers standing patiently in line, but that Sunday evening, for no particular reason, two trams trundled almost empty to the terminus together.

Sally, walking slowly in a dream-like trance, turned round at the brow of the hill, a hundred yards from home, to see Josie coming up behind her. Her mother was carrying a suitcase, letting it bang listlessly against her legs as if it was weighed down with books and not merely a change of clothing and a black chiffon nightdress.

Smiling, Sally took the case from her, laughing and swinging it free. 'You look tired, Mum. Did you have a lovely time? Oh, weren't you lucky with the weather? Tell me first what you did and then I've got something to tell you!'

'Your father's back.' Josie nodded at the front door, opened into the vestibule, with its inner door still devoid of its ruby red panes of glass. 'I thought he said it would be midnight before he got back. They must have knocked off half-way through the flamin' battle.'

She was so pale, so obviously depressed, that Sally's happiness evaporated into thin air. Suddenly an inexplicable sense of dread filled her, the lovely golden day fading as a small grey cloud covered the dying rays of the sun. Following her mother through the hall and into the living-room beyond she could feel her heart racing with an uneasy premonition of trouble to come.

'So you're back!' Stanley, his normally pale face burned brick red by the sun, stood by the fireplace, his heavy pack and his forage cap on the settee behind him, his rifle propped up against its side. 'Did you have a good time at Morecambe?'

he asked, with a twisted smile. 'Did Olive enjoy it as well?'

'It was lovely.' Josie took off her hat and ran her fingers through her hair. 'A nice change. Just what the doctor ordered.'

'And Olive's gone home now?' Stanley's voice was ominously quiet, but Sally read him as easily as if he had shouted the question at the top of his voice.

'Yes. Olive's gone home. I left her down at the station.' Josie picked up her case and plonked her hat back on her head, tilting it over her eyes and winking at Sally. 'The last I saw of her was her backside as she barged onto a tram.'

Sally's eyes swivelled sharply to her father's face, hoping to see the smile his wife's clowning always induced. But there was no smile, not even the faintest gleam of amusement in his eyes.

'Stop where you are!' He put up an arm. 'I haven't finished yet.'

'Yes sir!' Josie sketched a cheeky salute.

'Go up to your room, Sally.' Stanley spoke through set lips, and suddenly the sense of fear was there again, a tight sensation in Sally's throat.

'No,' she said. 'I'm not a child. I'd rather stay.'

Stanley nodded. 'Right. Then stay. Stay and listen. Listen well.' He tilted his small head so that she saw the working of his prominent Adam's apple. 'There was a raid last night. A bad one, and down the town a stick of bombs fell on a row of shops. Two of them got a direct hit, and one of them, madam, was yours!'

'Oh, my God!' Josie's face crumpled, and beneath the tiny hat perched comically over her eyebrows her face paled, leaving the round spots of rouge on her cheeks standing out in startling contrast.

'Your friend Olive was fire-watching.' Stanley clenched his hands into fists, raised them, then lowered them slowly to his sides. 'By a miracle she wasn't killed, not quite. But when they dug her out they left one of her legs behind, so you seeing her running for a tram was a bloody miracle, wasn't it?'

'You cruel bugger! You cruel, heartless bugger!' Josie rushed at him, only to have her wrists grasped. She stared in horror into Stanley's face. 'You trapped me! An awful thing like that happens and all you think about is catching me out!' She tried to jerk free but he held her from him, his whole expression clouded with a terrible disgust.

'It might have been *me*!' Josie screamed at the top of her voice. 'All right then, so I didn't go away with Olive, but what you don't know is that she stood in for me. It should have been *me* on fire-watching last night, but she did it for me! And I'll tell you something for nothing. I wish it had been me! I wish that bomb had finished me off proper so I would be out of this flamin' war, and I wish I'd stopped away because there's nowt for me here. There never has been and from now on there never will be!'

They were swaying together, one struggling to hold and the other to break away. Their mouths were opening wide as they shouted furiously at each other.

When Stanley let go suddenly, thrusting her from him in disgust, Josie staggered for a moment, lost her balance and fell, striking her head hard against the jutting edge of the sideboard. Then as she got to her knees, blood seeping from a cut on her forehead, Sally saw her grope wildly for the rifle, close her hands round it and lift it, pointing the muzzle straight at Stanley.

'Mum!' With a strangled cry Sally threw herself in front of her father. 'No! Please! Stop it! Both of you. Stop!' She was shaking violently.

Stepping forward, pinioning both her arms, Stanley swung her round to face him. She saw the bitter anguish in his eyes. 'It's not loaded, chuck.' He shook her gently. 'Now will you do as I asked before and go upstairs?' His face was grey. 'This is between me and your mother. Right?'

As she stumbled past her mother, Sally saw a face with all the laughter wiped from it. A middle-aged face with blood running down a cheek, past a mouth with the purple lipstick smeared and chewed.

For how long Sally sat on the edge of her bed she had no clear recollection. There was no way she could creep out on the landing to listen, to reassure herself that the shouting and the violence was finished. Instead she sat there, small and defeated, cocooned in her own web of total silence, numb with pain, rocking herself backwards and forwards.

When her door burst open and she saw Josie standing there, she got up slowly from the bed.

'Mum?' She took a step forward, but Josie backed away.

'There's been somebody sleeping in John's bed. Somebody who left this behind.' Holding out her hand she dropped a cigarette lighter onto the carpet. 'Seems I'm not the only whore in this house, in spite of what your father says.' Her whole body slumped. 'We only need to find out that your father's got Miss Shawfield at the office preggy and we would make a right trio, wouldn't we?'

Then, the crude joke over, she went out of the room, slamming the door behind her.

And Sally knew that the sweetness of her bluebell day had vanished as if it had never been.

Four

Stanley Barnes put his head back, closed his eyes, and stretched out his legs over the fluffy rug in front of the glowing fire. For that first week in August it had rained almost every day, but here in the cosy flat at the top of an old Victorian house he felt a creeping sense of peace.

The Russians were more than holding their own against the Germans. Their scorched earth policy was the admiration of every Britisher, and the 'V for Victory' sign was everywhere, a comforting indication to Stanley that his beloved country was a long way from defeat.

'London is simply amazing. I can't describe the feeling one gets when one sees St Paul's great dome rising from the ruins. We went to see Disney's *Fantasia* one evening and the music was glorious. When it comes up here you must see it, Stanley.'

He opened his eyes and smiled at the woman curled up on the rug with her back against the chair opposite to his own. Barbara Shawfield, a Clerical Officer in his department at Telephone House, had a quiet serenity about her, plus an almost antiseptic cleanliness, accentuated by the white collars she often wore tacked into the necklines of her dresses. It was the first time Stanley had been to her flat, but lately, at the office, they had gravitated together whenever possible, sharing the same table in the canteen and walking together through the streets to the tram stop.

'I ought to be going.' He settled more comfortably. 'But my daughter won't be home for a long time yet, and since my wife started on night shifts at the ordnance factory it's a case of her coming back in the mornings as I go out to work. A topsy-turvy life I suppose.'

Barbara tore her gaze reluctantly away from the tired, shabby man to stare into the fire. She knew all about his wife and his deaf daughter. She had had Josie Barnes pointed out to her once in the market and had been asking herself ever since how a man like Stanley could ever have married a woman so obviously out of his class. From her dyed hair to her pillar box red swagger coat, Josie had looked what she was – common. And lately he had worn an air of sadness, sitting at his desk, talking on the telephone, taking off his spectacles and rubbing his aching eyes. She had wanted to ask him if there was anything she could do to help. But sensibly she had bided her time, and now, to their mutual surprise, here he was sitting as she had so often imagined him in her flat, smiling at her.

'Please let me make you something to eat.' She nodded towards the tiny kitchen leading off the pleasant room. 'I've got a hoarded tin of prawns, and some tomatoes. It wouldn't take a minute to make a salad. That's what I'll be having anyway.'

'I don't believe you.' Stanley wagged a finger at her. 'A tin of prawns calls for a celebration, a sharing. I can't see you woofing them down all on your own.'

But him being there *was* a celebration, Barbara thought. She suggested a spot of music, feeling instinctively it was in keeping with his mood.

'Debussy? I always think that Debussy goes with rain at the windows and a fire in the grate.'

Stanley closed his eyes again and felt peace trickle through him in a warm tide. Yet even as he relaxed, his mind chewed over and fretted about the situation at home. Since that May evening when Josie had flown at him in a frenzy, she had slept in John's room, going off to her new job of work making sten guns and shell parts, wearing trousers and bundling her blonde hair up into a turban. Of the man with whom she had spent the weekend he had heard no more, and his wounded pride would not permit him to ask. They were strangers living together, if you could call it living. Even Sally had changed. There was a hardness about her eyes that had never been there before. If she wasn't writing long letters to her American she was out dancing with her friends from work.

Sally dancing! Going out alone and coming home alone as far as he could judge, slapping together a make-shift meal for them in the evenings, picking at hers, then flying off with her sandals in a paper bag. If it hadn't been for the companionship of his friends in the Home Guard Stanley felt at times he would have sunk into an unhealthy state of depression.

The music was so beautiful. If he wasn't careful the melancholy choking at his throat would spill out into his eyes. He was lonely. Why not admit it? He was achingly, dreadfully lonely. He opened his eyes to see Barbara at the gramophone turning the sound down, then turning to stare at him with a look of such sympathy and caring on her face that he had to blink the threatening tears away.

'Do you listen to Quentin Reynolds on the wireless?' She came to kneel down on the rug by his side, so close he could smell the sharp flower scent she used. Lily-of-the-valley, he guessed, and was reminded of how Josie had once told him it was her favourite flower. Because of that he had planted a clump in the back garden, in a patch dug over now for rows of Brussels sprouts.

'He's so funny when he addresses Hitler by his real name. Schicklgruber. He's so clever with a turn of phrase, don't you think? His voice gave me a positive thrill when he declared it unthinkable that a man by the name of Winston Churchill could ever bow the knee to someone called Schicklgruber . . .'

Stanley smiled. He felt his loneliness, his recent terrifying sense of inadequacy, leaving him as his deeply considered thoughts spilled into words. Words listened to and understood by a woman at his side. The music soared to haunting heights as the rain slid silently down the long window, and in the darkening room a soothing sense of warmth and tranquillity seemed to wrap him around.

'He was going to kiss me,' Barbara told herself when Stanley had gone. He had jumped up from his chair with a suddenness that had startled her for a moment. 'That lovely man. In another minute he *would* have kissed me. The kiss was there between us, I know it.'

She picked up the brown velvet cushion from the chair where he had sat, and hugged it to her, swaying gently backwards and forwards on her sturdy heels, seeing their heads drawing closer together and her eyes half closing in anticipation of the kiss that hadn't materialized.

At twenty-nine years old Barbara Shawfield had known only one man, and then in what she thought to herself as a purely spiritual way. Like Stanley Barnes, he had been unhappily married too. For four years she had anguished about him, meeting him now and again to hold hands across a restaurant table, drinking in his every word and expression as he assured her she was the only joy in his life, his one bright star. She had wasted long, lonely hours waiting for the telephone to ring, willing it to ring, but understanding when it didn't. His wife had been a semi-invalid, and so of course he couldn't leave her, but Barbara's love had sustained him through what he had described as his barren existence. To consummate their love would have despoiled its loveliness, he had said. She had believed that too until the day she had seen him out with his wife, holding her arm with tender solicitude as, heavily pregnant, she had made her way slowly along the pavement.

Barbara had cried for a month, grieved for six more, then on her promotion to the engineers' department at Telephone House had transferred all her longing to Stanley Barnes.

'Oh, my love,' she whispered. 'My own dear love.' She turned the record over, and to the background of Debussy took a precious egg from the cupboard and began to boil it for her supper.

The object of her affection was at that very moment hurrying down the road, with his dot-and-carry-one walk, to catch his tram, the brim of his dark brown trilby pulled low over his forehead. He was glancing at his watch, shaking his head and hoping he would be home in time for the nine o'clock news. Cursing himself for staying so long, but admitting how pleasing it was to have found a friend. There was no silly romantic nonsense about Miss Shawfield, he decided as he took his place at the end of a long, dripping queue. She was more like a man than a woman in her tweed skirts and tailored blouses, with her mouse-coloured hair scragged back into a sausage-like roll. For a fleeting second he wondered why she had never married? At thirty or thereabouts she must have considered it at times? As he moved his head a thin trickle of rain seeped down his neck. He cursed the apology for a summer, the non-appearance of his tram, and the war.

'Did you read where blackberries are to be fixed at five-pence a pound?' A stout woman in front of him nudged her companion and laughed out loud. 'I can just see thee and me queueing up for flamin' blackberries, even if there is any, which I doubt. Making jam 'bout enough sugar! Them silly buggers at the Food Office want their thick heads examining.'

'The woman next door to me got a pair of kippers from the Isle of Man,' her friend said.

'I thought it were full of foreign internals,' the stout woman said as the tram came into sight.

Oh, yes, Barbara Shawfield was a natural born spinster if ever there was one, Stanley decided as he boarded the tram. And if the pair in front of him didn't stop nattering and find a seat so the rest of the long queue could squeeze on, he would definitely miss the news. Besides, Sally would be wondering where on earth he'd got to.

Sally had stopped monitoring her parents' movements. Since the terrible scene between them that evening in May she had felt quite differently towards them somehow. Gone was the good-little-girl expression on her round face as her eyes had searched first one face and then the other for approval. Now the house was filled with a bitterness that was almost tangible. Josie's latent contempt for her husband showed itself in her raucous voice, and her broad Lancashire dialect was more pronounced than ever. Her dolly-blue eyes were hard as flint. She used the house merely as a place to eat and sleep in between her shifts at the factory and her weekend jaunts into town. She went out with her face caked with make-up and her too-tight skirts riding up as she walked.

Stanley, in desperation one night, had gone to John's room, telling her he was prepared to forget and forgive, and she had ranted and raved, telling him there was nowt to forgive and the blame for what she had done lay at his door, not hers. Sally had come onto the landing and seen them shouting at each other, and later, when she had crept down-stairs to find her father sobbing quietly into his hands, Stanley knocked her hand away. He had spurned her comfort, even mumbled at her without lifting his head, as if her deafness was an added irritation to his jagged nerves.

The letters from Lee were her only consolation. Before he left for Canada he had written to tell her he was deeply in love with her, and wanted to marry her. Not after the war finished, but maybe in the spring. And after the war finished she would sail to America, and at the farm in Texas he would teach her to ride a horse, and drive a car down long straight roads. And he would feed her with steaks as big as the biggest plate.

That August evening as the rain swept down outside she was reading, for the third time, his first letter since his arrival at a Royal Canadian flying training base in Ontario.

'After leaving the ship, we caught a train, with a stopover in Montreal. Boy, was that some experience, honey! For three hours I wandered around, and I can't find the words to describe the contrast to Great Britain. Imagine everything lit up, real pretty, and goodies in the lighted shop windows – things I reckon you've almost forgotten existed. Now, at the base, we've already gotten a start on flying training, which is great. You just wouldn't believe the kindness shown to the RAF boys by the Canadians! They treat me as if I were a Britisher! I suppose some of your accent must have rubbed off? I'm determined to make good grades so I come back as a commissioned officer. That's me, honey. A real go-gettin' American!'

He had ended by saying he had always dreamed of meeting a girl like her. 'A girl who always sees the funny side of this cock-eyed existence. A girl with dreams in her eyes and warmth in her heart. You are as soft and sweet as English summer rain, Sally. Don't ever change, okay? I want to come back and see you just the way you were . . .'

Sally looked through the window and pulled a face. Nothing soft about the deluge out there, overspilling the gutters, and nothing soft about her either. The girl who had run frantically away from David Turner, heart pounding with terror, existed no more. Twice since then she had fended off unwelcome attentions from dancing partners, refusing all eager offers to see her home and instead walking alone through the blacked-out streets, the soles of her feet still feeling the rhythm of the music.

Sally looked up from the letter to see her father standing in the doorway, shrugging off his wet coat before walking to the wireless and switching it on. As she went to fetch his cold meal from the kitchen she identified for a fleeting moment with her mother, recalling the times Josie must have experienced the same feeling of resentment at the sight of her husband, his small head inclined towards the speaker as he listened to the news.

'The Russians are killing those very same Germans who would have invaded *us*,' Stanley said at last, turning away from the set with reluctance. He sat down at the table and picked up his knife and fork. 'Is that a letter from David Turner?'

'From Lee,' Sally sighed. 'I haven't heard from David for ages. He's under no obligation to write to me. Why should he be? I haven't heard from him since his mother's funeral, as a matter of fact.'

'I thought you were good friends?' Stanley speared a pink slice of spam on his fork, and began to chew it absentmindedly.

'We are friends. But not *pen* friends.' Sally suddenly felt a pang of pity for the man going through the motions of eating the uninspired meal. 'The last letter I had from David read as if he had dictated it to a secretary. He's a strange sort of person. Inarticulate, almost. He doesn't seem able to express his thoughts at all.'

'And the Yank does?'

There was no way she could tell from how Stanley spoke whether he was joking. But his eyes weren't joking. Sally opened her mouth to answer but Stanley suddenly pointed his knife at her.

'I *know* Americans, and what I know of them I don't much like. They're brash individuals, all talk and no do. David Turner's worth a whole platoon of them. I'm telling you.' He jerked his head towards the letter. 'All sweet talk and most of it lies. What's he told you? That his father owns the Empire State Building in New York, or a hundred-acre ranch in Texas?'

Sally flinched. 'How many Americans have you met, Dad? Actually met and talked to?'

'None. But I *know* them.'

'Collectively?'

'Well, all right. So I'm generalizing. But I'm not having you getting mixed up with one.' He pushed his plate away. 'Stick to your own sort, love. Get yourself a boy you can trust. One with your own background. One who knows you and your family.'

'From down the road? Like David Turner?' All at once Sally's temper flared. 'Oh, Dad, you don't know how wrong you are! You don't know *anything*! You sit there making statements, passing judgement, as if you were God! You care about nothing but your flamin' news. You don't care anything about *feelings*. You don't even care about how Mum must be feeling! People do what they do sometimes because they can't help it. She was breaking her heart and you didn't even notice! She's suffering now just as much as the Russians and the Poles. And you can hardly bear to *look* at her! I love you both and I have to watch you hurting and destroying each other.' She nodded in the direction of the letter. 'And when Lee comes back I'm going to him. I'm not stopping in this house any longer. It's cold and dead, like you're cold and dead.'

When she got up and rushed from the room, taking the letter with her, Stanley sat for a long time at the table. The bitterness in Sally's young voice had shocked him. He fingered his moustache thoughtfully. And he was responsible for putting it there. Josie and he between them had destroyed Sally's taken-for-granted security, neither one of them stopping to think what they were doing to her.

Making his mind up quickly, he took the stairs two at a time and opened her door to see her curled up on her bed, the thin pages of the letter spread out around her on the counterpane.

'Look, love.' He walked over to the window and drew the curtains against the darkness and the driving rain. He switched on the light and faced her. 'Look, love. You can't be expected to understand. But you're old enough to try. Your mother and me.' He swallowed hard. 'We're going through a sticky patch, but things will work out all right. We've been selfish, I see that now, and what I said about the Yank, well, that was silly. When he comes back – *if* he comes back to this country – well, till then I'll reserve my judgement, right?' He smiled, the thin lines of his face lifting out of their customary sadness. 'And I don't feel like God. In no way am I as wise as God. And I don't pretend to be.'

'I can't hear you, Dad.' Sally picked up one of the closely written pages and began to read again. 'I'm sorry.'

Suddenly Stanley felt an almost irresistible urge to shake her. She had lip-read every word he had said. His little girl was behaving like the difficult adolescent she had somehow never needed to be. Sighing deeply, he left her alone, telling himself it was the only thing to do. But somehow he would force Josie to listen to him. He would show her that they weren't playing fair. Filled with a virtuous sense of righteousness, he cleared the table, piled the dirty dishes in the kitchen sink, then hurried back to switch on the wireless again. Colonel Britton was talking to the 'V' army again, advising them to go slow in all they did.

'Good man,' he muttered, nodding his head in total agreement. 'That will show the devils which side their bread is buttered on.'

In the office canteen of Duckworth Brothers the next morning the talk was all of Christine Duckworth's September wedding. Sally caught some of the words, then carried her plate over to a table by the window.

'What were they saying about Christine Duckworth? Did I hear someone say she was getting married?'

Sally had chosen the window table deliberately. Jean Davies was a plumply pleasant girl with a mouth filled with what seemed to be more than the normal quota of teeth, a girl always more than ready to tolerate Sally's deafness and interpret for her.

'In September,' Jean verified. 'To a family friend.' The teeth flashed in an engaging grin. 'The Duckworths are praying he gets leave. Otherwise our Christine will shame the lot of them by having to be married in a maternity smock.'

'No!' Sally remembered just in time to monitor the depth of her voice. 'I didn't know she was engaged.'

'She's not.' Jean poked around in her portion of potato pie

and forked a piece of meat triumphantly. 'He's called Nigel.' She pulled a comical face. 'He used to pick her up from the office before he got called up. I'd have sworn he was one of "those", you know? But it just goes to show.' Her smile was entirely without malice. 'Surely you've noticed Christine's waist-line? The way she belts her dresses in doesn't leave much to the imagination.'

Sally forced herself to chew and swallow the almost taste-less pie. Now that she had found out what she wanted to know she wished that Jean would get on with her own meal and stop talking. She appreciated the kindness and the toler-ance of the other girl, but once Jean got started there was no stopping her. The wide mouth opened and closed, a plump hand waved about in the air to emphasize a point, and the slightly bulging eyes glittered as she elaborated to her captive audience of one.

'You're too nice, Sally Barnes. That's your trouble. We're all surprised that Miss Duckworth hasn't got preggy long before this. They don't call her "The Forces' Sweetheart" for nothing. My guess is she's lucky she can pin the blame on Nigel whatever-his-name-is. At least he can keep her in the way to which she's accustomed. His father owns three mills out Bolton way, and they live in a house called Something Hall. There'd have been a right to-do if it had been a private in the Pay Corps or someone like that. Then the fat would really have been in the fire. They'd probably have got rid of it, knowing them. You know – booked her into a posh nursing home for a D and C for painful periods to get rid of it. I mean they say a baby is only like a little tadpole at that stage. People with money and an obliging doctor don't go to back-street abortionists these days, you know.' The friendly smile widened. 'You're not shocked, are you? Honestly, Sally, I realize you miss a lot not being able to hear. You just opt out, don't you? That's why some of the girls think you're a bit stuffy. But there are things you should know. And I'll tell you something else for nothing . . .'

On Sally's face there was nothing but an intent listening silence. Nothing to show the turmoil of her thinking but a dilation of her blue-grey eyes. She was remembering the night the bomb fell on David's house, the night when her brother stayed out all night with Christine Duckworth. She saw again the adoration in his eyes as he lifted a strand of Christine's auburn hair away from her ear to kiss her tenderly. She saw again the naked joy on his face when he came home the next morning as if he had returned from a happiness too much to bear.

And she remembered his last words to her: 'She's my girl now, Sally, and when I come back I'm going to marry her.'

Sally stood up suddenly, leaving Jean in mid-sentence, her mouth agape and her eyes stretched with surprise.

'Excuse me, Jean,' she said. 'I don't want any pudding. Excuse me.'

She walked quickly out of the canteen. She would really have liked more time to think, but already she knew what she had to do. She had to hear from Christine's own lips that she was going to marry some other man in September. And she wanted to ask if Christine had written to John explaining her broken promise. She sensed that something was very wrong, because in spite of what Jean had said, Christine Duckworth and her brother John had been drowning in love for each other that terrible night.

She quickened her steps, taking the stairs two at a time, running down the long corridor to Amos Duckworth's office. She was trembling with the realization of what she was about to do, but the fierce abiding love she had always felt for her brother was urging her on, making her strong and determined.

She saw Christine as soon as she opened the door, slumped in a black leather chair by the window of her father's office, smoking a cigarette and leafing idly through a magazine. A drawer of a tall filing cabinet was open and a pile of folders balanced precariously on top. There were papers everywhere, spilling from the folders themselves and littering the wide desk. As Christine swung the chair round she kicked over a mug on the floor by her side, and a thin trickle of coffee snaked over the carpet.

Christine's green eyes opened wide in astonishment. 'Sally Barnes! You've a cheek coming in here without even knocking! You know my father's away for a week, so if you want to speak to him you'll have to wait.' She indicated the spilled coffee. 'As you can see I was just having my lunch. So if you don't mind . . .'

With a violent twist of the chair she swung it round so that her back was turned, forcing Sally to walk round the back of the desk to stand by the window where she could see Christine's face.

'I came to see you,' Sally said clearly, then stopped, her mouth drying and her heart beginning to pound. Christine Duckworth looked terrible. It wasn't merely the thickening of her waist-line – you'd have to be looking specially to see that – but the cowed look about her. The beautiful reddish hair hung lifeless as if it hadn't been washed for weeks, and her nose, the distinctive Duckworth nose, seemed to have grown peaked and bony. All the arrogant confidence had somehow been beaten out of her, and the green glitter of her enormous eyes was dimmed into an apathetic dullness.

'I hear you're getting married, Christine.' Sally said the words bravely.

'And . . . ?' Christine's chin jerked up. She turned her head to stare out of the window.

'Have you written to tell my brother that?' Sally felt her stomach lurch. 'Before he went away he told me you were going to marry *him*. Have you written to tell him you've changed your mind?'

'You interfering little so-and-so!' Christine jerked upright in the swaying chair. 'I never liked you, Sally Barnes, and now I like you even less. How dare you ask me a personal question like that?'

'I dare because of John.' Sally clenched her hands into fists. 'He's a long way from home, and it's going to break his heart when he hears you're going to marry someone else. I'm not interfering. It's just that my brother doesn't fall in love easily.' She took a step forward. 'He's wanted you for years, and that night before he went away you gave him hope. He sailed with that hope alive inside him, and he deserves to know why you've let him down. John doesn't love easily, Christine. It's always been you. You must know that.'

For an unbelievable moment Christine thought she was going to burst into tears. They were there, choked in her throat as they had been for weeks now, frozen like the rest of

80

her into a terrifying acceptance of the way things were and the way they had to be. The room was very quiet – no sound at all even from the goods yard way below. She got up quickly, sending the chair spinning, to fumble with a folder on top of the filing cabinet, her back turned completely to Sally.

'I wrote to John last week if you must know,' she said quietly. 'I told him all he needed to know, and he'll understand. Now can I get on with my filing?'

'I can't hear you.' Sally felt the familiar rage of frustration. 'I'm sorry, Christine, but unless you turn round I can't hear you.'

Christine closed her eyes, feeling the tears behind the closed eyelids. It was too much, too bloody much having to repeat it. And why had she never noticed before how alike Sally Barnes and her brother were? The colouring was different, but there was the same open freshness about their faces, the same directness in the eyes. And who would have thought that little mouse of a girl would have found the courage to confront her like that? Deaf she might be, but a coward she certainly was not. A sudden overwhelming desire to push Sally bodily out of her sight overcame her so that she whirled round, her eyes sparkling with tears.

'I *have* written,' she shouted. 'So go away! Go back to your typewriter and leave me to manage my own life. Right?'

Sally hesitated, held out a hand, changed her mind and hurried towards the door. She walked down the corridor, down the stairs and into the main office, wanting nothing more than to creep back into her customary shell and immerse herself in her work, ignoring the curious glances being directed at her.

Jean came at once to stand by her table, her teeth and eyes shining with eagerness. 'Sally?' She touched Sally on her arm. 'There's an Air Force officer downstairs in reception asking for you. Where've you been? I've been looking everywhere.'

'For me?' Sally looked startled, trying to collect her thoughts. 'For me? An Air Force officer?' Then her bewildered expression cleared. 'David! It must be David!' She smiled at Jean's raised eyebrows. 'He's just a friend, that's all. Almost a relative. From down the road.' She glanced over her shoulder. 'If Miss Graham comes back, cover up for me, will you? I won't be long. Okay?'

With the feeling of desolation lifting from her heart, she ran quickly down the stairs into the wide reception hall at the front of the building.

The receptionist was busy at the switchboard, but over by the far window a tall boy in uniform with his cap held underneath his arm turned round when he heard Sally's footsteps on the parquet floor.

'Sally? Sally Barnes?' He looked somehow humbled and desperate as he held out a hand.

'Yes?' Sally looked into the boyish face and asked simply: 'It's about David, isn't it?'

'It happened at the end of last week.' The boy's brown eyes held a dreadful sadness. 'We'd been on a night bombing operation to Cologne. We'd taken a real hammering from flak.' He swallowed hard. 'No one actually saw what happened, but four planes failed to get back. David's was one of them.' He took Sally's hand and held it tight. 'He asked me to promise to let you know if ever anything like this happened. It's the least I could do, and I'm on my way home for a spot of leave anyway. Oh, God, I didn't mean it like that, as if I'd just dropped by. Oh, God, I'm sorry.'

'Thank you.' Sally felt the blood actually drain from her face, leaving her cheeks as cold as marble. 'David was my friend.' She stood still, staring into the embarrassed anguish on the young officer's face. 'At least his mother never knew,' she managed to say at last. There was a loud and shouting bitterness in her voice as she forgot to keep it low-pitched. 'I suppose that's one terrible blessing. That *she* never knew.'

'Can I organize a pot of tea?' The middle-aged receptionist came scurrying round from behind her counter, her homely face creasing into lines of concern. 'It won't take long.'

Five

As the great bomber turned and banked away from the city of Cologne, David knew with certainty that this time they would not be making it back home.

He had seen the fires, started by their incendiary bombs, shown as twinkling lights far below the starboard wing. The skipper had acknowledged the 'Bombs gone' call seconds before the flak came at them yet again, shattering the port engine and front turret. He had then pointed to the hatch, giving the thumbs down sign, and David's stomach had lurched, flopping over in his body as the bile rose in his throat.

Well trained, David obeyed the instruction immediately, sending up a silent prayer that the course he had plotted had by this time taken them clear of German territory.

By his reckoning he knew they should be over occupied Belgium, but for the moment all his concentration was centred on getting down safely and in one piece. His practice jumps were far in the distant past of his initial training, before the war in fact, when he had actually enjoyed the feeling of dropping through space. Now it was for real, and he gasped his relief aloud as his harness jerked at his body.

'At least the bloody thing has opened,' his mind screamed silently.

Through the black all-enveloping darkness he sensed rather than saw the ground rushing up to meet him.

'Bend the knees! Relax! Roll over!'

The remembered instructions pierced his muddled thinking too late. With a sudden terrifying crash he was down, feeling his left leg fold beneath him, and the branch of a tree tear at his face. A sharp blow to his head left him stunned, so that for a time he just lay there, vomiting wretchedly into a clump of grass.

In spite of the warmth of the late summer's night, he was shivering, his teeth chattering uncontrollably. The pain tore through him, and when he tried to raise his head, he fell back with a moan.

Half an hour later, a lapse of time which he would have sworn was only seconds, he managed to free himself from his harness and sit up. He blinked, trying to get his eyes to focus, but all he could make out was a blurred and uneven horizon fringed by strangely elongated top-heavy trees.

Far too dazed to remember to roll up and bury his parachute, he began to drag himself, inch by painful inch, over the rough ground. Instinctively he realized his duty was to go for cover. He shook his head from side to side like an injured animal, then felt the blood run slowly down his face, seeping into the fur-lined collar of his flying jacket.

Panting and retching, every inch a screaming torture, with his broken leg dragging behind him, he crawled for the next five minutes. Then he saw, not fifty yards away, a parachute hanging from a tree.

At first, in the darkness, it reminded him of the old net curtains his mother used to throw over her fruit trees to protect them from the starlings. So he must be in some sort of orchard. Maybe near a farm? Slowly edging his way closer, David felt his throat close in horror as he realized his mistake.

In the darkness, which seemed to be paling slightly, he saw the sightless eyes of his wireless operator staring straight down at him, set in a head lolling on an obviously broken neck. Vomit rose in David's mouth and he clenched his teeth to hold it back.

Jack Thomson, the joker in the pack, a boy with a wit as dry and coarse as emery paper. His pretty wife, back in Bolton, had stitched a Saint Christopher medallion inside his pocket so he had to be okay.

'You'll be okay, Jack. I'll get you down.'

David clawed at the air as his strength gave out. He sank back into the long wet grass.

When he opened his eyes again the sky was a pale milky

white. He tried to move his mouth and his jaw felt sticky with blood. The pain as he attempted to stretch out his leg sent shock waves of agony through him, tingling his armpits and bringing him out in a cold sweat.

He sat up, holding out both his arms to the body of his wireless operator. Some way, somehow, Jack had to be got down. Okay then, for Christ's sake, Jack was dead, but he couldn't go on hanging there. David knew the score, and the score said that dead aircrew had to be buried, or at least concealed from sight. He wasn't leaving him for the Jerries to find. Not old Jack.

David ran a hand over his gummed-up face. He had to see to Jack, then he had to set off himself, to God alone knew where, walking by night and holing up by day. He had to find a house.

'*Je suis Anglais . . .*' Oh, hell, what use was his matriculation standard French here? He wasn't even in France. Oh, hell, his mind had gone as numb as his face. He raised himself on an elbow, and the movement jarred his leg into agony. Whimpering, he lay down again.

Poor old Jack. Only the week before he had confided that before being called up he'd never left his native Lancashire.

'We always went to Fleetwood for the July Wakes week,' he'd said. 'We stopped at the same lodging house, me and Mam. And now Shirley's living with me Mam till the war's over. They get on a treat. None of the old mother-in-law lark there. I suppose I'm lucky, really.'

Now Jack's luck had run out, and he hung from a tree miles away from his mam and Shirley in Bolton. If David didn't get him down from that blasted tree he could swing there for days till the birds pecked at his staring eyes.

David gritted his teeth, rolled over onto his knees in a frantic effort to stand up, swayed for a moment, then fell face downwards into a black and velvety darkness.

'He's coming round.'

The voice was deep, rough-edged. White wrinkles fanned out from Fernand Colson's brown eyes as he showed tobacco-stained teeth in a satisfied grin.

By his side in the hayloft, his son Louis nodded his over-

85

large head up and down twice like a puppet. The flat planes of his face lifted into a smile as wide as his father's.

'He's waking up. The Englishman is waking up!'

Slowly David raised his swollen eyelids. He tried to move his leg, leaden now and weighted as if it was clamped in a vice. A wave of nausea beaded his forehead. The musty sweet smell of hay filled the air, and when he turned his head painfully he imagined he saw stars in a midnight blue sky.

He struggled to get the better of the deep languor creeping over him. Something was wrong. The last time he had seen the sky it was pearl white with approaching dawn. Jack's eyes, those terrible blank eyes, had stared at him, willing him to help. David frowned. Help him to do what?

Suddenly memory flooded back. 'I must cut him down. I have to . . . have to . . .'

Fernand Colson's understanding of English was limited to a few simple words, and he guessed that his own Flemish tongue would have as little meaning for the airman. But he tried. By gestures and a simple formation of words he tried his best:

'You must lie still, M'sieur.' He pushed David back gently with a huge brown hand. 'I have set it for you.' He pointed to the wooden staves holding the injured leg fast. 'I am not a doctor. Not medico. Your head needs stitching.' He made the appropriate signs. 'I have bound it tight. Do you think you could swallow some broth?'

The farmer smiled as he met David's pleading stare. 'You are safe, M'sieur. My son and I found you in the far field this morning.' He saluted. 'I am loyal Belgian. My wife is angry with me for bringing you here, but Fernand Colson will fight the Boche in his own way. I was in the last lot, and if the Germans think they can get away with it twice in my lifetime, then they are very badly mistaken.'

He muttered to his son, then as the top of the unnaturally flat head disappeared down the ladder, he went on: 'Louis is a good boy, but that is what he will always be, just a boy.' Fernand stroked his bushy greying moustache. 'We took your friend hidden on the back of the farm cart over the other side of Bruges.' His eyebrows lifted as David's swollen eyelids flickered at the sound of the last word. Fernand smiled. 'You know Bruges, heh?'

86

He mimed the actions of a hanging body from a tree. 'Over the other side of Bruges. Your friend. Heh? I am sorry, M'sieur, but it was necessary.' He flung out a hand. 'This is not a safe house, and if the Boche come – which they would surely do if we left your friend on my land – they would show no mercy.' Spitting on a finger, Fernand drew it across his throat. 'They are pigs, M'sieur.' He spat a stream of tobacco-stained saliva into the straw. 'I am just a farmer, but I will find someone to help you, never fear.' He made the noise of a train. 'Bruges to Brussels, okay? Over the border to Paris, then down the Pyrenees to Espagne. Heh? It is possible.'

David stared up into the walnut-brown face bending over him. There was a throbbing in his head like the beating of a tom-tom. Thump, thump, with a rhythmic persistence that brought the bile up into his throat. He felt more ill than he ever remembered. He had only understood the gist of what the farmer had said, but his head was spinning, his eyelids too heavy to lift, and it was strange how peaceful he was beginning to feel.

The flak was no longer ripping viciously through the interior of his aircraft; he was safe and the Germans hadn't found him. For a moment the faces of his crew came before him, laughing eager faces. They came and were gone . . .

When the broth came David was deeply unconscious once more. The flat face of Louis Colson crumpled in childish disappointment.

'He will drink the broth tomorrow.' Fernand nodded at his son. 'I promise you. He is going to live, this Englishman. You will see.'

Next day the broth was good but greasy. David turned his head away only to have his chin gently turned back again.

'You must try and drink a little. You have been without food for three days now, and it is important that you try.'

Francine Dubois smiled. At least her lips smiled, but her eyes, of a strange unusual blue, remained as hard as the moorland stones in David's native Lancashire. Her hair, barley pale, was caught back from her face with an enormous tortoise-shell slide, to hang down her back in a thick cluster of curls, and her skin, tanned by the summer sun, was the only colourful thing about her.

'It is essential that you eat, M'sieur,' she said again, and so to please her David allowed her to spoon a little of the broth into his mouth, then retched as a coarsely chopped sliver of onion caught at his throat.

'Your leg will heal,' she told David in a matter-of-fact way. 'But the wound on your head is worrying my father. It ought to be stitched.' She spooned another mouthful of broth between David's lips as she talked. 'The doctor was a good friend, but the Boche shot him two weeks ago for no other reason than being in the market place when they were rounding up ten men.' The spoon was dipped and raised once again. 'A German soldier had been found dead, murdered, and so ten men must pay with their lives. You would not understand.'

She put the bowl aside with a sigh. 'Your country has a pathetic ignorance of what life is like in Belgium now. The doctor was a wonderful man. He would have set your leg and stitched your head and you would be as good as new. But now . . .' She spread her hands wide. 'They are pigs, M'sieur. No, worse than pigs. At least animals have a kind of dignity. They have none.'

David struggled to say something that applied. But the pain in his head was beating him down into oblivion again. The girl's face, seen through the high unwashed window, was swimming in shadows, but there was so much he wanted to know, so much he *had* to know.

'Your English is very good,' he said lamely, at last.

Francine smiled a smile that merely tilted the outer corners of her wide mouth. 'Thank you, M'sieur. I was educated at a convent school in Bruges, then I worked in Brussels as a tri-lingual secretary until I married just before the war and the Germans came.' She stood up from her kneeling position in the straw, brushing her skirt down with her fingers. 'One of the last things the good doctor did was to provide me with papers saying it was necessary for me to live at home to work the farm and look after my mother. So now you see.'

'Now I see.' David nodded, fighting to keep his eyes open, wanting to tell her how grateful he was, how he would move on as soon as he was able, wanting to thank her . . . His head lolled and he was asleep, unaware that the girl remained where she was for a while, staring down at him with an expression that could have been pity softening briefly her cold blue eyes.

When Francine crossed the cobbled yard and went into the big farm kitchen the woman sitting in a chair by the wood-burning stove looked up from the crochet work on her lap. Her eyes never left her daughter's back as Francine rinsed out the bowl at the slopstone with quick deft movements before drying it and replacing it on the dresser.

'He is still there, the Anglais?'

'You know he is still there, Maman.' Francine opened the door at the side of the oven and peered inside. 'He will stay there until he can walk. Then we will see.'

Thin fingers whitened as Odile Colson tightened her grip on the crochet hook. Her nose sharpened with a mixture of fear and anger. 'Your father is mad! He knows what they will do to us if the Anglais is found. He knows what they will do to me! Her voice dropped to a whimper. 'Haven't we suffered enough?' She motioned to the stick by the side of her chair. 'Isn't dive-bombing a woman into a ditch when they first came, turning me into a cripple with the chatter of their terrible machine-guns, enough?' Hysteria crept into her voice. 'It is not my duty nor my privilege to defy those strutting brutes. I just want to be left in peace.'

She began a fierce rocking of her chair, leaning her head back as tears spurted from her eyes. 'And what about Gaston? Would he want you to risk your life – all our lives, this way? Is there no end to suffering?'

Francine closed the oven door with a slam. It was hard to keep her patience with the petulant whimpering figure in the chair, but she had at least to try. She went to kneel by her mother's side.

'Mother? I can't forget the day when the Stukas came either. I remember you as you were, and my heart aches for you. I stopped feeling anything after the news about Gaston came, but yes, my heart aches for *you*. I love you,' she whispered. 'And I want to protect and care for you, but the Anglais has to be got out of Belgium. For Gaston, and for what the Boche did to you, he has to fly again.'

Gently she shook her mother's hands between her own. 'Can't you see that? Father sees, and even Louis sees. This is our chance to score off them. We have to do this thing in order to keep our heads high. Mother? Are you even listening to me? We will beat the Germans. In our own small way we are going to beat them. I swear!'

Fernand and Louis came in from the fields, filthy, unshaven, tired, their faces and arms burned almost black by the hot sun.

'It's a good year for plums, Mother.'

Fernand glanced quickly at Francine before placing the overflowing bucket of ripe fruit on the table. 'See. If we jam it quickly we should be able to keep a fair amount for ourselves.'

'And what do we use for sugar? Heh?'

Odile began her rocking again, and Francine walked back to the stove.

The stew was browning nicely. She felt the need for fresh clean air, so with a reassuring nod at her father she went outside into the yard.

But the air was still with no comforting breeze to lift her hair away from her head. The sun was dying, and as it died it made a mosaic pattern of the pink tiles on the sloping roof.

Francine walked through the yard, past the corn barn and out into the farm field. The long grasses tickled her bare legs, and the distant fields, seen through the orchard, stretched far off to a slowly dimming horizon.

It was almost impossible to believe that German troops were stationed in the village beyond the fringe of trees. And yet Francine could sense their presence as vividly as if they marched towards her in their grey uniforms, arms swinging. The pain of remembering pierced her like the sudden thrust of a knife.

'Gaston!'

Whispering his name she began to run, over and across the fields, running until the breath came rasping in her throat. At the edge of the barley patch she threw herself down among the brittle snow-white tufts, and snatched the brown slide from her hair.

As her long curtain of hair covered her face like a blessing, she cried aloud her anguish. There were no tears. Francine

Dubois had forgotten how to cry.

It was a year since it happened, that was all. Just one year, and yet she could hardly remember Gaston's face in detail. She drew a strand of silken hair between her teeth and moaned. She could never forget Gaston's hands on her. Never. Never. His love-making had been ardent and tender as he caressed every single hollow of her body.

'My own darling,' he had whispered, his adoration rousing her to such exquisite pleasure that the whole world had dropped away.

'Oh, Gaston. Gaston . . .'

Francine got up slowly, fastened back her hair, and turned back to the house, a tall girl with rounded arms sun-kissed to a golden brown.

As she walked past the hayloft she glanced upwards to the high window. Oh, but he was so shy, the Anglais. With his brushed-back hair and neat moustache he talked as if he had a hot potato in his mouth, as all the English did. When the time came he would not let her down. For Gaston's sake, he must not let her down. But first he had to be restored to health. However much her mother ranted and raved, the Anglais had to stay where he was. It was a risk that had to be taken.

For David the first weeks passed in a haze of pain, dulled for the most part by the continual slipping in and out of sleep. The mild concussion saw to that, but as August moved into September he began to feel a restlessness that tormented him like an army of ants crawling beneath his skin.

Fernand had fashioned him a pair of crutches, and during the long days David would force himself to walk round and round the hayloft, testing his left foot gingerly on the sloping floorboards, praying for the day when the splints could come off. Taking care to keep well hidden, he would peer down through the window, staring out to where on a high ridge the poplars stood motionless, their leaves shimmering and grey in colour. There must be a road over there, he calculated, and saw himself walking down it, unmolested, unchallenged, en route for home.

Francine stayed longer with him now, watching him eat, smiling her tight dismissive smile at his acute embarrassment at the primitive sanitary arrangements.

'Bodily functions. Why the shame?' she said straight out, putting that little problem into perspective. He marvelled at her practicality, and wondered what had happened to make her so.

One wet September evening she told him. They were sitting well away from the window, and a tattered bedspread hung across the dusty panes.

'I am ashamed that we do not have you in the house after dark,' she told him. 'But my mother has made my father promise not to take the risk. The shrapnel that shattered her spine did more than paralyse her legs. It made her so alive to fear that she waits for the door to be kicked open. She cannot believe that the Germans will leave us alone. She cannot believe that they can be content with taking our eggs and our farm produce, and every Wednesday when my father drives the cart into town she sits and shakes with terror until he comes back.' Her voice faltered. 'She is remembering what they did to Gaston.'

'What did they do to him?' David put out a hand to touch her hand, only to see her flinch away as if the small gesture had the sting of a wasp in it.

'They tortured him,' she said. 'It was in the beginning when they were doing what they called "mopping up pockets of resistance". The evasion lines were already becoming efficient, and Gaston, as a design architect, was working night and day on forged papers. They were to be kept in a safe place, with only the name and photograph to be added. We knew then that allied airmen would soon be dropping from the skies, you see.'

The steel crept into her voice. 'Gaston was on his way to deliver a batch of documents. He was out after the hour of the curfew, because that night he had insisted on seeing me back to the small flat we shared on the outskirts of Brussels. I pleaded with him to let me go alone, but he wouldn't listen. The Germans on the whole had been leaving Belgian girls alone, but only the week before a girl we both knew well had been brutally raped by three of the bastards.'

David saw that her stare was fixed straight in front of her, like an epileptic when all sense of being has vanished. 'Don't talk about it if you don't want to.' He was so aching with pity he felt his eyes well with tears. 'I understand.'

'No! You do not understand! How can you?' Francine shuddered. 'Gaston was a gentle man. He was so gentle that at first, when we first met, I thought he had a feminine streak in him, but I soon found out that in his gentleness lay his strength. He refused to tell them anything, and so they broke his body, but they could not touch his mind. Then one day they had Gaston taken out into the street, and shot. I had heard they were taking a bunch of prisoners to a working camp in Germany, and I hoped . . . I prayed.'

David held his breath.

'I saw them drag him out from the back of a truck parked outside the building they had commandeered for their Gestapo Headquarters. I was in the Place that day. Oh, I don't know why. Just wanting to try to be near him, I suppose.' She was silent for a moment. 'They rounded up all the people there, the passers-by and even the children. To watch, you see. To watch and learn what happens to anyone who defies them.'

'Gaston's hair used to grow down into the nape of his neck. It was fine hair, fine like a baby's, but when they shot him his head came open. I saw it. And I'll never stop seeing it, whenever I close my eyes.'

David squeezed his own eyes tight shut to block out the horror. His arms enfolded her, holding her close, straining her to him, making her agony melt into him.

Then, with a terrible wail, her control snapped and the tears came.

At the beginning of the following week the Germans came. David heard the noise of a motor-cycle engine and pressed himself close to the wall near the window overlooking the yard.

Because the weather was still warm a broken pane of glass had not been filled in. He found that by straining his ears he could hear what was being said down below.

There were two of them, thick-set men, burly in the field-grey uniforms. They shouted at Fernand in a mixture of German and bad French. Both Fernand and Louis, on their way back from their work in the fields, wore sacking round their shoulders as a protection against the morning drizzle, and as they stood close together they looked like a couple of country yokels. Fernand's head was bent, and Louis was already casting darting glances in the direction of the hayloft.

David felt his muscles tense with fear.

'You!' The German corporal pointed a finger at Fernand.

'I am farmer. Fernand Colson.'

The taller German looked up to the sky as if seeking patience. 'I can see you are farmer. I asked you your name.'

'Sorry.' Fernand returned the German's insolent stare coldly, then to David's horror Louis lifted his big head and glanced fearfully over his shoulder, straight in the direction of the hayloft.

'And him?' A finger was pointed at the quivering man-child.

'This is my son.'

Again the flat eyes darted towards the loft, and as David felt the sweat breaking out from every pore in his body the German stomped towards Louis and flicked a contemptuous finger into the massive chest.

'You! Why do you keep looking over there?' He stared over Louis's shoulder, and David flattened himself against the wall, every nerve alive and quivering. Louis was moaning now, rocking himself from side to side.

'I haven't done nothing!' he sobbed. 'Father! Tell him I haven't done nothing!'

Fernand cut in angrily, and David marvelled at his courage. 'Do you not have "children" like my son in Germany? Ask *me* your questions. You cannot expect straight answers from my son. He is terrified of you. Even the colour of your uniform frightens him. Can't you see?'

'I didn't do nothing.' Louis's voice had thinned to a pleading whine. 'Do not cut my throat. Please . . .'

David closed his eyes. So that was the ploy Fernand had used to silence his son, and now it looked as if his words were having an entirely opposite effect on the poor fuddled mind. He glanced round the loft for means of escape and found none. The only way out was down the rickety ladder, and even if he managed to negotiate that with his splinted leg, the way out led directly into the cobbled yard. He was trapped, and they were trapped, the whole of the Colson family who had risked their lives in keeping him there. They would be shot, each one of them, even the mother who had prophesied this day would come. He felt the bile rise warm and bitter in his throat.

'Would you like a bowl of turnip soup?'

He heard Fernand's voice, strong and deep. He smiled at his son's red moonface. 'Go in and tell your sister.' He gestured towards the open farmhouse door. 'There will be bread hot from the oven. You look as if you have come a long way. You are welcome to share our meal.'

'Antwerp,' the German said. 'We thought we were on the road to . . .' He took a small map from his pocket and scrutinized it. 'We want to get to a place called Diksmuide. Can you put us on the right road?'

David let out his breath in a long sigh. Dear God in heaven . . . they were lost, that was all! The Boche in their smart grey uniforms, on their motor-cycle, had merely lost their way. Oh, dear God, it was funny . . . If it wasn't so terrible it would be laughable. He leaned slightly to the side and saw the two Germans following Fernand across the yard, the thought of turnip soup and hot crusty bread turning them momentarily into human beings. They even stopped at the door and wiped their feet in their shiny leather boots on the scraper by the open door.

'Mother?' David heard Fernand call out. 'We've got two visitors. For lunch.'

It was not over. Far from it. For the next half hour David stood exactly where he was, pressed against the wall, his eyes slewed round to the window. He imagined them sitting round the table in the farm kitchen he had never seen, Fernand playing the host, Francine holding the newly baked bread against her, as she sliced. He saw the mother, imagined her dark and brooding as her daughter had described her, and he saw Louis's strangely ovalled eyes giving his childish terror away.

When he heard them clatter out into the yard again he looked down, shaking his head to blink away the sweat that was running down his forehead and into his eyes. He saw the

Germans slap Fernand on the back; he heard their loud laughter as they kicked the motor-cycle's engine into life. And he saw them drive away, a hand raised in a farewell gesture that looked, to his disbelieving eyes, like a Hitler salute.

'Root beer,' Francine told him three minutes later, appearing suddenly through the open hatchway. 'My father had three flagons stored away. He plied them with it, and we watched them drink it like water, swigging it down like the swines they are.' She came to him and David slid down to the floor and pulled her close. 'They couldn't guess how strong it is, and my father kept filling and refilling their glasses. Oh, God, they got redder and redder till I wondered how they would ever be able to walk.' She began to laugh, snorting through her nostrils, till her nose and eyes ran together. 'My mother looked as if she was going to die of fright, and Louis . . . oh, God . . . Louis! My father told them that to make sure his son never wandered out after curfew he had explained that the Germans would slit his throat.' She gulped for air. 'They thought that was funny! They yelped with laughter. Oh, David! Why aren't you laughing? One of them even clicked his heels and kissed my hand before they left.' She held up a hand, roughened by the hard work on the farm, and waved it about in front of her face. 'To think the day would come when this hand would feel the touch of a German's lips! Oh, God, it's so funny! So funny . . .'

David kept on holding her, straining her close until with a last hiccough the sound of her hysterical laughter died away. With a deliberate determination he was calculating how soon he could discard the unwieldy crutches, test his leg without the splints, and perhaps with the aid of a stick get away. He frowned. He would go by night, walking as far as he could, putting as much distance between him and the farmstead as was possible. Then he would hole up by day and hopefully move on.

It wasn't working out at all in the way he had been told it would. There must be Belgians who were in touch with the army of resistance, but it was gradually becoming clear that Fernand Colson didn't know of any. Or was it his wife who had persuaded him not to trust anyone? Had she pleaded with him not to give their secret away? Not even to one of his own countrymen?

'I know Diksmuide,' he told Francine when she had regained some semblance of control. 'I was sixteen when my mother and I came to Belgium to find my father's grave.' He moved slightly to ease the pins and needles in the arm she was lying on. 'We went out in a bus to somewhere north of the Somme. Arras?'

Francine nodded, snuggled closer to him and closed her eyes.

'I'm suddenly so tired,' she said.

'Rows and rows of white crosses,' David went on. 'We went to see the trenches, and there were duckboards laid across them. We saw some barbed wire red with rust. Then one day we went to Diksmuide. There was a statue on the cobbled square of a Belgian general who had besieged the town continuously for four years. I remember there were quiet streets and closed white painted doors with the windows shrouded in net curtains and filled with pot plants. It seemed so peaceful.'

'And now it's all happening the same.' Francine sat up, pushing the heavy weight of her hair away from her flushed and damply swollen face. 'How silly it all is. How stupid and silly and utterly pointless. Oh, David . . .'

She lifted her face. When he kissed her he tasted the salt of her tears, and when he moved his hand to caress the back of her neck the silken weight of her hair flowed across his wrist.

'I do not want you to make love to me, David,' she whispered. 'But I would like it if you lay with me.' She pulled him down to lie pressed closely to her. 'Just to be held, that is all.'

So David held her.

They stayed like that for a long time with the sounds of the September afternoon drifting up from the yard below. For the moment there was nothing in Francine either of hate or contentment, but the terror was slowly drifting from her mind.

And David? As the resolution to get away hardened in him, his expression was that of a dreaming boy. An English grammar school boy, reared to discipline, ever conscious of wanting to do the right thing. He thought of his home and the pristine cleanliness of it, with the cricket and tennis club no more than a stone's throw away. He saw himself dressed in white flannels with a cravat tucked into the open neck of his shirt, walking down the road carrying his tennis racket underneath his arm. He saw the rough lane leading to the pavilion and the courts beyond, and he saw Sally Barnes, her curly dark hair tied up in a blue Alice band, sitting on a stile and waving to him, her round face bright with the vivacity of innocence. He remembered swishing with his racket at a cluster of weeds, as he talked to her. He remembered the shape of her round brown knees, and the way her cotton frock had rows of wavy braiding round its hem.

'Were you ever afraid when you were flying, David?'

He came back with an effort to reality, and smiled into the top of Francine's head. 'I was once grounded for a while,' he told her. 'Lack of moral fibre, they used to call it, but now that we're at war they're kind and send us somewhere for a resting period until we're mentally fit to fly again. It won't happen to me again. Never again.'

'Why?' she asked. 'How can you be so sure?'

He frowned and bit his lip, struggling to overcome his natural sense of reticence and his aversion to divulging his innermost thoughts.

'Because at first I was, I suppose, an idealist. At the beginning I was filled with a sense of burning patriotism, saving my country, you know, that sort of thing.'

'And you're not now?'

'Now it's my job,' he whispered, groping for the right words to convey his meaning. 'This war is going to go on for a long time yet. I, that is my *mind*, cannot accept the callousness of slaughter.' He smiled. 'I'm a Lancastrian and a Lancastrian in the main thinks straight ahead, not in a curved line, making excuses and working out reasons. If I were really brave I'd chuck it all in and become a conscientious objector, but even if I found the courage to do that I know I'd find myself wanting to be back in the thick of it again. I think about my mother's wasted life for all those years after my father was killed, and I try to work up a good thick lather of hatred. But all I can feel is the sadness of the sheer futility of it all. And in the meantime the war goes on.'

'It doesn't make a lot of sense to me, either, David.' Francine pushed him from her gently, then kneeling up in the straw by his side lifted her arms and secured the heavy curtain of her sun-bleached hair in the nape of her neck again. She smiled her bleak little smile. 'I don't mean that what you said doesn't make sense. It makes a lot of sense.' She bent down and laid her lips sweetly against his for a moment. 'You are a nice man, David Turner.' She flipped the disc at his throat. 'Your Sally, the girl you talked to when you had a fever, is a lucky girl. I hope she loves you madly.'

To her surprise she saw the deep blush creep up from the Englishman's throat to stain his cheeks with colour.

'I haven't told her yet,' he mumbled. 'She doesn't know.' He sat up and fiddled with his belt. 'I blotted my copybook with her, and we don't seem to have hit it off since then.'

'Blotted your copybook?' Francine's face was a study of bewilderment. 'My English isn't good enough for that. But you must marry her, David. When you go back that is what you must do. At once. Okay?'

'Bang on,' David said, and they smiled at each other, closer than if they had indeed made love lying there in the musky-smelling hay.

And when David ran a finger down the apricot softness of her cheek, when he leaned forward and kissed her swollen eyelids, she did not know that he was saying his goodbye.

In October the weather broke at last. David chose his time carefully. Wrapping the food he had stored for the past two days in a piece of old sacking, he climbed slowly down the ladder, feeling his way, letting his good leg take the strain, clutching his bundle and the stick Fernand had fashioned for him from the branch of a tree.

It was very different walking outside on the rough ground from his daily deliberate circling of the hayloft. His leg ached intolerably, and his head throbbed with a rhythmic pounding beat.

Away from the farm he made for the open fields, avoiding the road winding like a dark ribbon in the direction of the nearest village. Fernand had given him an old coat to use as a bed covering, and he had buttoned this over his uniform, threading two of the buttonholes with string where the buttons were missing.

Without papers he knew that he must avoid the towns at all cost, and with no clear idea of where he was heading he stumbled on, catching his coat in bramble hedges, keeping to his intention of putting as much distance as he could between himself and the farm before the light of dawn streaked the sky.

He found an empty farm building with the walls broken and pitted, and crouched in a corner, his ears alert for the slightest sound. He opened the bundle and gnawed at a piece of bread, and swallowed a little of the water in the green glass bottle he had found discarded in a pile of hay in the loft which he hoped was now at least five miles behind him.

His trouser legs were torn by the brambles as he had stumbled and crawled his way through the long night, and he smelled to high heaven from the cow pat he had fallen into in his frenzied search for shelter once daylight came.

He was exhausted and knew it would be foolish to sleep. Maybe when the morning came and he could risk a quick survey of his surroundings, maybe then . . . He stretched his eyes wide and tried to pinpoint his exact location. Francine had mentioned Bruges. He concentrated on remembering the long-ago time he had spent there with his mother.

There were – had been – the bells of course, and the café with a red-checked gingham frill round the wall. He remembered a large tureen of thick soup on the table, and a sort of dish moulded into the shape of a fish. There were tiny birds in cages, and one day they had gone on a trip down the canals, past seventeenth-century houses leaning almost into the water. Tall spires of churches, and a stone cat set in the middle of a grassy courtyard. That he remembered well, because he had taken a photograph of it with his new box camera.

His head drooped onto his bent knees. And somewhere, not all that many miles from here, his father's grave, one of thousands, with his mother weeping, her hand on his shoulder. He recalled his embarrassment, and the way he had automatically snatched his school cap from his head, feeling the sense of drama called for by the moment.

Surely there was drama too in the fact that the soldier's son was here, a victim of another war, fighting the same enemy, but this time determined to stay alive. Determined to stay awake.

His eyes closed, his legs twitched, his hands unclenched, and as the grey light crept over the fields, he slept.

He jerked awake at the sound of a voice. He raised his head and saw a man looking down at him, a slight man with some sort of deformity pulling his head to one side. David instinctively drew the coat closer round him and tried to stand up, only to feel the man's hand on his shoulder, pressing him roughly back against the wall.

As David hesitated the man's hand shot out to tear aside the front opening of the coat, revealing David's RAF uniform, and the brevet sewn above the flap of his top pocket.

'Name, rank, number?' The question was asked in very bad, very broken English.

David's heart sank. 'Turner, David. Flight Lieutenant. 164308.'

'Squadron?'

David shook his head. 'Turner, David. Flight Lieutenant – '

The man sighed. 'Very well. You have given me enough for the moment.' He kicked the sacking bundle aside. 'Fasten your coat and follow me. No speaking! Right?'

'I follow you,' David said, and reaching for his stick staggered after the man into the wide sweep of fields, pale green now in the early morning mist.

There were clouds drifting over the inevitable rows of mushroom-topped trees; a wind was blowing and already it was obvious that the day was going to turn wet and stormy.

They turned into a field dark with fresh-ploughed furrows, and as David tried to negotiate the uneven ground his left ankle twisted and a pain like a red-hot needle ran up his leg. Hearing him cry out, the man turned and smiled, and his smile sent a shiver of fear down David's spine.

Was he a loyal Belgian? Or was he taking David now to hand him over to the Germans? David stopped for a moment, glancing round, assessing his chances of making a break for it, dismissing them as nil.

He could see smoke rising from chimneys hidden by the

trees of an orchard, trees bare of fruit, with apple leaves scattered in dank wet mounds.

It was like the end of everything – or it could have been the beginning. The man turned round again, motioning David to move more quickly. As David stumbled and almost fell, the smile flashed again, mirthless and uncalled for, twisting his mouth into a devilish grin.

Six

By November German troops were still bogged down outside Leningrad and fighting hard on the outer perimeter of Moscow. The weather in England was cold and damp and there were shortages now of practically everything. Pears were two shillings a pound, and on a never-to-be-forgotten day for Sally she saw a zinc bucket in the window of a hardware shop, and bore it home in triumph to her mother.

Stanley Barnes, crouched over his precious wireless set late one evening, heard a recording of Nazi sadism in a concentration camp reported by a doctor from Frankfurt. The described brutality filled Stanley with horror, and not even the news that the Italians in the Mediterranean were being routed could cheer him up.

Sally received a letter from the young airman who had called at the works to tell her that David was now officially reported 'Missing, believed killed'. The short letter had such a resigned fatalistic ring about it that Sally was filled with a deep sadness as she read the stilted words. So correct and proper, she thought bitterly, as if the writer had considered himself duty-bound to inform her of any eventuality. It was just the kind of letter David himself would have written, hiding his true feelings, phrasing it as if it were a school essay.

For a brief moment she saw him, standing as she had last seen him at the cemetery gates after his mother's funeral, straight and tall, hair sleeked back, his neat moustache brushed into line. It was impossible to erase his memory from her mind even if she had wanted to, and every night before she slept she prayed that he might still, somehow, be alive.

Lee's letters were very different. Even the airgraphs, photographed and reduced to a minute size, brimmed with the sound of his laughter and his capacity for seeing everything as a kind of game.

'Hi!' he had written from Canada, sending her an over-tinted card from Niagara Falls, showing the Rainbow Bridge with a technicoloured rainbow spanning the water. 'By the time you get this I will be on my way back. Are you ready for me, Sally, honey?'

Oh yes, she was ready for him. She was more than ready for the mere sight of him. The vivid blue of his eyes and his way of laughing with his head thrown back, sudden explosive laughter that she felt as a tingling in her ears. That dark November, laughter was in as short supply as the tiny luxuries of life, things which not long ago had been thought of as necessities. Like a zinc bucket spotted lying unbelievably in the centre of an ironmonger's shop window.

On the fourteenth of the month Lee disembarked with two thousand RAF personnel at Greenock. Rushing impulsively to the nearest telephone he actually dialled Sally's number before realizing that to the girl who had occupied his heart and mind all the time he had been away a telephone call was an impossibility. For the first time the enormity of her disability was brought home to him and he banged his fist against the sides of the call-box in an agony of frustrated impatience. The idea of passing on a message through either of her parents he dismissed entirely. After so many weeks of longing it would be an anti-climax he couldn't stomach, not at the moment.

The entire contingent boarded a train for Bournemouth, and Lee wrote immediately from the family hotel where he was to be billeted for a time not yet specified.

'I had forgotten the queues, honey,' he wrote, 'and the goddamned black-out, but I'm comfortable here. There's maid service, would you believe it! I might just change my mind about the class system yet. Now that I'm an officer things look kinda different from the other side of the fence.'

At the end of his second week he wrote to say that already the enforced waiting time was dragging. 'It's boring the pants off me, Sally. After the stiff discipline over in Canada I don't have enough to *do*! The weather has turned fine, and Bourne-mouth is a vacation resort in spite of everything, but I find it all so goddamned boring! But in December, honey, maybe in the first week of December, I'll be getting leave. So you hurry and tell that boss of yours the war effort will have to carry on without you for a while. Why? Because you're going to meet me in London, that's why!'

'He's an American,' Stanley said. 'That's why he talks daft about you going down to London to meet him. Distances mean nothing to them. I once heard tell of a Yank who drove three hundred miles there and three hundred back, all on the same day. They're mad, the lot of them. I remember them in the last lot. Just the same.'

Sally shook her head. 'Now, come on, Dad. You've never talked to an American, ever, have you? You can't generalize; it isn't fair.' She wrinkled her nose at him. 'Unless a man's a Lancastrian and follows cricket in summer and football in winter he's no good. Oh, and it helps if he's Church of England or Methodist, and isn't too keen on the Irish. An' you can just about tolerate him taking his tie off on his holidays, but only just.'

'Well, you're not going anyway, so there's no point in arguing, is there?' Stanley glanced at the clock on the mantelpiece and began to unlace his Home Guard issue boots. 'If you're not coming up to bed just yet, remember to leave the front door unbolted for your mother. She goes to that blessed factory in the dark now and comes home before it's proper light. Cheese and flippin' rice, that's the second time in a week this bootlace has broken. They couldn't be more fragile if they made them out of liquorice chews.'

He wasn't going to admit it, not even to himself, but Stanley Barnes was a frightened man. It wasn't just the war and his only son being in the thick of it out in the Middle East, though those things were bad enough. No, it cut deeper than that.

It was his home life that seemed to be tumbling in disorder around him. Josie, his wife, well, she had always had a hard side to her but now her tongue was as sharp as a new razor-blade. She never wore anything but trousers, even at weekends, and in his opinion God had given women bottoms that were better disguised in a feminine flutter of skirts. She was still sleeping in John's room, so his so-called sex life was apparently finished. He frowned as the bootlace refused to knot the way he wanted it to. Not that sex had ever bothered him much. He accepted that he wouldn't even make the starting post as a Casanova, but damn it, at their age, should it matter?

It wasn't money that was the trouble either. Josie was earning more than she had ever earned at that dress shop; Sally was handing over more than a fair share of her wages, and altogether they were better off financially than they had been for years.

He finished repairing the lace and, straightening up, met his daughter's direct gaze. He felt a muscle twitch at the side of his jaw-line. Once he could have laid down the law and Sally would have immediately acquiesced, listening to him in her own special way, nodding in agreement and seeing his point of view. She had been his beloved daughter, the apple of his eye, the veritable corner-stone of his existence. The joy of his life, he supposed wryly.

They had never meant to be a divided family, but from early on it had always been Josie and John, Sally and him. Siding two against two, even matching in appearance. John was the one who had inherited his mother's colouring and flippant way of speaking, while Sally took after her dad, dark of hair and eyes, with a bright untutored intelligence that no university course could have instilled in her. Now she never seemed to want to talk to him about the books she read, or have him explain the way the war was going. The war for Sally was that unseen American and his avalanche of letters and airgraphs plopping through the letter-box almost every flippin' day.

Now he had to talk to Barbara Shawfield at the office when he wanted to discuss what he had heard on the wireless. Her comments on what Professor Joad had said on 'Any Questions?' last week about his disbelief in astrology had put that old know-all into place. Barbara was a great believer in the stars. She had told him that he was a typical Capricorn, stolid and set in his ways, a man of integrity.

Stanley blinked. He wished Sally would stop looking at him like that as if she found him wanting. All *he* wanted was a bit of peace in his own home, his meals on the table at the proper time, his work and his Home Guard duties, and his women-folk sticking to the roles the good Lord had intended them to play.

'I'm going to London,' Sally said clearly.

'No, you're not,' Stanley said with equal clarity.

'You can't stop me.' Sally knew this was the wrong tack to take, but said it just the same.

'Can't I?' Stanley widened his eyes at her, trying to keep his voice light. 'Till you're twenty-one, my lass, I can stop you doing anything. While you're under my roof you do as I say.'

Sally put a hand to her forehead in a dramatic gesture that sent a flick of irritation across her father's face.

'You're not exactly Mr Barrett of Wimpole Street, you know, Dad. Queen Victoria's been dead a long time. It's nineteen forty-one, remember? And there's a war on. Lee may be posted overseas when he joins his squadron, then soon he'll be on operations.' Her soft voice was suddenly bleak. 'The odds are so much against them once they start that.' She got up and actually twisted her hands together in distress. 'Look what happened to David Turner. We were only friends, me and David, but I keep thinking about him, and I wish sometimes I'd been kinder to him. But with Lee, I don't intend to have any regrets, not now, or ever. I shall wait until he sends for me, then I will go.'

There was a vulnerability about her that made Stanley's heart contract with love. She seemed to have grown thinner lately, and her eyes had a bruised look about them as if she hadn't been sleeping too well. Suddenly he was blustering: 'You won't be safe on the train on your own.' There was an infinite compassion in his expression. 'What about the announcements? You won't be able to hear them. And the stations – they've taken all the names down.'

'I won't have to change trains. You know that. I'll get there all right.' Joining her hands around her knees she rocked herself backwards and forwards. 'I know what's bothering you, Dad, but I have to make my own way. You can't keep me wrapped up in cotton wool just because I'm deaf.' She stopped the rocking and looked straight at him.

'You're only really happy when I'm not going anywhere, aren't you? I can go to work and I can come home, but you'd like to keep me where you have your eye on me.' Her voice rose uncontrollably the way it always did when she was troubled. 'You have to stand back from me, Dad! If I hurt myself or make mistakes, or get lost, then that's fine, because the next time I'll do better. You have to stop *smothering* me!'

'Then I'm coming with you.' From the depths of his abject misery and misunderstanding, Stanley blundered into the unforgivable. 'I'm not having you standing up in the corridor of a train all that way. I'm not having you landing down in London with nowhere to stay, finding yourself marooned on Euston Station in the black-out with your luggage and that American chap not turning up. If you're set on going then I'll take you, see you settled in a decent hotel, then when you've introduced me to this Yank and I've sized him up I'll come back.'

Immediately, when it was too late, he realized his mistake. Sally jumped to her feet, her rosy cheeks even redder with anger. Her voice, so carefully monitored most of the time, came out in a hoarse wail.

'*You're* the deaf one, not me! You haven't been listening to a word I said! I am *nineteen*! If I'd been a boy I could be flying a plane or serving in a submarine! As it is I could be married, with a baby, or even two or three! I could be working away from home, living in a room and fending for myself. I'm *grown up*, Dad, and you want to take me on a train, and hold my hand, and keep my ticket safe in your wallet . . . Oh, God, I can just imagine the look on Lee's face if I turned up with you in tow! It's laughable! If it wasn't so pathetic it would be funny!'

Then just as quickly as her anger had flared, it seemed to evaporate. Sally shook her head from side to side, more in pity than harsh despair. 'Oh, Dad,' she whispered, her voice at its normal low pitch again, 'those days when you could boss me around have gone. I am going to think for myself, and act for myself, and if it makes you unhappy then I am truly sorry.'

There was an incipient bald patch on the top of his head; there was a sleeveless fair-isle pullover underneath the open battle-dress top, and these two homely ordinary things wrenched at her heart-strings. Conditioned over the years of her childhood into wanting to please this beloved father of hers, Sally was finding her metamorphosis into defiance difficult to cope with. But the war was going on and on. David Turner was just one of the growing list of casualties, and she was sick of the grey drabness of everything. It was unpatriotic to grumble, people were ordered to smile and take it on the chin, but Lee was back in England, he wanted to see her and not even her father's obvious distress was going to stand in her way.

'I'll finish unravelling this jumper, then I'll come up,' she said tonelessly. 'I never liked this lacey pattern anyway. I'm not a very good make-do-and-mender, but I'm saving my coupons to buy a new swagger coat for when I go down to London. I don't suppose . . . ?'

'You can have any coupons I've got left.' Stanley got up from his chair and stood looking down at the daughter he had once been able to guide and advise knowing with certainty that she would listen and see his point. Now there was this unknown Yank who only needed to crook his little finger to have her rushing to meet him. 'I don't know what your mother will have to say,' he muttered.

Realizing Sally hadn't heard, he stretched out a hand to touch her wrist in the old familiar way, drawing it back as he changed his mind. 'It doesn't matter.' He turned and limped towards the door, leaving his boots set side by side beside his chair.

'Oh, to hell with it all!' he whispered as he climbed the stairs, and his tone held a bitterness alien even to his own ears.

'Is your journey *really* necessary?'

The phrase, first dreamed up at the beginning of the war to discourage civil servants from going home for Christmas, was blazoned on a poster in the station entrance.

'Yes, it is,' Sally nodded at the poster, gave a twitch to the saucy little maroon felt hat secured to her head by a band of elastic underneath her hair, adjusted the collar of her new grey swagger coat, and joined the scramble of pushing passengers on the platform.

An hour later there was still no sign of the train, and looking round the crowded platform Sally decided that they would be lucky if even half of them got on the train, let alone found a seat.

There were servicemen dragging bursting kitbags, civilians lugging cases, and a general air of good temper and resigned tolerance that made Sally, in a sudden unexpected pricking behind her eyelids, feel proud that she was British.

The euphoric mood was short-lived as the London train backed into the station. Even before it jerked to a halt the smiling Britishers turned into a frightening shoving mob, elbowing their way into the compartments. Hesitating only briefly, Sally dived in, clutching at the carefully positioned hat as she felt it knocked sideways. A soldier trod on her foot whilst another pushed her roughly from behind. With one foot precariously on the high step Sally could see that the compartments all along the carriage were full, with servicemen and women hurling their kitbags onto the racks and claiming their seats in a spirit of good old 'Bugger you, Jack, I'm all right.'

With travellers surging in through the other doors, Sally saw with dismay that the corridor was already packed solid.

'They'll have to get off,' somebody shouted, and as she lip-read the command Sally's mind was made up.

Using her case as a battering ram, she barged her way into the train. Three soldiers opened a door and almost fell inside. The first one, with a smile of triumph, took up his position on the lavatory seat, and the other two sat down on the floor, tipped their forage caps over their foreheads and settled themselves for sleep. Sally, taking advantage of the man-oeuvre, stood with her back against the door jamb, planted her feet apart and prepared to stand firm. The seething mass trying to get past her all seemed to have extra-sharp elbows or kitbags with unidentified objects which jabbed into her, but, red in the face, her small jaw set in fierce lines of determination, she refused to move.

Over two hundred miles away down in London, Lee would be waiting for her, and if they tried to make her get off the train then it would have to be on a stretcher, she decided, because they would have to render her unconscious first!

'The whistle's been blown, so why the flamin' heck don't they set off?' A sailor with a pock-marked face lumped his kitbag on top of Sally's case. 'At this rate it'll be dark before we get to London and I've a train to catch to Southampton. Turn your back, love. The Gestapo's here!'

The guard, making the most of his hour of glory, was walking down the long platform, chivvying people off the train. 'We can't set off, tha knows,' he shouted. 'There's some of you lot come for the train after this. There's some of you only going as far as Crewe,' he scolded. 'Now come on, missus, it's servicemen first. There's a war on, tha knows!'

'Who d'you think you are? Adolf Hitler?' the woman shouted back.

At last the train started, leaving a furious knot of people on the platform. Sally breathed a deep sigh of relief. Standing all the way to London was nothing compared to the unthinkable possibility of watching the train depart without her. She felt feverish and light-headed. The train made two unscheduled stops even before reaching Crewe, and unbelievably a few more passengers squashed themselves into the corridor, treading on other people's feet, arms pinioned to their sides, leaving Sally propped against the lavatory door, her head swimming. She began to feel sicker by the minute.

But all the time the train was getting closer to London, its wheels clattering over the rails, taking her nearer to Lee, now Pilot Officer Lee Willis, a man she hardly knew. A foreigner, in spite of his British uniform.

When darkness fell the compartments were lit dimly by a boxed-in central light fitting. Blinds were drawn down over the windows, but in the corridors the darkness was almost complete. From time to time a fairly steady stream of passengers literally fought their way to the toilet, forcing the three soldiers to emerge from their comparative comfort to perch on top of a handy kitbag or weld themselves to a standing passenger until their bolt-hole became vacant once again.

Sally had long ago given up all hope of trying to reach her sandwiches in the case now hidden beneath piles of other people's luggage, and the sailor had given up trying to make conversation with her. Mistakenly deciding that her small set face and lowered eyes were indicative of shyness or reserve, he slid down to rest his forehead on his knees and fell into a jerking, open-mouthed sleep.

At long last the small stations of Hertfordshire were gliding past the darkened windows. The train whistled its way through the Watford tunnel, and the weary dishevelled passengers began to stretch cramped limbs. Sally felt beads of sweat form on her upper lip. Soon she would be seeing him, and whatever boats she had decided to burn were about to burst into flame.

Moving like a sleep-walker she was carried along the platform by the stream of exhausted travellers, her case bumping against her legs. She walked through to the ticket barrier, and out into the station foyer, and saw Lee waiting anxiously in a sea of faces, his blue eyes scanning the crowds, looking more English in his new Air Force officer's uniform than any American had a right to do.

'Hi, there, Sally, honey!'

Suddenly overcome by a terrible shyness, she could only stare at him. 'I'm sorry the train is so late. I don't know if I'm right, but we seem to have come half-way round England. It was so crowded you wouldn't believe.'

'So it seems.'

She looked very different in her grey swagger coat swinging from a yoke across the shoulders. The last time he had seen her she had been wearing a flowered summer dress with short puffed sleeves. Her hair had cascaded down her shoulders in wispy curls, but now she had rolled it up somehow underneath the saucer hat, making her look older, and so much a stranger that his heart sank.

'You look real smart,' he said. 'Give me your bag and we'll go find a cab.'

She handed the case over, then fell into step by his side. He seemed to be shorter in height than she remembered, and broader of shoulder. His heavy greatcoat was almost Russian-style in length, and his new cap was already squashed down and perched at a jaunty angle on his corn-yellow hair. He had a rolling way of walking, almost as if he were walking on the shifting deck of a ship. Sally frowned and chewed her lip.

Why had she never noticed these things before? She felt a weight of depression settle on her shoulders. His letters had been just words, after all, making her laugh, brightening the grey drabness of her days. Now she was painfully aware of his 'difference'. Almost as if he were a stranger. He was unlike any other man she had ever known, and having known so few it was surely pointless to begin to look for details of similarity. He was of a different breed, a stranger from a land over three thousand miles away, a land of cowboys and film stars, chewing gum and being familiar with strangers.

'I could stay at the YMCA,' she told him when they were seated side by side on the back seat of a taxi. 'I mean the YWCA.'

He patted her hand, his smile showing his perfect white teeth and the dimples in his cheeks. 'It's okay, honey. I've booked us into a hotel. Separate rooms. Okay?'

They were half-way through their meal, sitting alone in a corner of the dining-room, eating fried spam and mashed potatoes flanked by watery Brussels sprouts, when Sally looked across at him and recognized with relief the crazy laughing American she had remembered from what she would always think of as their own bluebell summer.

'What have they *done* to this so-called food?' he grinned, spearing a yellowed sprout on his fork. 'I know a charcoal-grilled steak can't be come by, but do they have to boil the stuffing out of the darned things?' He put the sprout back onto his plate. 'Okay, okay, don't tell me. There's a war on.' His eyes twinkled. 'What have you done to your hair, honey? For a minute I couldn't believe it was you back at the railroad station.'

'Tucked it into a top cut from one of my stockings. An old laddered pair,' Sally confided, then she blushed. 'Thanks for the lovely presents in my room. I've never seen stockings like that before, and the . . . the other things are beautiful.'

'I should think so considering what I had to pay on them to get them into the country.' Lee pushed his plate to one side and leaned his elbows on the table. 'I had to guess your size for the nightgown and the slip. I hope they fit okay.'

Sally lowered her eyes to her plate as she thought about the oyster satin nightgown, cut on the cross, with a halter neck.

She remembered seeing Betty Grable in a film wearing one very similar, or was it Veronica Lake? The cream winceyette pyjamas sprigged with forget-me-knots in her case were hardly to be compared.

'Oh Lord,' she thought, and wished she wasn't quite so hungry. It was embarrassing eating so heartily with those blue eyes watching her every mouthful.

'What are we going to do tomorrow?' she asked. 'You won't believe it, but this is the first time I've been to London. North Wales or the Yorkshire coast have been as far as my father was prepared to go.' She smiled. 'He looks on London as the city of vice. Could we walk round the West End? I'd love to see the shops in Oxford and Regent Streets.'

'If you'd like to do that, honey, then that's what we'll do.' Lee reached across the table and took her hand. 'There's no need to be afraid of me, Sally. I don't know what your father has told you about Americans, but we're not all hell-bent on stealing a young maiden's virtue.' He jiggled her hand up and down. 'You look exhausted. My guess is, the right place for you right now is bed. Then tomorrow we'll start out fresh. Okay?'

Sally nodded, too tired to argue, too filled with conflicting emotions to be able to think of anything else but the single bed in the room at the top of the four-storey hotel. She could still feel the vibration of the train wheels clacking on the rails, still see the blacked-out stations gliding by the dark windows, still see that first uncertainty in Lee's eyes when he had seen her walking towards him.

'Yes, tomorrow,' she said, wanting to weep without knowing why.

In Piccadilly Circus the famous statue of Eros was boarded up, and covering the boards were yellow and blue posters. 'Save in War Savings' the ring of onlookers were ordered, and Lee pointed to the huge drawing of sailors signalling the same message in semaphore.

Sally was beside herself with excitement. Here she was, in London! With the man she loved standing beside her. It was all too much. Sentimental tears filled her eyes as she clung to Lee's arm. A good night's sleep in the strange hotel bed had

114

brought back the warm colour to her cheeks, and her hair, unfettered now by the stocking-top, clustered round her vivacious smiling face.

They had already walked the length of Oxford Street and Regent Street. She had exclaimed over the clothes in the shop windows, calculating their worth in clothing coupons, sighed at the prices. She had seen servicemen of every nationality, crowding in the big stores, eager to spend their leave money. Gripping Lee's arm hard she had read the flashes on passing shoulders. Poland, Canada, Norway, New Zealand and South Africa, and at one point two Czechs crossing the busy road deep in conversation.

It seemed as if the whole of the Allied Forces were represented there on that bright morning. Staring up at Eros, she turned her face up to Lee.

'I once read in a book that if you stand on the steps of Swan and Edgar's over there for long enough someone you know is bound to walk by.'

'Is that so, honey?' His own face reflected her happiness. He nodded to himself, more than content that the subdued girl he had met at Euston Station was no more, leaving in her place the lovely girl he remembered from their last time together.

'That's Leicester Square down there, honey,' he told her. 'Last spring that whole area was bombed and set fire to. Like your city of Liverpool.'

He pushed his cap further to the back of his head. 'You'd never believe it when you see all these people strolling around, would you? Shall we go down there and get in the queue for a movie? It's *Gone with the Wind* showing right now.'

'Oh, Lee. Look at poor old Shakespeare!'

Sally pointed to the statue, damaged and bomb-scarred. 'I wonder what he would have made of all this?'

The queue moved forward slowly. 'I never rated him all that much,' Lee confided. 'We read him in the eighth grade, but I guess he only registers when he's acted in the theatre. I know he just about bored the pants off me.'

'Me too.' Sally giggled. 'Aren't we awful?'

The film lasted for three hours and forty-eight minutes. The cinema was packed, and even during the interval the majority of the audience stayed in their seats as if totally mesmerized. When the lights came on and Lee told Sally she was the dead spittin' image of Vivien Leigh, she said she wished she could endorse his flattery by swearing he was Clark Gable's double.

'But I cannot tell a lie,' she said, her whole face crinkling into laughter.

And the following days were equally laughter-filled. Hand in hand they walked for miles, absorbing the beauty of the war-torn city, stopping to stare at famous landmarks, walking on once more, then stopping again.

'I can't imagine Park Lane with the railings round the park.' Sally waved an arm. 'If you didn't know they'd gone for salvage you could imagine this was a wide road out in the country. London keeps surprising me all the time.'

Following directions pointed out to them by a newspaper seller, muffled against the cold by pieces of sacking tied round his old legs, they wandered down the middle lane of Covent Garden.

'Rhubarb!' Sally gasped. 'And crates of apples! Look, Lee, it says Canada on the boxes. It's like a fairy grotto, isn't it?'

'If you discount that fair-sized bomb crater, honey.' Lee sniffed. 'Strikes me it's being used as a dump. I reckon someone ought to have filled that in.'

'We're fighting a war!' Sally told him, raising her voice a little. 'On our own soil, for heaven's sake! Would New York be as tidy as I'm sure it is if bombs had fallen on it?' Then she wrinkled her nose at him. 'Sorry, love, that was unfair. But even that dump looks good to me. I want to go back with so many memories of what I've seen that they last me for a long, long time.'

Lee swung her round to face him. 'I want you to remember *me*!' He bent his head and kissed her. 'That's the most important thing, sweetheart.' For a moment they clung together till the freezing wind wrapped a piece of packing paper round their legs. They drew apart, still laughing.

On the day before Sally was due to leave for home, a winter sun, round and red as one of the Canadian apples, hung in the sky over London.

'What would you say if I told you I'd like to go to church,

honey?' Lee touched her nose gently with his finger. 'I haven't suddenly gotten religion, but back home Sunday was always church-going day, and I guess I'd like to go with you. Would you mind?'

They walked the short distance to the badly bombed church of St James's. Sally felt the ache of tears in her throat as she saw the extent of the damage to the centuries-old church. The usual smell of decaying walls was almost hidden by the stronger smell of charred wood and disturbed earth. She saw Lee's lips move in awe as he read the inscription on the only plaque untouched by fire:

'William Van de Velde the elder, who died in 1693; and of his son who died in 1707.'

'Holy smoke!' Lee mouthed, and Sally stifled a giggle.

When they knelt down to pray, Lee peeped through his fingers at Sally's bowed head. A wave of tender caring suddenly engulfed him as he tried to imagine the isolation of her totally silent world. For him the service had been marred by the sounds of cars and taxi-cabs hooting their way along Jermyn Street, but for Sally there was nothing.

'But that's not why I love her,' he told God in all seriousness.

At nine o'clock that night he heard on the hotel wireless that American bases in the Pacific had been bombed by the Japanese.

'We're in!' he told a startled Sally, bursting into her bedroom without knocking, his previous gentlemanly behaviour forgotten. 'Roosevelt will declare war. He can't fail. Oh, boy oh boy, what will old Colonel Lindberg have to say now? We can't hold back any longer! We're in! We're in! You'll see!'

He was as excited as a young boy, his blue eyes shining, his fair hair standing on end as he ran his fingers through its short silken stubble. He seemed not to notice that Sally, about to change into a warmer skirt and jumper for their proposed walk to a Regent Street café for a farewell drink, was standing in front of him wearing a skimpy pair of camiknickers.

'There seem to have been a lot of casualties,' he told her, suddenly serious. 'The Japs will have had themselves a field day if they dropped bombs on Honolulu.' He came towards her and pulled her into his arms, then remembering held her away as he went on: 'Australia will have to wake up now. And what about those Japs we saw in church this morning? They'll have to hide their yellow faces now, honey, that's for sure!'

When Sally reached behind her for her dressing-gown on the bed, he held it out for her, helping her on with it as if it were a coat, words bubbling out of him, the elongated dimples at the sides of his mobile mouth coming and going, his eyes blazing with excitement.

'Do you mind if we stay in?' he wanted to know. 'We can get a bottle of wine maybe, and keep the radio on.' He nodded to the set at the side of Sally's bed. 'There isn't one in my room, believe it or not, and there's bound to be more news. They said there'd be more on the midnight bulletins, but there may be more before then.' Kneeling on the bed, he twiddled the knobs, groaning with disgust when the sounds of a Palm Court orchestra filled the little room. 'It means you too, honey. Your Mr Churchill swore that if America was involved in a clash with Japan, then Britain would join in "within the hour". Oh, boy oh boy, did you ever believe that it would actually happen?'

With an almost motherly expression on her face Sally watched him prowling round and round the small room, the muscles of his broad shoulders rippling beneath his blue shirt. His excitement was infectious, and yet suddenly she burst out: 'Lee! Stop and think! It's marvellous news, but don't forget it also means total war and that means your boys being killed. Stop waving a flag and just *think*!'

'What's gotten into you, honey?' He was genuinely bewildered. 'God damn it, the war's as good as over!'

Sally shook her head at him. 'Okay. You go and get the wine. We'll stay in and listen to the wireless. Who knows? Old Hitler might have decided to throw the sponge in already!'

Lee shook a mock fist at her as he almost ran from the room, and even before he came back Sally knew what would almost certainly happen.

She had no clear idea of what to expect. At school, then at the office, she had struggled to lip-read as her friends whispered their experiences, but unable to join in had accepted that they regarded her as some kind of retarded freak.

She had never seen a man naked, not even her brother, but she remembered with awful clarity the terrifying hardness of David Turner's body as he had ground himself up against her.

Lee had never treated her roughly. His kisses had always been slow and sweet, and when her senses had responded he had put her from him, smiled at her with his blue eyes and trailed a finger down her cheek. Sally frowned and bit hard at her lip. Tomorrow she was going home. Lee was moving on to the final part of his training before, like David, he went onto operational flying. She trembled and rubbed the tops of her arms.

Lee wanted to marry her. He had said so over and over again. He was going to take her back to America. In his heart he was confident this would come to pass, because unlike David he seemed to be immune from fear, assured of his own immortality.

David knew the odds, but Lee refused to consider them. Sally shivered.

'Flying is so wonderful, honey,' he had told her. 'I like it best early in the mornings when we fly through the clouds. Up there is the sun, and down there the clouds are like snow raked up with a garden fork.'

'And when you fly at night?' she had wanted to know.

'Still beautiful. Okay, sometimes you're lonesome just sitting there watching the dials. I tell you, honey, it's guys like your friend down the road who do all the hard slog. It's the observer who has the brains of the outfit. Me, I'm just the driver of that darned crate.'

It was at this point that Sally had almost told Lee about David. Missing, believed killed. The words had been there, but such a feeling of terror had gripped her heart she had let the moment pass.

If that should happen to Lee . . . Sally looked over at her case on the luggage stand by the bedroom door. The oyster satin nightgown was inside, folded into slippery silken folds. For a brief moment she considered putting it on, then her northern sense of humour came to her rescue.

'This isn't a picture, and you're not Joan Crawford sending her man to his almost certain doom,' she told herself, and when Lee burst into the room waving two bottles aloft, she was laughing softly to herself.

'I can't bear the thought of you going back tomorrow.'

There was only an inch or so of the rough red wine left in the first bottle when Lee told her that. They were sitting close together on the bed, and as Lee pushed her gently back Sally knew a sudden brief moment of fear. Then, as his hand moved slowly over her breasts, she wound her arms round him to draw him closer.

'How lovely you are, Sally.' His voice held a quiet wonder, and because she could not see his mouth Sally heard nothing. She knew he was murmuring words of love and even at that moment of surrender she felt an aching frustration because his tender words were lost to her.

'I want to make you happy,' she whispered. 'For the rest of my life I want to be the reason for your happiness.'

Her sweet flat little voice with the unusual inflections in its rise and fall was stilled. The tears were stinging behind her closed eyelids, but soon the pain ebbed into a sensation of such intensity she felt she could die of it.

'Oh, Sally . . . my own darling Sally . . .'

Lee held her close when it was over, murmuring his love until they fell asleep.

They slept, drugged with wine and love, right through the midnight news on the wireless.

Held close in each other's arms, they were totally oblivious of the solemn voice of the announcer telling of bombs falling on far-away islands in the sun.

Seven

'Christmas!' Josie wailed. 'What am I supposed to give him for food? Fed on the fat of the land, Yanks are. He'll expect a turkey with all the trimmings, and God knows what besides! And where's he going to sleep?'

She sat down at the kitchen table and gave Sally a baleful look. 'There's only our John's room, and I'm in there.'

'You can move in with Dad, surely? It's only for the one night.' Sally slewed her eyes ceilingwards as if begging for patience. 'I'm going to *marry* him! Don't you want to meet him, for heaven's sake? You'll like him, I know that. You can't help liking Lee. He's special, you'll see.'

Josie stared at her daughter in disbelief. Where was the good little girl they had moulded, protecting her and unwittingly cramping her development as surely as if they had bound her feet with bandages. It was startling, to say the least, to see the way Sally had come back from London a changed person. Her face seemed all upswept curves, with the closed-in look gone completely. It was as though even her former vivacity had been all a pretence. Josie raised her shoulders in an exaggerated sigh, remembering the days when she herself must have looked like that. In the days of her loving, when a phone call from Bill could send her flying to meet him as if flamin' wings had been taped to her heels. Now, since the weekend at Morecambe, nothing. Bloody nowt.

For a while she had made up excuses for his silence. Reasons like, well, like his wife had contracted an incurable ailment, so terrible that they had given him his discharge to look after her. Or that he had been killed drilling his men on the seafront at Morecambe, waving his hands above his head to warn them as a lone German fighter swept in from the sea to dive-bomb. Unlikely, maybe ridiculous, but just possible, she had told herself in despair.

But the truth was, she knew now, that Bill had been plain scared off. When she had told him she was prepared to leave her husband, that had put the lid on it. Good and proper. For ever.

'I don't know what your father will say,' she grumbled, reaching for a packet of cigarettes, taking one out, then shaking the packet as if she refused to believe it could possibly be empty. 'You know what he's like about Americans.'

'And the Irish, and the Welsh, and anyone who comes from south of the Wash,' Sally reminded her. 'Well, he's going to have to get used to Americans. Lee says this country will be full of them before long. The girls at work say there's going to be a US army base not far away from here, so there'll be thousands of them.' She waved a hand at the cloud of smoke hiding her mother's face across the table. 'You'll love it, Mum. There'll be dances, lots of them. Wouldn't you like to start going dancing again?'

'With Olive and her one leg?' Josie refused to be cheered. Puffing doggedly at the cigarette she pulled the collar of her dressing-gown closer round her throat. 'He'll expect a fire in his bedroom, and where would I get the coal? Even if there was a fireplace in John's little room. Americans like over-heated rooms,' she added darkly, 'and showers and toilets. They're years ahead of us.'

'He *has* stayed here once, remember?' Sally was just going to add 'the weekend you went to Morecambe', but one look at her mother's set face stopped the words in her throat. 'Mum? Lee lives on a farm. He told me they have wood-burning stoves. It's not as if we live in a back-to-back house with the lavatory in the backyard. And even if we did, it wouldn't matter to him. He's not a snob.'

'Before I married your father I lived in a house like that.' Josie dredged up a long shuddering sigh. 'We shared a toilet with the family next door, and a lot of dirty buggers they were. It was just a wooden seat with a hole in it, and a flap let into the wall for the muck men to shove a rake in. It used to be my job to tear the newspaper into squares and thread a string through the corners, and the boy next door used to write rude things on the whitewashed walls. I remember once he wrote: "Even the King shits".'

'Mum!' Sally realized that when her mother was at her crudest it was usually because she was doing it purposely, for a laugh and to shock, but now there was no gleam of humour in the bleak blue eyes. And her mother's brand of honest vulgarity without its qualifying laughter *was* offensive, Sally decided, then was immediately ashamed.

'I want you to like Lee,' she said quietly. 'It means a lot to me that you at least *try* to like him. He's miles away from home, and soon he'll be going on operations. Mum, listen! He told me that now America is in the war he could be asked to transfer to the United States Army Air Force, but if that happens then he's going to fight it all he can. He won't do it unless they make it official. He's been in this war right from the beginning. In the worst of the fighting in France before its capitulation. He was with the American Volunteer Ambulance Corps, and at one time he was fighting with a Free French squadron. That was when he knew he wanted to fly. For us. For *England*. Lee is special, Mum. You'll see.'

Josie squinted through the smoke at her daughter's face, glowing with love for this unknown Yank who one day would take her away. The blue eyes narrowed. Away from this godforsaken hole where it rained every other day, where even when the war ended life would go on in a dreary monotonous round of work and sleep.

'What do you want me to do? Put a flamin' flag out?' she said, hating for a moment the sight of that naked face with the eyes shining with happiness and the mouth pleading for understanding.

'A woman at work knows somebody who might know where there's a goose going,' she said at last. Then she turned her head away from the blazing gratitude on Sally's face.

'I love you, Mum.' Sally came round the table and kissed Josie's powdered cheek. 'I knew you'd manage to come up with something.'

'As the chorus girl said to the bishop,' Josie said, her eyes hard and unsmiling again.

*

They were waiting for him when he came striding up the road from the tram terminal, walking with that rolling movement of the hips, his RAF cap pushed to the back of his corn-yellow hair.

'That's the doorbell, love.' Stanley nodded at Sally, put his newspaper aside and stood up, fiddling with the knot of his tie. Josie stared into the fire, trying not to see the way Sally rushed from the room. Christmas was hell for those who had lost somebody, she had already decided, preferring to think of Bill as dead, lying beneath a wooden cross in some foreign field.

'It's real nice of you to have me visit, sir.' The American shook hands with Stanley, and immediately Josie saw why Sally was the way she was about him.

The Yank was the best-looking young man she had seen in a whole month of Sundays. Handsome in a totally masculine way, with his bright gold hair and his flashing white teeth. And his eyes, when he turned and shook her hand, were as blue as a postcard sky, and he was so clean . . . the cleanliness of him made you blink. Surely his uniform had been tailored in Savile Row! It fitted him like a kid glove, not a wrinkle anywhere. She smiled at him and went on smiling, even when he let go of her hand and sat down next to Sally on the settee. If he was an example of what was coming over, then life might be worth living after all. For a brief moment a glimpse of the old light-hearted Josie was visible in the small powdered face, then the mask came down again as the hardness crept back into her expression.

'You're stationed near Oxford now?' Stanley leaned forward, questions at the ready, trying with his usual good manners to set the Yank at his ease. Josie curled her lip. Any minute now and he'd be going on about Anglo-American relations and Lend Lease. Josie got up and excused herself, murmuring something about the dinner, willing Stanley to follow her through into the kitchen and knowing full well he wouldn't. She crossed the hall, her behind swaying in the too-tight skirt, conscious of the fact that the Yank had stood up as she left the room.

'He knows his manners, anyroad,' she told herself, and reached into the cupboard for a hoarded tin of plums and another of cream.

'I only got there the other day,' Lee was telling Stanley, sitting down again when Josie had closed the door behind her. 'But I've done a bit of exploring already, sir.' He put an arm round Sally's shoulders and drew her to him. 'You can't tell there's a war on if you don't spot the odd air-raid shelter. The colleges and the churches look as though they've been there for ever and intend to go on being there. Your Oxford has a serenity unlike any of our university towns in the States.' He grinned. 'But I guess the results are equally as good. You just take education at a slower pace. Anyway, I was most impressed.'

'So some of our towns and institutions haven't impressed you, then?' Stanley fingered his moustache, his thwarted love of argument for argument's sake getting the better of his judgement. 'I'd be interested to hear your impressions of us, Lee.' He winked at Sally, unaware that she was holding her breath and shaking her head at one and the same time. 'Come on, lad. Let's hear what you really think about us.'

Sally fled to the kitchen, and stood picking nervously at a succulent piece of roasted goose, only to have her hand smartly slapped. Mild hysteria shone from Josie's blue eyes.

Sally came to stand close. 'Dad's in his element. He's doing his best to get Lee to criticize England, and Lee is falling for it. But what Dad doesn't and won't understand is that Lee would laugh off similar comments about his own country. Mum? Are they arguing? Can you hear anything? You'll have to go through and do something. I'll die if Dad starts a row.'

'Chop them carrots,' Josie said, forking roasted potatoes onto a dish, while keeping an eye on the gravy thickening nicely on the top of the stove. 'Then go through and tell them to sit down at the table. We don't want it getting cold.'

'I expect you have food parcels sent over?' Stanley, carving the goose, looked over the top of his spectacles at Lee. 'I remember in the last war your lot never seemed to be short of anything.'

Sally's eyes slewed quickly to Lee's face, then relaxed as he winked at her.

'No, sir. Not me. There are a lot of Canadians on my squadron and they get butter and candy and cakes sent over pretty regularly, but I told my folks not to fret. Candies and stuff like that don't bother me none.'

'Don't hold back, love.' Josie passed him the dish of browned potatoes. 'We don't mind starving for a week after you've gone back.'

Just for a second, bewilderment passed like a shadow over Lee's face, then he grinned. 'I'm just about getting used to the English sense of humour, I guess, but it had me worried at first.'

'Lancashire humour is very down to earth,' Stanley stated, raising his eyebrows fractionally as Lee refused the gravy and began to cut up his meat with quick movements before transferring his fork to his right hand. 'And I'll tell you another thing. This country might seem a bit disorganized compared to yours, but we're proud of our defects, own up to them and then go on and win. We don't shout the odds first.'

'No, sir.' Lee nodded seriously. 'I grant you that, but don't you agree that what seems to be lack of initiative in some of the lower ranks could be because they've been made to feel second class for too long? Both at home and in the Forces. They sure spend a lot of energy in grumbling.'

'The English have *always* grumbled!'

Sally held her breath as her watchful eyes told her that Stanley's voice was raised. Josie was giving him black looks across the table; the carefully prepared food on their plates was growing cold, and any minute now her parents would launch into one of their bickering insulting exchanges. She glanced quickly at Lee, but his face showed no embarrassment. To him it was merely an interesting discussion, and he was totally unaware of the undercurrents of bitterness crackling in the air like thunder.

'Lee's father is a farmer, and his grandfather was a Methodist minister.' Sally's soft flat voice held a tone of pleading, which turned to desperation as Josie threw a baleful glance in her husband's direction.

'Methodists? Oh well. You've come to the right shop, lad. Sally's father here was brought up as a Methodist. Anything enjoyable was classed as Sin. No dancing, no drinking, not even a pack of cards in the house.' She smiled at Lee to pretend to him that what she was saying was teasing. 'A right funny religion I reckon Methodism to be when a game of rummy sets you on the road to ruin.'

'My wife likes her little joke.' Stanley winked at Lee who nodded politely, while Sally stared down at her plate, her eyes shadowed with despair.

But it wasn't a joke. Josie's jokes were spiked with bitterness, edged with barbed insults, and Stanley knew it. Any minute now and they'd be at each other's throats like a pair of fighting cocks, only stopping when one of them drew blood. Sally choked on a mouthful of food. It was Christmas, and Lee was here for such a short time. Soon he would be walking with his crew out to a big black bomber lined up with other big black bombers round the edge of an airfield. He would climb aboard and the ugly monstrosity would trundle into position like a lumbering great bird before rising into the air on its way to Germany. Flak would come at them, blinding, maiming; Lee would push up his goggles from a face wet with his own blood. The odds against him surviving were so small as to be hardly worth considering. He was brave, so foolishly brave. She knew instinctively that Lee would never crack as David Turner had cracked. But up there in the dark night sky he would be as vulnerable as the most nervous.

She glanced at her mother's tight little face beneath the floss of white-gold hair. She looked across the table at her father, trying to hide his hurt behind a barrage of forced sarcasm, and for a moment she hated them both.

'And you've never found yourself to be the odd man out?' Stanley was making an effort. 'I mean with you being the only American in your particular little lot?'

'No, sir.' Lee's blue eyes twinkled. 'At first there was a kind of veiled antagonism. At the beginning most of the men had come straight from home postings. They resented the power wielded over them by a certain Corporal Whiteley, but I was used to it. You can get used to being called a Yankydoodle after a while.' He grinned. 'The worst time was when I left a newspaper cutting from back home lying around. The heading was: "A gallant Texan flies with the RAF". That took a bit of living down.'

'I should imagine it did.' Stanley pointed his knife at Lee. 'We don't talk that kind of language in England.'

'You sure don't,' Lee said, completely unrattled. 'It took me a while to figure out that "bloody wizard" or "good show" meant very good etcetera. And I had a few problems with "shooting a line" and "putting up a black", but we understand each other pretty well now.'

Sally, trying hard to follow the unsatisfactory conversation, her eyes darting from one impassive face to another, caught Josie's triumphant nod.

'That's telling you!' it told her husband.

Immediately Stanley stood up, pushing back his chair, throwing his paper napkin down on the table. Then to Sally's horror he walked swiftly from the room. She felt misery tighten like a hard knot inside her. Surely, surely, Stanley wasn't making one of his dignified exits like he always did when his wife's taunts and black looks got too much for him to take? She put out a hand and felt it immediately gripped in Lee's firm grasp.

'It's only the doorbell, honey,' he said, and she closed her eyes in relief.

'It's a funny time for anybody to call, at dinner time,' Josie said. 'It's not the milk because we got extra for the holiday, and I paid him then.' She widened her eyes at Lee. 'Is it right that you don't have your milk delivered in the States? That you have to drive to a shop for it?'

Lee nodded. 'That's right, ma'am. But being on a farm, that don't signify. We get our milk as easy as turning on a faucet.'

'Faucet?' Josie was flirting now. 'He's a long time.' She glanced at her husband's plate. 'Well, at least he'd finished. I'll fetch the pudding in. Just pass me your plates, it won't take a minute.'

She was standing with the plates in her hand when Stanley came back into the room. He stopped on the threshold, his whole body curved into a line of misery. Sally's heart skipped a beat as she saw the telegram held loosely in his hand. She sat upright in her chair, her eyes wide in a face suddenly drained of all its fresh colour.

'Dad?' Her voice cracked. 'What is it? What's wrong? Are

you all right?' But she knew. She knew what was in the telegram before Stanley spoke. Her mind screamed in terror. 'Oh, no! Please God, no! Let it not be that . . .'

Stanley limped over to the table, putting his hand on Josie's shoulder, pulling her up to hold her still. Sally's eyes searched his mouth, her heart thumping now with a racing fear.

'It's John. He's been killed. In Libya. On a commando raid. He's been killed in action.'

'But he wasn't a commando!' Josie's voice rose in a scream. 'He was in bomb disposal! Not the commandos. It's a mistake! He wouldn't go in the commandos, not without telling us.' Her eyes hardened as she pushed herself away from Stanley's arms. 'It's that girl! That Christine Duckworth! He must have joined when she wrote to tell him she was getting married. It's her fault! The bloody snobbish bitch! My son wasn't good enough for her, and now she's killed him!' Her voice rose hysterically. 'An' she won't even care! She won't give a damn! Not her!'

'Oh, love . . .' Stanley stretched out his arms again, but Josie knocked his hands away with a fierce swiping motion. 'Don't you tell me I'm wrong! He loved that girl from the moment he first set eyes on her.' She began to back away from the table towards the door. 'The last time I spoke to John on the phone he told me he was going to marry her. An' she threw him over because he hadn't got no pips on his shoulder. She broke his heart.' Her eyes flashed scorn. 'When she wrote to him he decided to get himself killed! I know! *I know!*'

When she rushed from the room Stanley turned pain-dazed eyes onto Sally. 'Let her go, love.' His voice was flat but firm. 'She's wrong, but it might help her. She has to blame someone. That's the only way she can bear it.'

Sally trembled as the horror of it rose inside her. Her mother was speaking what could so easily be the truth. She felt Lee's arms come round her. John might have been killed even if he had never set eyes on Christine Duckworth, but Josie would never believe that.

'Oh, Lee . . . Oh, Dad . . .' She twisted round and getting up from her chair, tears blinding her, groped her way into her father's arms. He stared at her blankly, wrapped in his own pain.

'He was my son too.' His eyes slewed ceilingwards. 'But she won't see that. At a time like this she still has no time for me.'

'Dad!' Sally stared at her father, seeing, even through her anguish and her tears, the weakness and selfish demeanour of the broken man standing in front of her. Her fingers tightened on his arms. 'Don't you think you ought to go upstairs?' She turned to Lee. 'Don't you think he ought to go up and see to her?'

'Sally's right, sir.' Lee spoke with a firm decisiveness. 'I guess she needs you right now.' He looked round at the remains of the Christmas meal on the table. 'I figure I ought not to be here, sir. Not right now.' He picked up the dish with the carcass of the goose congealing in a layer of fat. 'I'll take Sally into the kitchen and we'll tidy up some. Then if there's anything you want me to do – any messages – just say so.' He put out a hand to Sally. 'Come on, honey. You come with me. Okay?'

In the kitchen, folded close in Lee's arms, the tears flowed down Sally's cheeks. She could taste their saltiness as they ran past her open mouth.

'He was so full of life and fun,' she sobbed. 'Always laughing.' She raised an anguished face. 'He used to put a record on the gramophone and dance with my mother, twirling her round till she went dizzy. He was so clever with his hands.' She nodded towards a row of cupboards high on the kitchen wall. 'He put those up because he knew my father can't even knock a nail in straight. Everybody liked him, Lee. Everybody.'

'Sh . . . sh . . .' Lee smoothed the curly fringe back from Sally's forehead, one half of his mind on what Sally was saying and the other half trying to concentrate on what was happening upstairs.

'Let me in!' Stanley's voice rose higher as he pounded on a door. 'Josie? Open the door! *Unlock* the door! Josie? Do you hear me? The panic in his voice spiralled downstairs.

'This will kill my mother,' Sally whispered. 'John was the apple of her eye. She adored him. Oh, God, this awful war! She'll never lift her head up after this.'

When Stanley came into the kitchen he seemed to have aged twenty years. Limping over to the table he sat down, burying his face in his hands.

'She's locked herself in the bathroom,' he whimpered into spread fingers. 'Won't even answer me.' He lifted his head and looked straight at Lee. 'It's no use, lad. I know my wife, and she won't come out of there till it suits her. She's crawled into a hole, gone into a corner away from us. We'll just have to let her be.'

'What's happening?' Sally came round the table and forcibly pulled her father's fingers away from his face. 'Dad? I can't hear you! What's wrong with Mum? Tell me!'

'There's nothing wrong with her that we can put right.' Stanley lifted a ravaged face. 'She doesn't want you, and she doesn't want me. The only one she wants at this moment is John, and nobody can fetch him back.' Tears filled Stanley's dark eyes. 'We just have to let her be.'

'Where is she?'

Lee marvelled at the patience in Sally's voice. Young she might be, his little English sweetheart, but in this moment of crisis her strength was twice that of the defeated man slumped at the table.

'What is she doing, Dad?' Sally gripped Stanley's bowed shoulder. 'In her room?'

Wearily Stanley shook his head. 'No, not in her room. She's shut herself in the bathroom and shot the bolt on the door. She won't speak to me. She doesn't *want* me, lass. That's all there is to it.'

'Lee?' Whirling round, Sally held out a hand. 'Come upstairs with me! We've got to get in to her! If we have to break the door down we have to get in!'

She ran out into the hall, pulling herself by the bannister rail, her feet scarcely touching the stairs. Grasping the handle of the bathroom door she rattled it gently at first, then with increasing panic.

'Mum?' Her eyes were wide in the terrified pallor of her round face.

'Mum? It's me, Sally. Open the door. Please!'

She turned to Lee. 'Is she answering?'

He shook his head.

'Is she moving about? Can you hear anything? Anything at all?'

Putting his head close to the solid door, a door built in the twenties and made to last, Lee held his breath for a second. 'I'm not sure, but I think I can hear water running.' He stepped back. 'Move away, honey. This won't take a minute.'

The narrow landing did not give him much of a run, but the months of training had left the American fighting fit. With a well-aimed kick the door shuddered and the flimsy bolt gave.

The water in the bath was just beginning to flood the diamond-patterned oilcloth on the floor. It was pink water; that was the first thing Sally noticed as she stood on the threshold, unable to move, a hand holding still the strangled scream rising in her throat.

Her mother's head rested on the side of the bath, the blonde hair sleek to her skull as if she had tried to drown then changed her mind. Her hands were spreading tendrils of red through the water. She was fully clothed.

'She's cut her wrists!' Lee turned off the tap, and bending over lifted the still figure up into his arms. 'Go tell your father to call the hospital for an ambulance! Quick! She's alive, honey. She's alive!'

But by the time the ambulance came Josie had sunk into unconsciousness nearly as deep as death itself. Stanley hovered, helpless in his anguish, watching as Lee bound Josie's wrists, telling Sally what to do, cursing when the ambulance took twenty minutes to arrive.

'God damn it, man, what kept you?' Lee followed the stretcher out to the door. 'Go on, sir.' He pushed Stanley through the door. 'You go with them. I'll follow with Sally. We'll get a cab. Go on!'

'You'll never get a taxi. Not today. Not at Christmas.' Stanley, ineffectual to the last, turned a piteous face as he stumbled down the path. 'Better stay here with Sally. Better . . . far better . . .'

'We'll get transport, sir. Okay?' Lee stood bareheaded in the pale afternoon sunshine, an arm round Sally. 'Go on, sir. Please.'

'He's too gentle.' Sally stood by the telephone, watching dazed as Lee did exactly what he had said he would do, and rustled up a cab. 'Oh, how could she do it, Lee? Especially now?'

'*Because* of now,' Lee said, putting the receiver back on its stand. 'Her mind couldn't take it, so she did what she could to shut it all out.' He pulled Sally into his arms and kissed her on her trembling mouth. 'Now go get your coat, okay? Your momma's going to be okay.'

Suddenly he pulled her close again with a desperate urgency. 'I can see you're going to need me around, honey.' His blue eyes darkened with love. 'And that's where I'm going to be. Around as much as I can, and when I get settled and stop moving about – when we're married, you're going to come and stay near me.' He looked into her eyes. 'It can happen, honey. A guy can have his wife near the base.' He traced her mouth with a finger. 'Your momma's not going to die. She's going to be okay, and your dad will look after her.' He smiled. 'They might not be getting along too good, but in his own way he loves her. You know that.'

'She had another man. A soldier.' Sally reached up and clasped his hands as they lay on her shoulders. 'She went away with him, then he chucked her, and it left her feeling . . .' she groped for the right word 'It left her *diminished*. You know?'

'And your father hasn't forgiven her?'

'I don't think he's ever mentioned it.' Sally felt her eyes begin to burn again. 'They just hurt each other. All the time.'

The sound of the doorbell stopped Lee's reply.

'The cab's here,' he said hurriedly. 'Ready, honey?'

They sat round the fire until late that night, Lee and Sally on the settee together and Stanley opposite them in his chair. There was no uncomfortable embarrassment about the American. He had slipped into easy familiarity as though he had belonged to the Barnes's household for years. Already he knew his way around the kitchen, and kept disappearing then reappearing with a tray of tea.

'She'll be out of the hospital in a few days, but what then?' Stanley shrank down into his knitted cardigan, droopy from many washings, the knot of his tie unloosened, even his small moustache following the downward lines of his whippet-lean features. 'Hearing about John was only the final straw. She's been depressed for a long time.'

He stared into the fire. 'I wish you'd known her a year ago, lad. Always cracking jokes, and going out dancing.' Stanley reached for his pipe. 'I know some folks thought it strange for a married woman to go out dancing, but she *needed* to be gay and happy. I suppose some thought I was weak for letting her go and saying nothing, but Sally's mother was different. She needed people round her all the time; she liked bright colours, music – not my kind of music – but I understood. At least I thought I understood.'

He was pretending the soldier had never existed, Sally told herself. After that first initial outburst, when Josie had come back from Morecambe and he had caught her out, her father had pushed it to the back of his mind. And now was certainly not the time to remind him of it.

A coal shifted in the grate, throwing up flames that made shifting shadows in the darkened room. Sally knelt down on the rug, feeling the heat on her face as she took the firetongs and put the coal back into place. She could still see her mother's eyes as she lay in the high and narrow hospital bed, desperate blue eyes mirroring her damaged spirit. She wondered how much of the gaiety and sometimes crude light-heartedness had been a cover for a desolation that had always been there?

When she took her place beside Lee again, the brightness of her own eyes told him she was near to tears.

He took her hand and held it for a moment against his cheek. 'I wish I didn't have to go back in the morning,' he whispered.

'We'll be all right.' Sally nodded her head up and down twice, then flinched as Lee searched her eyes for a long moment.

'God damn it! You English slay me. You crucify yourselves trying not to say what you really mean and think!' He turned to Stanley. 'Forgive me, sir. It's impertinent of me to speak my mind. It's just that the stiff upper lip mentality has me bugged, I guess.'

'What other way is there, lad?' Stanley sucked at the stem of the empty pipe. 'The English, and in particular northerners, don't and never have worn their hearts on their sleeves. It's our way, and the only way we know.'

The piece of coal fell from position again in a shower of sparks, and this time no one moved to put it back.

'The trouble with you Americans,' Stanley said as if to himself, 'you have no depth. It's all a matter of roots, I suppose, roots that don't go deep enough.'

He got up, bending to knock out the empty pipe against the bars of the grate. 'Put the guard round and see to the front door before you come up, will you, lad? I'll see you before you go in the morning.'

'See how it is?' Sally's smile tore at Lee's heart-strings. 'He doesn't even give me the responsibility for locking the front door if someone else is there.'

'He's okay.' Lee pulled her close into his arms. 'Oh, love, my little love, you look worn out. C'mon. Let's just sit here awhile.' He put up a hand and smoothed the hair away from her hot forehead. 'You were born to be cherished. Don't you realize that?'

'I realize how much I love you.' Sally closed her eyes, snuggling deep into his shoulder. 'What would have happened if you hadn't been here today?'

'I'll always be there when you need me,' Lee said softly, and the words, unheard, hung for a moment in the stillness of the firelit room.

Barbara Shawfield heard the news as she tucked a stray strand of her mousey hair into the neat roll encircling her head before the mirror in the downstairs cloakroom at Telephone House.

'Poor little Mr Barnes. It was bad enough getting the telegram, without his wife trying to commit suicide like that. He looks like a loser, though. I've always thought he looked like a loser. I'm surprised he's come into the office today.'

'I'm not!'

Heads turned towards Barbara, as, flushing red, she faced the small knot of clerical workers. 'Mr Barnes would have come into work the day *after*, even if it hadn't been the Christmas holiday. He's like that. It doesn't surprise me in the least!' She walked swiftly from the cloakroom, opening the door with a flourish and letting it swing back of its own accord.

It was only five to nine, but Stanley would be there at his desk. She climbed the stairs that had been the servants' stairs when the offices were a family mansion, her jaw thrust out and her pale eyes glistening with emotion.

Christmas had been a barren time, and if that was sacrilege bordering on blasphemy then she couldn't help it. The other woman always paid; she had accepted that a long time ago. The wireless and her records had been poor company. Twice she had lifted the receiver and dialled Stanley's number only to replace it when she heard the ringing tone. If he had answered she would have murmured 'A Happy Christmas!' that was all, but at the last moment her courage had failed her. Barbara, more than a little breathless, reached the top floor.

But it wasn't going to fail her now. If any man needed a shoulder to cry on then that man was Stanley Barnes, and she was here – with all the frustrated burning love inside her. She was here!

Stanley was staring at an overflowing in-tray on his desk when Barbara burst into his room. He looked up, mildly surprised, as she closed the door behind her. Then he snatched off his reading glasses to see her better as she sagged against the door, panting hard.

'Ah . . . Barbara . . .' Stanley nodded. 'Please don't say anything, dear. Not yet. I need your concern, God knows, but these past few days . . . I think I've been to hell and back.'

It was too much to bear. Barbara felt as if her soul was melting. 'Oh, Stanley . . .' With three long strides she was across the room, hands outstretched, her mouth wrenched into a twisted shape by the force of her emotions.

For a disbelieving moment Stanley thought she was going to hurl herself onto his lap, but as he leaned as far back in his chair as was possible without tipping it over, Barbara perched herself on the edge of his desk. Bending down, she took both his hands in her own.

'Why didn't you let me know?' He saw her eyes redden as they filled with tears. 'Why didn't you come to me? You said I was your friend. I would have done anything . . . anything at all to help.' She leaned even further forward. As her dignity crumbled away his own reasserted itself, but Barbara was past noticing anything that might have stopped her gushing flow of sympathy.

'It's beyond comprehension how your wife could do a thing like that when you needed her most. Oh, Stanley, when I heard about it all just now my one thought was to get to you.'

She squeezed his hands hard. 'Please, my dear, let me share your grief.'

With a determined effort, Stanley managed to free his hands from the damp clinging fingers. Pushing back his chair he limped over to the window, leaving Barbara sitting foolishly on the edge of the desk, a carefully darned ladder in her stocking snaking down from her knee to disappear beneath the laces of her sensible shoes.

He hardly saw her. Cringing from the embarrassing show of emotion from a woman he had genuinely believed wanted nothing from him but friendship, he felt angry and dismayed. He stared down at the well-kept lawns fringed with darkly dripping rhododendron bushes, and asked himself what he had done to deserve this. Cruelty had never been a part of his make-up, but what he had to say must be said quickly, and now, before anyone came into the room. Stanley ran a finger round his white starched collar.

Josie's attempt at suicide had done more than jerk him out of his complacency; it had shaken him to the depths of his being. For as long as he lived he would never forget the sight of his wife's face on that hospital pillow. Without the habitual layer of make-up, Josie's cheeks, washed clean, had seemed more transparent than pale. Her arms with the bandaged wrists had been stretched out on the bedspread, reminding him, as if the reminder was necessary, of what she had intended to do. Nothing could bring John back, but he had almost lost his wife as well, and as God was his judge he intended to try to make it up to her.

Turning round, he spoke quietly to the tearful woman who sat watching him devotedly.

'My dear. You must not upset yourself on my behalf.' He took out a white handkerchief and blew his nose, wanting to let her down gently, feeling for the right words. 'I want you to know that you will always have a special corner of my heart, and under different circumstances, well, who knows?' He opened both hands wide, then bent down to pick up the handkerchief as it floated to the floor. 'I am not worthy of your touching concern, believe me . . .'

Barbara slid from the desk. How good this dear little man was. So much a man of integrity, a real Capricorn. Striving to be loyal to the wife who wasn't fit to tie his shoelaces. She understood. Never by word or deed would she compromise him, ever, in any way. But in trying to kill herself, Josie Barnes had bound her husband to her side for ever. Barbara sighed deeply. It was all so beautiful, so inevitable and so very beautiful.

Moving across the room, she put a hand on Stanley's arm and kissed him lightly at the corner of his moustache. Now it was her turn to make the ultimate sacrifice.

'Remember me with love,' she whispered, then turning swiftly ran from the room at a graceless plodding run, the welt of her grey cardigan showing peg marks from hanging on the line over her bath, the seam of her left stocking not quite straight.

Back in the downstairs cloakroom she locked herself in a lavatory to indulge in a few scalding tears. Then she wiped her eyes and pushed the handkerchief, with its spray of forget-me-knots embroidered in the corner, up the sleeve of her cardigan.

Her head was held high as she emerged. Let the girls in her department notice her red eyes and think what they liked. What did they know about anything, anyway? It took a woman of her age and sophistication to understand the real meaning of love and sacrifice.

On her way down the long corridor she almost bumped into Mr Armitage from Accounts, a tall stooped man with fine hair receding from a high domed forehead, and an invalid wife at home with a dicky heart.

'Ah . . . Miss Shawfield.' He made a little side-stepping movement. 'Did you have a pleasant Christmas?' His pale eyes were only briefly focused on her, but Barbara felt her spirits lift at once.

'Have you heard about poor Mr Barnes's dreadful Christmas?' She lifted a hand to tuck a stray wisp of hair back into the sausage roll. 'Life can be very cruel, can't it, Mr Armitage?'

When she went to her desk five minutes later there was a gleam in her eyes, a gleam which would have made Edwin Armitage, Clerical Officer, choke on his morning coffee biscuit had he even begun to guess what lay behind it.

Eight

'Sally? Sally Barnes?'

Christine Duckworth, now Christine Myerscough, very heavily pregnant, hating every inch of her grossly distorted figure, saw Sally hurrying to catch her tram. She called out to her.

'Oh, God, I'd forgotten she was deaf!' Christine, muttering to herself, started a lumbering run along the pavement, her swagger coat flying open to reveal a turquoise woollen smock hanging in gathers from a pointed yoke. The coat was made of what was called teddy-bear material, an apt description for the hairy garment which seemed to accentuate rather than conceal her enormous stomach. Christine, in spite of her tall willowy figure, had not carried well. When she touched Sally's arm the smaller girl had difficulty in keeping her eyes fixed on Christine's face. She felt a sense of shock as she saw the puffed eyelids and dulled eyes of the girl whose beauty had once been breathtaking.

The weather had turned very cold. The sky was low with the promise of snow to come. Sally had managed to buy a packet of soap flakes on her way to the tram and was clutching it, unwrapped, to her chest, bearing it home in triumph, anticipating her mother's face when she handed it over.

'Christine! I haven't seen you for ages. How are you? I thought you were staying down south somewhere with your husband?'

'I was.' Christine hesitated. Oh, God, this was going to be more difficult than she had thought. There was a defensive look on the glowing face of the girl in the red bobble cap, as if she was remembering their last meeting way back at the end

139

of last summer. Oh, God, why had she bothered? Christine tried to pull the coat together at the front, and forced a smile.

'I saw you, and I wondered . . . I just wondered if you had heard from Johnnie lately? You know? Whether he's still where he was, and how he's keeping?'

To her surprise, Sally simply stared at her, completely and obviously taken aback.

'You mean you haven't heard?'

'Heard what?'

Sally frowned. 'Well, no, you wouldn't have if you've been away.' She stared at the ground for a moment, then lifting her head looked straight into Christine's face.

'John is dead, Christine. We got a telegram to say he had been killed in action. I'm sorry. It seems an awful way to tell you, but well . . . I'm sorry.'

'Oh, my God!'

Christine's eyes opened wide, her jaw sagged, and her next words seemed to be forced through frozen lips.

'Johnnie dead? Oh, dear God! Not Johnnie! I don't believe it! I won't believe it! He swore he'd come back . . . He *promised* me.

'Promised *you*?' Sally couldn't help it. There was more than a touch of her mother's acidity in her voice. The self-control she had practised so assiduously since the telegram came now broke as she stared at the girl swaying before her on the busy pavement. 'You broke your promise to John a long time ago. Remember?'

'He *can't* be dead,' Christine said distantly. She was crying now, very quietly, so softly it was hardly noticeable. The fluffy coat had fallen open, and to balance herself she was swaying back on her flat heels, her stomach encased in the turquoise wool as rounded and huge as if half a barrel had been clamped to her front.

She began to shake. 'Oh, Sally. Help me! I feel so ill. I think I'm going to faint . . .' She clutched at Sally's arm. 'Don't leave me . . . please.'

'Hold on to me and we'll find a taxi.' Sally glanced round her at the hurrying Saturday lunchtime crowds, heads bent against the snow-spiked wind. Could no one see that they needed help? She looked at Christine's ashen face, and urged her on. Round the corner there was a taxi rank with a lone car waiting, its driver hunched over the wheel.

When she helped Christine into the back of the taxi she saw that the colour had come back into her cheeks. Christine still looked terribly ill, but as she gave her address to the driver Sally sensed that some of her old arrogance was seeping back.

'I'll come with you,' Sally offered, but, sunk deep into the voluminous coat, Christine moved her head slowly from side to side.

'No, thank you. I'll be fine. Really.' As if suddenly remembering Sally's deafness she lifted her head and repeated the words, moving her mouth in an exaggerated way. 'I'll be fine. Thank you for helping me. Thank you.'

'I'll see to her, chuck.' The driver, a man in his sixties, with grizzled hair and a noble Jesus profile, grinned at Sally. 'I've had four of my own. I'll see she's okay.'

Nodding, Sally stepped back, the packet of soap flakes still clutched to her chest. She lifted her free hand to wave, but Christine stared straight ahead, a bright wing of hair falling over her averted face.

It was snowing in earnest now, thick flakes falling like feathers from a leaden sky. At the tram stop, joining the long queue, Sally moved the precious packet to a place of safety inside her coat. Her mind was in a turmoil as she accepted the truth of what she had only half suspected. Obediently she shuffled forward with the women with shopping-bags and the workers going home from their morning stint in factories and shops.

Sally moved like a clockwork toy, shut away in her silent world, seeing and remembering her brother's face that May morning after the bomb had dropped down the road killing David Turner's mother. Almost without realizing what she was doing, she closed her umbrella as her part of the queue moved underneath the tram shelter. In spite of everything, there had been a look of uncontrollable joy on John's face that morning. As if he had been to heaven and was finding it hard to come down to earth once again. Sally frowned and chewed her lips. She suddenly wanted to weep for him. Right there in the pushing crowd she wanted to cry her pain aloud, but she could not do that, not here and now. So she stared dumbly in front of her, the snow blowing in on her face, pricking her cheeks and stippling her eyelashes.

'Christine is *my* girl now,' John had whispered. 'We're going to be married when this lot's over. Be nice to her for my sake, our kid.'

Sally pushed her way onto the boarding platform of the tram. All the seats were taken, but it didn't matter. Standing in the gangway, fumbling in her handbag for her fare, her mind was filled with a growing sense of unreality. She bowed her head, the certainty of what she had once only suspected frightening the heart out of her. There wasn't a single coherent thought in her head, only the truth shouting itself aloud.

Christine had given herself away. Christine's baby was John's baby. Sally did not need to do sums on her fingers to know that. Her brother was dead, but soon his child would be born. It was a suspicion and a secret she had to keep for ever. It was immeasurably sad; sad and yet wonderful. Sally suddenly felt as if her beloved brother was still alive. She bowed her head, the force of her emotions overwhelming in their intensity.

When she let herself into the house, Josie was in the hall, a hand on the bannister rail, one foot on the bottom stair. Her hair, showing an inch of undyed brown roots, hung uncurled round her small face. Her wrists were still bandaged, and there was an air of such desolation about her that Sally hurried forward, holding out the packet of soap flakes, offering them with love, willing even a single spark of pleasure into her mother's blank stare.

'See! They're Lux! If we're careful they should last us for ages.' She started to unbutton her coat, shrugging it off and holding it away from her. 'I'll go and shake it at the door. The snow's sticking, and the wind's that cold even my goose-pimples have goosepimples!'

It wasn't much of a joke, but it was a try. Sally held out her hand. 'Don't go upstairs, Mum. Come and talk to me while I'm eating my dinner. You can go for your rest afterwards.' She covered the hand on the bannister rail with her own. 'Would you like me to do your hair this afternoon? You can tell me what to do. I promise I won't let you turn green or anything. Mum?'

Josie slid her hand away and started to climb the stairs. Half-way up she turned her eyes full of a terrible accusation on her daughter.

'Mum? What's happened?' Sally started to follow, but Josie waved her back.

'Sometimes somebody comes back from the dead. You think they're dead and one day there's a knock at the door, an' when you answer it they're standing there.' She turned her back, climbing the stairs like a woman of eighty with an arthritic hip. 'But then it's not your son. An' you know it will never be your son.' Her voice was flat and final. 'It can never be your son, because *he's* dead. Proper dead. *Proper* dead!'

Sally opened the door of the living-room, and then felt as if her heart had stopped.

'Hello there, Sally!' The tall man in Air Force uniform smiled, coming towards her with hands outstretched.

'David!' Sally closed her eyes to stop the floor coming up to meet her. 'David Turner! I'm dreaming! I have to be!'

There were the lines of hardship and deprivation on his thin face, and as he talked Sally saw the shyness was still there. It was a reserve so alien to Lee's frank way of speaking, so different from Lee's jokey way of expressing himself, that Sally found herself for the first ten minutes comparing the one to the other. Then she hated herself for the comparison.

'All this time, David.' She sat opposite him, smiling, wanting to go on smiling. 'It's unbelievable. So wonderful. Oh, I can't tell you how wonderful it is just to see you sitting there.'

'And you,' he said. She saw him glance at her left hand. 'Your mother told me you were going to be married.' He looked away, then, as if remembering, turned back to face her again. 'He's a lucky man.'

'Thank you.' Sally suddenly felt the tall young airman's shyness affecting her. 'Lee is an American,' she said stiffly. 'From Texas.'

They were silent for a while, then David said gently: 'I am sorry about John. Your mother told me.' He hitched at the crease in his trousers. 'She's taken it very hard.' He swallowed. 'Well, of course she has. That was a stupid thing to say. What I mean is, she is very . . .'

'Bitter,' Sally said at once. 'She cut her wrists, David. It wasn't just a cry for help. She really wanted to die.' She moved restlessly in her chair. 'My mother has changed. It will be a long time before she can accept anyone else's happiness.'

'I saw that in her face when she opened the door.'

'Yes, you would.' Sally tucked a stray curl behind an ear. 'Oh, David, I can't tell you how marvellous it is, you coming back like this. I was so sure I would never see you again.'

'Bad pennies always turn up.' David looked down at his shoes. 'There were times when I doubted it myself, I can tell you.'

'Tell me what happened.' Sally felt the familiar sense of unease as David glanced quickly towards the door. Was it the telephone in the hall? Someone at the door? David caught the look of uncertainty on her face and felt again the almost forgotten impulse to cherish this small vulnerable girl. He spoke quickly and clearly to reassure her.

'It must have been next door. I thought I heard a noise, but your father is out on Home Guard duty, so your mother says.' He smiled. 'It's okay. I was mistaken. It's nothing.'

'Then tell me,' Sally said once again, and her face took on its listening look, so familiar to him.

'Well, I baled out over Belgium, then I was hidden in a hayloft by a farmer and his family.' David stretched out his left leg to the fire, flexing the injured muscles. 'My leg was broken and I had a head wound, and a fever, so they kept me hidden until I could walk.'

'And then?' It was like getting blood out of a flamin' stone, Sally thought, with a sudden warming feeling of pure affection.

'I left the farm,' David said simply. 'I walked through the night, then I was picked up – that was where the miracle came in – by a loyal Belgian who was a member of the Resistance.' He paused, remembering the terrifying moments when he had stumbled across the stubble field, dragging his injured leg behind him, not knowing whether he was following friend or foe. 'I didn't know it then, but I was in for a long bout of pneumonia, and without drugs of any kind I was ill for a long time.' He touched his forehead where a long scar, faded now to a purple weal, stood out against the pallor of his skin. 'I was almost over the pneumonia when this got infected somehow, and it didn't help when they were forced to keep moving me on from one hiding-place to another.'

He shook his head slowly from side to side. 'Sally . . . I know we've had the bombing here, but we don't know, believe me we don't know, what they are suffering over there. We *have* to rescue them. Somehow, sometime, when the time is right we have to go in force and liberate them. Their bravery is . . .' He lifted his hands. 'Oh, God, it's indescribable! As far as I know, not one family paid the price for helping me, but then I wouldn't know. They kept moving me on, even once when I was delirious. I remember being hidden underneath a load of manure in a farm cart.' He grinned. 'Not to be recommended for someone running a high temperature.'

'Then eventually . . . ?'

'Eventually I was taken by train, believe it or not, down through Vichy France, then to the Spanish border. Over the mountain passes by a Spanish guide, on to Lisbon, and home.'

'When?'

'Last week. I spent a week being medically examined, questioned, then leave.' He smoothed the back of one hand with the fingers of the other. 'I should have written to you, but I wanted to . . . well, I wanted to surprise you. And anyway,' he added quickly, 'I had to come back to see to things here, about the house. You know.'

It was hard having to look at her all the time. It was almost impossible to keep the truth hidden when grey eyes searched your face all the time. David desperately wanted to get up and walk away from her. Just for a moment, maybe to stare through the window – anything. She had been in his thoughts every waking minute. He had imagined the day when he would turn up out of the blue at her door. Her eyes would widen, she would come into his arms, he would hold her away from him and tell her how the memory of her had kept him sane. There would be no more holding back. Francine had made him see that the time for holding back was gone. Whatever was to become of him, Sally had to know how much he loved her, how he had always loved her since the time she walked past his house on her way home from school, navy-blue coat flying open, striped tie anchored into place by her form badge, shapely legs encased in long black woollen stockings.

'That poor deaf girl,' his mother had said, but there had been nothing even bordering on pity in his feelings for Sally. To pity her would have been an insult to her own bright courage. No wonder the unknown American had fallen in love with her. David glanced round the room. There was no sign of a photograph anywhere, but he knew what the Yank would be like. Closing his eyes briefly he conjured up the image of a broad-shouldered, grinning slob, chewing gum and showing large tombstone teeth.

'Are you all right, David?' Sally's voice seemed to come from a long way away. 'What's going to happen about your house? Will the compensation mean you can start afresh somewhere when it's all over?'

With an effort David jerked his mind back to reality. 'After the war's over? You know, that's something I never think about. There's too much to do first.'

'You won't be flying again?' The question was more a statement of fact, and for no reason he could fathom David spoke more sharply than he intended to.

'Of course I'll be flying again! Why not? It would kill me to be some desk-bound wallah. Especially now.' He tapped his left leg. 'That's as good as new, and when I've joined my new squadron it'll be action stations again.' He smiled. 'It's a good life if you don't weaken.'

There was nothing Sally could say to this quiet inarticulate man. His shyness was still there, but now there was a determination and a bitterness about him which hadn't been there before. The last time she had been in his company for any length of time he had been all taut nerves, his hands dancing on his knees like bony spiders. His unexpected vehemence startled her when he suddenly said: 'I have to go back, Sally. For the sake of so many people I have to go back. There was a pal of mine. I left him hanging dead from a tree.' His words

146

spluttered out passionately. 'My blood's up, Sally. It was tough luck on old Jack, but I've got to see to it that he didn't die in vain.' He smiled. 'I'm up for a gong. Imagine! *I* survived, so they give me a gong. Jack died, so he gets sweet Fanny Adam. There's justice for you!'

When he stood up suddenly Sally looked round, startled to see her father coming through the door wearing his Home Guard uniform, both hands outstretched in welcome, his face a mixture of shock and delight as he saw David standing there, unbelievably alive.

In the afternoon, when David had gone, Sally pulled on her wellingtons, tied a woollen pixie-hood round her hair and set off for a walk. She went past the flattened spaces where once four houses had stood and turned down the uneven road out to the fields which were grey with the slush of half-melted snow.

The wind was fierce, biting at her in angry gusts, so she walked with head bowed as it blew stinging sleet at her, turning her nose into a cherry.

Miraculously there was a sun, hovering over the horizon, as round and red as a child's ball. When she reached the reservoir she stopped and looked down at the thin layer of ice covering the dark water like a ruffled skin. The scene was so desolate, so devoid of even a vestige of warmth, it seemed to be part of the sadness deep inside her, cold and without hope.

The meeting with Christine, then with David, had left her mind in a turmoil of whirling thoughts, and the progress of the war too seemed to be locked in frozen immovability, neither side making any discernible gains or losses.

She thought about the countries across the English Channel, suffering not only the cold and despair, but also the added dangers of German occupation. As David had said, they were paying the price, locked in with an enemy who would show no mercy.

She felt a sense of shame at her elation on finding the packet of soap flakes. For that tiny space of time she had been happy; in spite of everything she had known an upsurge of joy. Men might be lying frozen on the Russian Front, buried deep in drifts of snow, and yet her own little world had been brightened by a cardboard carton of Lux flakes. She shivered, thrust her hands deep into the pockets of her coat, and turned for home.

There had been a strange shadow on David's thin face. A sort of death wish, as if he knew and accepted that his days, once he started operational flying again, were numbered.

She trudged on, burying her nose in the upturned collar of her coat. She grieved for the friend who had lost so much . . . his mother, his entire crew, and his home. Tears pricked behind her eyes as she saw again the look on David's face when he said his goodbyes to her at the front door.

'I don't suppose I'll be seeing much of you from now on.' His chin had been lifted in the shy mannerism she knew so well. 'Me joining a fresh squadron, and you getting married. I don't suppose I'll be back this way all that often.'

'But you'll write?'

He had smiled then, a strange smile moving only his lips and leaving his eyes empty and sad.

'Your American's a lucky bastard. Tell him I said so.' Balling his hand into a fist, he had punched her gently on the side of her cheek. 'Take care, Sally. Take good care.'

And before she could tell him that *he* was the one needing to take care he had walked away, back erect, down the path and away down the road, not even turning to wave.

Stanley noticed his daughter's red and swollen eyelids the minute she came into the room. But he said nothing, merely stared into the fire, keeping his thoughts to himself.

Nine

'You mean you've made up your mind about leaving Duck-worth Brothers?'

Reluctantly Stanley put down his newspaper to stare at Sally. He tried not to look as exasperated as he felt.

What the heck had got into her now? Taking off his reading glasses, he plucked nervously at his moustache. He hated change, couldn't abide it, and the way things were going this war was changing everything, even his home life.

John was dead, Josie was moving round the house like a zombie since the doctor had signed her off as unfit for work, and now Sally was upsetting the apple cart again.

It had been a terrible week, with Singapore falling to the Japanese. Even Mr Churchill had sounded depressed as he described it as a great English and Imperial defeat. Out in Libya the Allies were on the retreat, and to cap it all German battleships had had the nerve to sail brazenly up and down the Channel.

There was a scab on the bridge of his nose, the result of a collision with a lamp post in the black-out. He fingered it morosely.

'I can't understand your reasons for wanting to leave a safe, steady job, Sally. You don't come within the Essential Work Order, not with your little disability. Why swap and change now?'

'I needed a change.' Sally leaned over and actually patted his hand. 'Come on, Dad, don't look so worried. I'd have joined the WAAFS if that had been possible, so the way I see it this is the next best thing to being in the Services.'

Stanley glared at her. 'But that place you're going to is two tram rides from here, plus a long walk at the other end.' He frowned so that the line above his nose deepened. 'I've seen some of the girls coming home from that factory, and they're rough. Not a bit like the girls you're used to working with in your office.' Angrily he rustled the paper on his knee. 'Why waste your typing? What will you be doing, anyway? Working on a machine? Because in your case that could be dangerous. Surely you can see that?'

Sally's eyes twinkled. 'I'll be filing. When I went yesterday they took me into the room where I'll be working to show me. There's nothing to it as far as I can see.'

Stanley's expression of gloom lifted visibly. 'A filing clerk? Oh, well, I suppose that's office work at least. Things could be worse.'

'They are,' Sally told him cheerfully. 'I won't be filing letters. Oh, no. The things I will be filing are called "heels".' With a thumb and forefinger she demonstrated their size. 'About this big, with a raised ridge on each one. I have to smooth it off with a tool like a big nail file. I'm paid so much a thousand so it's up to me. I think they're bits of tanks, but the technical side won't come into it. Each of us is responsible for our own particular piece of whatever it is.'

'Cheese and flippin' rice!' Stanley exploded. 'Is that what you went to a grammar school for? Is that why you had all those private lessons in touch typing? Give me one good reason why you're throwing your education away, then.'

'There's a war on, Dad.'

'I *know* there's a flamin' war on! And what you're laughing at I don't understand. You'll be laughing on the other side of your face before you've done, Sally Barnes. Just you wait and see. And one of these fine days you'll come to admit it. Mark my words!'

He disappeared behind his newspaper, a bewildered man who at that moment felt his whole world was toppling down, leaving him isolated and all at sea.

It was certainly no picnic working in the large factory spread out in huts with corrugated roofs over almost an acre of ground. Sally sat on a long bench in a long narrow room, windowless and lit by glaring lights suspended from the

150

ceiling. The drilling machines were in the centre, and from where she sat she could see the women drilling holes in heaps of oblong-shaped brass plates, their heads swathed in turbans to keep their hair from the whirling machinery.

Even though the noise of the machinery was no more than a muted hum in Sally's damaged ears, there was a constant pounding in her head. The hours were longer than any hours she had worked before, but it was the repetitive monotony of the work she found wearing.

Take out a small 'heel' from the box on her left, file it smooth with quick deft strokes of the big file, then drop it into the box on her right. Over and over. Over and over, one after the other, fingers aching but mind wandering free.

She knew and accepted that to have continued to work at Duckworth Brothers would have been impossible, suspecting – well, *knowing* – what she did about Christine's baby. She had even resisted the temptation to write and tell Lee about it, sensing that the decision must be hers alone. She had only, like countless other women in war-time, exchanged a comfortable way of life for one much harder, and if her motivations were not purely patriotic, well, what did that matter?

Raising her head she saw that the girls were singing at the tops of their voices, enjoying the music blaring from loudspeakers set high in the walls. If it was 'Music While You Work' then it must be half past ten, she decided, lowering her head again, cocooned in her own little world of throbbing silence, her familiar shell of solitude.

It was a ten-hour day. She arrived in the dark and went home in the dark. In Lee's last letter he had accepted this as perfectly normal and reasonable. Sally smiled as she remembered his exact words: 'The truth is it must have taken a war to wake your country up to the fact that long hours and hard work should be accepted as normal. We Americans have *always* worked hard.'

Sally could just see him saying it, his wide grin and twinkling eyes making the unpalatable truth more acceptable. He mentioned the Canadians and New Zealanders on his camp, and their moans about the 'sawdust' bread and the soggy boiled vegetables. 'Maybe when they see your country in the spring they will learn to love it as I do – in the meantime, it's flying almost every day and, oh boy, am I enjoying that!'

The file in Sally's right hand was stilled for a moment. Lee had told her it would be months yet before he was ready to fly on operations, but she could only guess at the danger involved in mastering the craft of flying a heavy bomber by night. David Turner had told her a long time ago of the incidence of accidents during training, and in spite of Lee's eagerness to get to grips with what he called those 'winged office blocks' he was so vulnerable she could hardly bear to think about it.

'The plane I'm flying has a cruising speed of 140 mph. Below average nowadays. Peanuts,' he had written. 'I ought to be so goddamned happy, but without you near me, how can I be?'

Sally turned round startled as the girl sitting next to her touched her arm. 'Time to knock off, love. The hooter's gone. It's dinner time.'

That same evening, in the local paper under the heading of Births, Marriages and Deaths, was an announcement:

'At Springcroft Nursing Home, to Christine and Captain Nigel Myerscough, a son, Peter John.'

Sally felt the blood drain from her face, then looked up startled as Josie tapped the column with a finger.

'Reading the Hatched, Matched and Dispatched again, are you, love? You're getting as bad as me. I always look to see if my name's there, and if it isn't then I know I must still be alive and kicking.'

It was only a poor attempt at a joke, but for a moment something of the old Josie was reflected in the dulled blue eyes. Quickly Sally closed the paper.

'One of the girls at work has got engaged to a Polish airman. It's going to be dried egg cake all round tomorrow. I just wondered if it was in the paper,' she lied. 'She's been engaged twice before, so maybe they didn't think it worth the bother.'

'We never got engaged, me and your father.' Josie held out a hand for the newspaper. 'Is there anything in about that girl being murdered down by the flats? I don't like you walking home alone these dark nights. Murders seem out of place somehow when there's a war going on. There's enough killing without anyone taking it up privately.'

'I walk in the middle of the road swinging my torch, and if anyone crept up behind me then I'd shine it straight in his face.'

Josie opened her mouth then closed it again. Sally wouldn't be able to hear if anyone *did* creep up behind her. She wouldn't hear now if a whole regiment banged the front door open and marched up and down the hall. A piece of coal fell with a clink onto the tiled hearth, but Sally's eyes never flickered. In spite of the grief that Josie nursed like a child held close to her heart, in spite of the despair seeping through her very veins, she forgot herself for long enough to identify with the solitude that was part of her daughter's daily existence. The ice round her heart melted a little as she surveyed her daughter in silence. A warmth of compassion flooded her starved soul as she tried to imagine how it would be to turn on a tap then have to *look* to see if water was coming out. To walk in high heels along a pavement and hear nothing. To dig in the garden with a spade which never rang against a stone. To see people jump up to answer a silent telephone; to live in a padded cell, and to accept so readily a misfortune that to hearing people seemed insurmountable.

Suddenly Josie was consumed with guilt. Wrapped in her own mourning she had forgotten this other child of hers. This small girl, tired half-way to death, with great bruised shadows beneath her eyes, who crept out of the house in the mornings and came back at night too weary to eat the slapdash meal prepared by a mother who couldn't be bothered even to try and make the most of rationed food. Josie swallowed a great lump that seemed to have formed in the front of her throat. Stanley was just as bad. In his own way he was enjoying the war, revelling in the feeling that the whole country was banded together against the Germans. With his Home Guard pals he was reliving the last war, exchanging reminiscences, supping billycans of tea, like in the trenches, but far more comfortable in the evacuated junior school they used as their headquarters.

The lump in Josie's throat hurt so much that tears sprang unbidden to her eyes. She had never even acknowledged the truth that Sally might be truly and deeply in love with her American. Josie tried to remember his face and failed. He had been friendly, she remembered that, but after the telegram came he had been obliterated from her mind as thoroughly as if he had never existed. David Turner had come back from the dead and she had rushed away upstairs, hardly able to look at him.

Raising her head she was shocked to see how much Sally's face had changed over the past few weeks. It was a sad face now with all the vivacity and animation drained away. It was almost as though something in that newspaper, slipping now from her knees, had upset her.

Impulsively Josie leaned across the hearthrug, holding out her hand. When Sally gripped it convulsively, the tears behind her eyelids spilled over to creep slowly down her cheeks.

'Oh, love . . . Oh, Sally . . . I've been such a bad bugger. I've never thought how you must be feeling. I've been that sorry for myself . . .'

Josie began to cry, noisily and without restraint. Sally immediately came to kneel down by her chair, pulling her mother's head to rest against her, patting and soothing, murmuring words of comfort, whispering them over and over again.

Sally didn't cry. She dare not, and the trying not to was terrible. Her face was closed up tight as she fought the overwhelming desire to tell her mother about Christine's baby. It might not be true. Even her thoughts were being carefully controlled. But if it was, and she were to speak her mind, then Josie Barnes would find a way to hold her baby grandson in her arms, even if it meant dragging the whole Duckworth family down. Sally set her face firm against any further emotion.

But she could not help wondering what Peter John Myerscough looked like. Peter *John*, she thought, then put the thought from her with resolution.

Captain Nigel Myerscough, resplendent in his well-fitting uniform, stood outside the glass-fronted nursery in Springcroft Nursing Home and stared into the sleeping face of his little son.

The baby was being held up by a nurse. She had picked

him up from a cot lined up with other cots as if for kit inspection, in the large airy room overlooking the lawns edged with winter-bare trees.

Nigel smiled and nodded. The baby seemed particularly unwrinkled, although its face did resemble a sponge. Nigel supposed that was because Christine had gone three weeks or more over her time. He wished the nurse would put the baby back so he could stop smiling and nodding. If the truth were known he felt a right Charlie standing there trying not to look embarrassed.

'Very good,' he said at last, then immediately thought, what a damn-fool thing to say. 'Thank you, nurse.' He turned on his heel and walked down the corridor to his wife's room, his slouching gait at distinct variance with the smartness of his uniform.

Head inclined, he was about to rap politely on the door before entering when he turned to see a sister beckoning to him from a room further down the long corridor. With her hair scragged up into a white cap and a figure shaped like an avocado pear, she was hardly the type to raise one's blood pressure a single notch, Nigel thought uncharitably, but he went where she beckoned, surprised when she closed the door behind him.

'Captain Myerscough?' She stood before him, hands folded over her starched front.

Nigel nodded. 'Yes, Sister?' He shuffled his big feet on the well-worn carpet. There was something ominous in the way the nurse was regarding him with her pale blue eyes. His rose-madder complexion paled slightly. Was she about to tell him that his son had something wrong with him? That the boy was mongoloid or something equally unacceptable? For a moment he was shaken out of his habitual diffidence. The baby's head *had* wobbled a lot, and his face had the round-ness of an embryo Winston Churchill, but then hadn't he been told that *all* new-born babies looked like the great war leader?

'Your wife.' Sister Kelly stepped back a pace to avoid craning her neck. The captain must be six foot four at least. In his stockinged feet, she decided. 'It isn't an unusual state of affairs, but she's rejecting her baby.'

'Rejecting it?'

Sister Kelly nodded. For no reason at all she had taken an immediate dislike to the gangling, stoop-shouldered young man standing before her with his mouth wide open. She knew his sort. Cushy job in peace-time working his way up in Daddy's firm; cushy job in the army, not an ounce of leadership in him in spite of his public-school upbringing. They deserved each other, she decided. Captain Myerscough and his spoilt and pampered wife lying back on her pillows and refusing to breast feed.

'Mother is refusing to breast feed!' she said, her voice ringing with ill-concealed scorn.

'My God! Is that all?' Nigel let out a nervous laugh. For a minute the silly woman had had him worried. 'Well, for heaven's sake, Sister, *I* was bottle-fed, and it didn't exactly stunt my growth, now did it?' He laughed again, then smothered the laugh behind a hand as the sister quelled him with a cold glance. 'It would be bad enough if it was merely the feeding,' she added. 'But mother doesn't even want to *cuddle* her baby. We keep him in the nursery of course, but mother refuses to give him the bottle. In all my years of maternity nursing I've never come up against such a total rejection.' Sister Kelly shook her small head mournfully. 'I was wondering if you could throw some light on the position, Captain? When you go back off leave and we discharge mother and baby in ten days' time, it won't be a very happy situation unless things have changed very much for the better.'

Nigel wished the silly woman would stop referring to Christine as mother'. His wife had given the impression that the swollen protruding stomach was in a strange way a completely unconnected part of her.

'My God! What do I look like?' she had grumbled. 'I can't wait to get my figure back. I haven't seen my bloody feet for a month. If men had to have babies the human race would die out.'

'The baby wasn't planned.' He stared over the sister's left shoulder. 'Bit of a surprise to both of us, eh?' His narrow face widened into an apologetic smile, causing Sister Kelly to clamp her lips tight.

'A silly man,' she whispered, watching him amble along the corridor, then she thought about Mrs Hardcastle lying bravely in her bed after losing her third baby with projectile vomiting. Swearing she would try again. 'There's no justice,' Sister Kelly told herself, going back into her room.

'Decent little chap, eh?'

Nigel sat down on the little hard chair drawn up to his wife's bed and tried to find a place for his long grasshopper legs. Christine looked positively blooming, or were the spots of colour on her high cheekbones more indicative of a fever? By no means a sensitive man – even his doting mother could never have described him as that – there was a certain brittleness about his wife that put him immediately on his guard. To offset his unease he laughed out loud. 'Sister tells me Mother Myerscough is being a naughty girl about feeding.'

'She thinks I'm a cow!' Christine plucked at the ribbon ties of her pink bedjacket. 'I've felt like a cow for months and months, and now she expects me to *behave* like one.' The green eyes flashed. 'There's a woman in the next room with a premature baby and no milk of her own.' Christine shuddered. 'Sister Sourpuss wanted me to do what she called expressing my milk into a bloody jar for it. But the more you pump – oh, my God! – the more the flamin' stuff flows, so I refused.' She glared at Nigel, forbidding him to laugh again. 'The whole thing sickens me. Disgusts and nauseates me.'

Nigel shifted uncomfortably on the chair, moving his long body as if by doing so he could change the subject.

'Did it hurt much? Having the baby?'

'Oh, my God!' Christine slid down the high-piled pillows. 'Never again!' She turned her face to the window. 'Whoever said nature steps in to make a woman forget the pain immediately it's over, needs his head examined. It was bound to be a man. I've dreamed every single contraction over and over.' Her voice shook. 'Do you know what that barbarian of a doctor did to me? He came in and stitched me up without even a whiff of ether!' She moaned and moved her legs in the high white bed. 'They're sticking out of me like barbed wire, those bloody stitches. Come to think of it, he probably used

157

bloody barbed wire! "Just a little prick, mother," he said. My God! I wish someone would sew his whatsit up for him, then he'd know!'

A tiny nurse in a pleated cap put her head round the door, then withdrew. Nigel wished with all his heart that she had come in and done whatever it had been she intended to do. He was at a loss, the way he was always at a loss when Christine got herself into this mood. He patted his pocket for his cigarettes, then remembered where he was. His pleasant face struggled to form itself into what he hoped would be an acceptable expression. He wasn't afraid of his wife. On the contrary, when she was in a different frame of mind they had fun together. He enjoyed having a beautiful girl to show off. It tickled him when she was in one of her 'Oh, my God!' moods. He wondered if he dared risk a cigarette? But this was different. There was no point in him trying to say the right thing. Whatever he said would be wrong. He sighed and fingered his flourishing moustache.

'A rum thing happened the other day,' he said at last. 'We were on manoeuvres on the cliffs and three Focke Wulf 190s came in at wave-top level. You could almost see the friggin' pilot's underpants. They dropped four 250-pounders, one on a farmhouse. The farmer and his wife bought it. Blown to smithereens.'

'And?' Christine continued to stare out of the window.

'Just thought you might be interested.'

She turned round. 'Well, I'm not. I got the impression it was safe down there in Cornwall. Is that supposed to make me feel better?'

'It was only a hit and run raid,' Nigel said lamely. 'Probably a training run for the Huns. They have to get their practice in somehow.'

When he had gone, promising to come back in the evening before leaving to rejoin his unit, Christine sat up straight in bed, wincing as the stitches sent a thousand needles pricking where it hurt most. Pushing a vase of snowdrops to one side she reached for the bedside telephone and dialled a number.

'Yes, who is it?'

The voice was flat and disinterested. Christine took a deep breath.

158

'Mrs Barnes?'

'Yes?'

'This is Christine Myerscough.' Christine heard the sharp intake of breath, then went on bravely: 'I'm in Springcroft Nursing Home.' She wetted her dry lips. 'I'm speaking from there. Can I speak to Sally, please?'

There was a moment's silence. The same nurse put her head round the door only to be waved impatiently away. 'Are you there, Mrs Barnes?'

'Aye, I'm here.' Josie found she was gripping the receiver so hard that her knuckles ached. 'Sally's at work, but even if she was here she couldn't talk on the telephone.'

Christine frowned. Oh, my God! She had forgotten Sally Barnes was deaf, and in her agitated state she had forgotten it was the middle of the afternoon when someone like Sally Barnes was sure to be at work, anyway. She felt the strength draining from her.

'It's Saturday tomorrow. Do you think Sally would come and see me?' Every pore in Christine's body seemed to be oozing sweat. The binder round her swollen breasts tightened like a tourniquet. She could feel the milk seeping through. 'It's terribly important, Mrs Barnes. I have something to tell her. Please, Mrs Barnes.'

Josie held the receiver away from her ear and glanced at it with distaste. This was the girl who had broken her son's heart. This boss's daughter with her lah-de-dah voice who had chucked her son for an officer stationed somewhere safe in England, so she'd heard. A chinless wonder who would come back as a director in his father's firm, while John – Josie's lovely laughing son – was buried somewhere out there, with sand blowing over his grave. If they had found enough of him to put in a grave. Josie felt anger suffuse her face with a hot wave of passion. The pent-up bitterness in her exploded. Her grief came up, choking her throat and welling into her eyes. But for this girl, her John would never have volunteered for the commandos. He wouldn't. He loved life too much to do a thing like that. 'I'll come back, Mum,' he had promised in that last phone call. 'I'm only going where I'm going to get my knees brown. Anyway, I'll be a lot safer riding a camel than that motor-bike you used to worry about so much.'

'Are you still there, Mrs Barnes?'

Josie shivered as the high voice with its cut-glass accent brought her back from that imagined far-off country where the sun shone down from a sky hazy with dust, with flak guns mounted on half-tracks, and where British soldiers dived for their slit trenches as German tanks rumbled towards them over the spreading sand. She had seen it all on the newsreel at the pictures only the week before when Stanley had persuaded her to go to be taken out of herself. And then she had had to be helped from the cinema, leaning on him as if she were ill, because never in the most horrendous of her nightmares could she have imagined it to be as terrible as it was.

'You'll tell Sally then, will you?' Christine's voice was higher still now, with a hysteria that Josie was in no condition to recognize.

Gripping the receiver till her knuckles paled, she shouted into it, the Josie she had once been, triumphantly alive for a fleeting moment.

'Piss off!' she shouted, then collapsed sobbing into the nearest chair.

When they sent for Captain Myerscough and asked him whether he would mind returning at once to see his wife as she was in an emotionally disturbed state, Nigel put down the whisky he was drinking with his father-in-law and uncurled himself slowly from the low chair.

'It's nothing to worry about.' He trundled to the big front door of the house set high on a wooded hill, Amos Duckworth following behind, his long face anxious beneath his thick greying hair. 'Something to do with hormones after a birth, they said. I'll be back as soon as she's calmed down.' He ran lightly down the steps to where his blob of a sports car crouched on the gravel like an angry red beetle. 'You know Christine.'

Amos waited until the car, filled with black-market petrol, zoomed down the drive, Nigel with his gauntlet-gloved hands on the wheel, driving it as if he were on the last lap of the Monte Carlo Rally. Then he went inside and closed the door.

'That baby was a mistake,' he muttered to himself, pouring

another whisky. 'And I don't mean its conception. I mean in being born at all.' He took a long swig of the amber liquid. 'And you're an unnatural grandfather, Amos Duckworth, because your feelings haven't been right about it from the start.' He drained the glass then glanced at its emptiness in surprise. 'Give our Christine a doll she didn't want as a child and she'd chuck it right back at you. Give her owt she didn't want and her reaction was always the same.' Pushing himself out of the well-padded chair he made a wavy bee-line for the whisky decanter again – a bewildered man who had only wanted to give his only child the best of everything, laughing at her tantrums and easing her out of her sulks with gifts he could well afford.

The whisky missed the glass and dribbled over his white shirt cuff. He mumbled to himself, a habit he'd always had when troubled: 'Amos, there's something in this baby set-up that doesn't quite add up. Not in my book it doesn't.'

Nigel, roaring down the almost deserted road on his way back to the nursing home, was equally flummoxed. He frowned. The baby had come at a most awkward time. Stationed in the West Country, he saw the war as a game played round a table, with the officers winning all the tricks and the lesser ranks losing and cheating when one's back was turned. His public school background had turned him into a good leader, and if only Christine could have stayed on with him she would have been reasonably happy. His pals had gone a bundle over her, and damn it, they could have gone on having a whale of a time together. She didn't mind lazing about doing nothing for most of the time. She *liked* doing nothing, for Pete's sake. And now she'd have to stay up north with the baby, and he'd miss her. He'd miss her like hell.

He turned a corner on two wheels. They were okay, him and Christine. Or had been, till he slipped up. Then for a while she'd gone all funny on him. Nigel slapped the wheel hard. He'd always seen that she was okay, so what the hell had gone wrong? There had only been one weekend when it could have happened, and he could have sworn she'd be all right. He remembered reading once that the only safe form of birth control was total abstinence. He snorted. Whoever the geezer was who'd said that, could say it again!

The little red car swung into the drive and drew up in front of the nursing home in a spatter of gravel.

Sister Kelly had meant to have another word with Captain Myerscough. His wife had interrupted the other mothers at their six o'clock feed. Sobbing and wailing and refusing even to try to have her bowels moved.

'My God!' she'd screamed. 'Take the bloody thing away! It's like sitting on an iceberg!' And poor little Nurse Tamworth had rushed from Mrs Myerscough's room vowing she wasn't going to stay and be clocked one with a bedpan.

But for the twenty minutes the captain was closeted with his wife, Sister Kelly had been kept busy dealing with a labour that looked as if it was going to end up as an emergency caesarian. So all she saw of Nigel was his back as he strode down the corridor, passing the nursery without even a cursory glance.

'Heaven preserve me from mard women!' the sister grumbled, her crêpe-soled shoes making angry slapping noises as she marched into Christine's room, her back ramrod straight and the light of battle in her eyes.

Mrs Myerscough had another visitor later that evening. A small girl who looked as if she had come in straight from work in slacks, raincoat and a bunch of dark curls sticking out from the front of her turbanned head.

'I never thought your mother would pass on my message.' Christine, calmed and settled with a dose of Sister Kelly's tranquillizing medicine, was sitting up in bed, hands folded over the neatly turned-down sheet.

'She thought better of it.' Sally stood at the foot of the high narrow bed. 'I came straight here.' She looked at Christine apprehensively, then spoke quickly. 'She sort of blames you for John joining the commandos like he did. She is convinced he would still be alive if he hadn't done that.'

'Oh, my God!' Christine began to gather the sheet between her fingers, pleating it like a fan. 'Oh, my God!'

Christine Myerscough, née Duckworth, looked a sorry sight. Used to staring frequently and admiringly into mirrors, it was obvious to Sally that she had not taken a long hard look at herself for a long time. If she had done so she would have screamed in dismay.

162

The auburn hair hung lank round hollowed cheeks. Anguish stared from eyes dulled with despair, and her mouth, innocent of lipstick, was compressed into a thin hard line.

She said softly: 'I can't take the baby home, Sally.' If Sally could have heard, the voice would have sounded as if it came as an echo, disembodied, unreal.

'Why can't you take him home, Christine?' There was a kindness in Sally's eyes as she watched the other girl carefully, a kindness tempered with concern. Sally waited. 'I know what you are trying to tell me, Christine. I think I guessed a long time ago, but you have to tell me yourself. Okay?'

'You see,' Christine said, in the strange far-away voice, 'we decided we didn't want children, Nigel and me. I have no maternal feelings whatsoever, and if that makes me into a freak, then that's what I am.' She turned her head away.

'Please look at me when you speak,' Sally said in her flat little voice. 'I can't lip-read you if you don't.'

As obedient as a hand-controlled puppet, Christine turned her head back again.

'I know my marriage would go to pot if a baby started mucking things up. It must sound awful to you but I've had a long time to think about it all. Nigel deserves better than a cuckolding, even though he'd have made a rotten father.' She went on almost absently. 'We are both basically bone-idle, selfish and altogether rotten, I suppose. I want to join Nigel again down in Cornwall as soon as they let me out of this mausoleum, and with any luck we can whoop it up together till the war's over.' She nodded. 'If there should be any rumours about going abroad, Nigel's father is all ready to step in. His mill is making uniforms for the Services, you see, and with him being on more than nodding terms with a Cabinet Minister who shall be nameless, Nigel could be out at a stroke of a pen. Essential war work. Don't look at me like that, Sally. I told you, we're a rotten lot.' She said abruptly: 'The baby is Johnnie's. I've told Nigel.'

There! It was said, and the enormous relief brought the tears up from where they'd been frozen for a long time. Christine let them come in great gulping sobs, making no attempt to wipe them away.

'You guessed, didn't you?' Christine raised her head.

'And what did your husband say?'

'What I thought he'd say.' Christine groped underneath her pillow for a handkerchief. 'He blew his top at first, then when I told him it was just the once, and that I was drunk, and that your brother was on embarkation leave, he calmed down.'

'And were you drunk?'

'No.' Forgetting the stitches, Christine moved restlessly then moaned. 'No, we were both quite sober.' She put the handkerchief to her face, remembering the night when the bombs were falling, when nothing had mattered but the two of them, holding each other tight, whispering words of love, clinging, promising, totally abandoned to a passion that had shattered with its intensity. 'You won't believe this, but I truly loved Johnnie. Until he went away, and I found out I was pregnant. I was going to tell Nigel when he came on leave. Then I started to think. Don't ask me why – something to do with me imagining a life with your brother, having more babies and making-do-and-mending, I suppose. Having the baby here, with him in the Middle East – oh, God, I couldn't face it. It was much easier all round, for everyone concerned, for me to marry Nigel and let him think it was his.'

'And could it be? Christine? Could it *possibly* be?'

'No, not a chance. I'd had a period after Nigel.' Christine broke out into fresh sobs. 'When I met you that day and you told me Johnnie had been killed, I wanted to die. Then I thought I'd done the right thing, but I hadn't. The baby would remind me every day of its life what an awful muddle I'd got myself into. It would remind me of Johnnie, and oh, God, I daren't be reminded of him! I've forgotten him, I *have* to forget him, can't you see? I can't see his face any more, nor remember his voice. And that is how it's got to be. For me to go on being rotten, which is the only way I know, I can't be reminded of your brother. Ever!'

Sally moved round the bed to stand looking down at Christine's bowed head. A growing sense of excitement was moving inside her. She restrained herself from putting out a hand to touch Christine. What had to be said had to be said calmly and without emotion clouding her words.

'What about your parents? It's their grandchild, Christine.'

The bowed head jerked up. 'Nigel will have told them by now, and they . . . oh my God, they're in their late fifties, for crying out loud! Mummy's not likely to give up a single one of her blasted committees to look after my little by-blow. She's the top brass in the Guides, didn't you know, and if it's not Inner Wheel it's VAD on her mind. I can just see her waking in the night to change a shitty nappy.'

'Nigel's parents?' Sally's voice, no longer under her normal stringent control, came out as a croak.

'Separated.' Christine blew her nose. 'Oh, it's not official. They still live under the same roof, believe it or not, but they go their separate ways. Mrs Myerscough told me straight out what a fool I'd been when I told her I was pregnant. And *that* was when she thought the baby was her son's. Now that she knows it's a little bastard she'll be even more delighted than ever.'

'So . . . ?' Sally said, in a tone so harsh that had she been able to hear it it would have horrified her.

'So . . .' Christine said, then looked away from the fierce little face beneath the blue turban, the strength suddenly ebbing from her as if it had been siphoned off by Sister Kelly's hypodermic needle. 'Oh, God, I'm tired.'

'May I see the Myerscough baby, please?' Sally stopped a nurse outside the nursery. 'I know it's on the late side, but may I?'

'Are you a relative?' The nurse was on her way to supper but something in the uneven lilt of Sally's voice prevented her from quoting the rules and giving a blank refusal.

'I'm his auntie,' Sally said proudly.

'We're having him!' Josie gripped Stanley's arm hard. 'They don't want him and we do! You heard what Sally said.'

Stanley prized his wife's fingers gently away from his wrist. 'Steady on, love. It isn't as clear-cut as that.' He stroked his moustache, chewing the situation over, considering, worriting, wanting time to think. 'Suppose Sally here has got the wrong end of the stick? Suppose Christine changes her mind? It won't be the first time a girl has offered her baby for adoption then gone back on it.' He chewed on nothing for a long moment. 'Besides, are you sure you want to start with a baby at your age?'

Winter sleet dashed against the blacked-out window. Exasperation gripped Josie in a vice. 'Hell's bells and buckets of blood, Stanley Barnes! What do you mean, at *my* age? I'm young enough to have a baby of my own!' She moved away from him abruptly, making for the door. 'I'm going to ring old Amos Duckworth up and tell him we're coming round. Then first thing in the morning I'm going to see my grandson! Our John's baby. Oh, stop standing there like a fart trapped in a bottle! Just for once do something decisive. There's nobody having that little lad but me! I'm his grandma, and you're his grandpa, you great soft ha'porth!'

'Stop it, woman!' Stanley followed her into the hall. 'Sleep on it, for God's sake! The Duckworths have enough to chew on tonight without us turning up uninvited.'

As Josie picked up the telephone, he turned to Sally standing quietly by the fire. It occurred to him suddenly that if this wild scheme came to fruition it could impose the kind of solidarity on his family that had been missing for a long time. He had seen Josie sliding ever further into a depression he could do nothing to prevent, and now, with Sally's startling news visibly shaking Josie out of her morass of frustration and despair, it was as though the wife he loved had been restored to him, vibrantly alive once again.

Wordlessly he held out both hands to Sally, palms upward as if in supplication.

'Now who's set the cat among the pigeons?' the gesture said.

Sally saw them off at the door, heads bent underneath a shared umbrella; and going back inside she said a fervent prayer over a covered plate of spam and potatoes keeping warm atop a pan of gently boiling water.

She asked God to let it work out right, and begged His forgiveness for interceding on His behalf. When her hunger was satisfied and a little warmth had seeped back into her bones, she took a pad of paper and a fountain pen out of the sideboard drawer and began a long letter to Lee.

'You are not going to believe this,' she wrote, oblivious to the rain now dashing against the window pane in a torrent of fury.

Ten

'Stanley Barnes! It's a wonder you don't have aerials growing out of your ear-holes, the time you spend with your head in that flamin' speaker!'

Because Josie spoke with a nappy pin clenched between her teeth, Sally failed to catch the words, but by the way her father wrinkled his nose and smiled she knew the remark had been a teasing one.

The Myerscough baby, soon to be the Barnes's baby once all the papers had been signed and red tape sorted out, lay on his back on Josie's knee. His mottled legs were waving and thrashing about, and he was staring up at her with what, to the besotted, could have been interpreted as a cross-eyed devotion.

'The first refugees from Singapore have begun to arrive over here.' Stanley spoke directly to Sally, accepting with equanimity that, for the moment, powdering his little grandson's bottom occupied all his wife's attention. 'From the reports it sounds like our lot were playing bridge and tennis and dancing the nights away right till the Japs landed.' He tut-tutted his disapproval. 'We had our guns pointing out to sea, but the little yellow men came in overland.' With obvious reluctance he switched the wireless off. 'Makes you sick to think of the Union Jack being pulled down for the Rising Sun flag. Java will be the next, mark my words.' He reached for the comfort of his pipe. 'They're right bastards, those Japs. A chap at the Post said he'd heard they were bayoneting our soldiers in Hong Kong then leaving them to lie on the ground unburied.'

His pipe going nicely, Stanley leaned sideways and tickled

the baby's head, running a finger round its Friar Tuck fringe of brown hair. 'One good thing about it, little chuck, you couldn't care less, not so long as you get your bottle at the right time.'

At a nod from his wife, he passed over the feeding bottle, testing the contents first by shaking a few drops onto the back of his hand. 'Want me to do it, love?'

'No fear.' Josie guided the rubber teat into the baby's wandering mouth. 'You let air in last time, then who was it had to get up twice and wind him?'

Sally watched them carefully, her eyes slewing from one face to the other. She was writing to Lee, the notepad on her knee, only needing to lower her head to shut herself away completely from the conversation.

'I can't wait for next weekend,' she wrote. 'I may have to work Saturday morning, though. Boy-friends coming on leave don't merit special time off. We've to treble our output before the end of the month! So it means still more overtime.' She chewed the end of her pen for a moment, then went on:

'They lined us all up in the canteen yesterday and showed us a film. It was about tanks we're helping to make going into action against the enemy. I tried to imagine one of the little fiddling things I file being part of those great monstrous things, but it was hopeless. Maybe it's as well. If I realized I was helping to make an end product geared to kill and maim I think my thousand-an-hour output would slow down. Is that terrible? I wish my ideas about the enemy were as clearly formulated as my father's. He's a gentle man and yet to him they are all so much fodder, to be killed as quickly as possible. But surely — surely, Lee, some of them are just ordinary young men like John? Are they *all* riddled through and through with evil?'

She looked up to see Josie winding the baby while Stanley cleared away all the paraphernalia necessary for bathing and feeding a tiny baby.

'Leopards don't change their spots,' she wrote, starting a fresh paragraph. 'My mother hasn't suddenly become a different person since John's baby came to live here. But she's much happier. Before she was without purpose, now it's as though she has put the clock back and is bringing up John again. Do you believe in miracles, Lee? Because from now on I certainly do.'

'It's like a miracle,' Lee told her as they sat close together round a corner table in the saloon bar of a public house out on the main road the following Saturday evening. 'I never thought it would come so soon, honey, but apart from a flight-engineer still to be roped in, the crew I'll be flying with is all rounded up.' He took a long sip of his warm beer and grimaced. 'All volunteers, so they know what they're at. Now it's up to me to weld us into a kind of family. We depend on each other entirely. See?'

'You mean regular airmen?' Sally tried to hide the creeping sense of dread holding her still. She couldn't take her eyes off him. He had blown into the house like an invigorating wind, scattering presents, chucking the baby under the chin, sparring verbally in his good-natured way with Stanley, flirting with Josie, then whisking Sally off in the single-decker bus to a place where they could talk and be alone.

'Nope, not regulars,' he said. 'My navigator was an architectural draughtsman in civvy life, and the rear gunner kept a stall on a London street market. The wireless operator held a first-class boat pilot's licence before the war. He can read morse like you read a book. He's a Canadian, honey, as smart as they come. There ain't no flies on a single goddamned one of them! We did a two-hour trip over Scotland last week and we ran into a German raid – an unexpected bonus. There was flak coming up, but we never saw even the tail whisker of a Hun. The rear gunner came out of his turret as cold as if he'd been shut in an ice-box.'

Sally felt as if her smile might crack at any minute. She remembered David Turner telling her once about his own crew. All eager beavers, raring to go. Imbibing the atmosphere so completely that they saw themselves almost as a race apart. Boasting amongst themselves about their squadron scoreboards, dicing with death and glorying in it.

And now Lee was all set to join their ranks.

'When will you actually start operational flying?' Taking a sip of her beer she watched his face carefully over the rim of her glass.

169

Lee shook his head mournfully. 'We've still got fifty hours of scheduled flying to do out of the seventy laid down in the rule book, worse luck.' He grinned. 'It's my job to keep those guys happy till then. You know, raise their morale so they don't get too goddamned bored. We're all raring to go, Sally, and believe you me, it's not true that the English all have placid temperaments. They're like a bunch of fire-crackers with their fuses lit and no place to explode. It's routine stuff day after day. Check and double check till we can all do our respective jobs with our eyes closed. But they rate me now, honey. Even the Limeys rate me pretty high. I reckon they realize I know what I'm at.'

He stared round the crowded bar. 'I don't rate *this* place all that much.' He took a cigarette from the packet on the table and lit it. 'Me, I like to drink my ale in a place where Queen Victoria slept on her way to somewhere or other. Or Oliver Cromwell. Didn't he hang out somewhere round here?' Without waiting for a reply he pulled a heavy glass ash-tray towards him and flicked the cigarette vaguely in its direction. 'The kind of place I go for has sloping floors and oak beams spanning the ceiling. This one's pretty new, isn't it?'

Through his eyes Sally saw the dark red carpet with its geometrically designed whirls and triangles in royal blue, the glass tables with their chrome legs, and the hunting murals on the walls. She nodded. 'I don't suppose anyone of note sleeps here. Only commercial travellers with their cases of samples, though I suppose *they're* all in the Forces now.' She leaned sideways and kissed him lightly. 'I'll have you know, however, that this is a very posh place. Only the best people come here.'

'But of course,' Lee said promptly. 'One day when I'm dead they'll put up a plaque. "Lee Willis drank here."'

A small drifting shadow flitted across Sally's mind, then was gone in a second as Lee pulled her to him and traced a finger down her cheek.

'Remember that old inn where we stopped over last summer? The day we rode our bicycles out into the country-side and forgot to pick bluebells?'

'Do you remember an inn, Miranda?' Sally said softly.

'Miranda?'

170

'Poetry, love.'

'Ah, poetry.' Lee dismissed poetry with a shrug of his broad shoulders. 'Now that old inn was how I see England. Places like that link this country to its past, all kinda interwoven. You're going to miss that when you live over in Texas after the war.'

Sally shook her head, glanced over to the bar then swiftly back, feeling her face flame.

'Oh, no!' She twisted round in her seat. 'Don't look now, but that girl with the army officer – the girl on the high stool – that's Christine Duckworth, I mean Myerscough. You *know*. Baby John's mother. Oh, Lee, she's the last person I wanted to see!'

'Why?' After a quick glance, Lee covered Sally's hand with his own. 'There's no call to get upset, honey.'

'I'm not upset. I'm *embarrassed*.' Sally moved her hand away. 'Surely you can see why? If anything happens now to make Christine change her mind, it will kill my mother. There's nothing made properly legal yet. Oh, suppose she sees me and suddenly decides she wants the baby after all? She's quite capable of doing that. You don't know her.'

'Oh, but I do honey. I met her once only briefly, but that was enough.' A flicker of impatience showed in Lee's blue eyes. 'Stop looking so stricken, Sally. You were bound to meet her sometime some place. Anyway, she's seen you and they're coming over, so relax. Okay?'

Christine was transformed. With her figure back to normal, there was a radiance about her that slewed all eyes in her direction as she led the way to their table. She was wearing a scarlet woollen dress, princess style, with a fur coat swinging from her shoulders. Her hair was burnished to the exact shade of a copper warming pan, curving forward onto her carefully rouged cheeks. Green eyes shone with amusement as she smiled at Lee.

'Well! If it isn't the American! A bit dryer than the last time we met, n'est-ce-pas?'

The tall man following on behind, carrying their drinks, tripped over what could only have been the pattern in the carpet. 'Whoops!' Nigel beamed at his wife. 'Sorry, darling, it's all right, no damage done.'

Lee stood up, holding out his hand. 'Nice to meet with you again, Christine.' He turned to Nigel. 'And this is . . . ?'

'My husband, Nigel.' Christine made the introduction hurriedly before sitting down, choosing the seat next to Lee. She was smoking a cigarette, and before she spoke again she blew out a stream of smoke. 'We're off in the morning at first light. Down to Cornwall.' She laughed loudly. 'Nigel's wangled enough petrol, thank God. I couldn't face the train with everyone breathing up each other's nostrils. Hell's bloody bells, it would probably take us a week to get there.'

She drained her glass and set it down again. 'What are you two drinking? Nigel, be a lamb and fill us up. And if the man says the gin's off, tell him to squeeze the bottle. I'll have it with limejuice this time.'

Sally watched Nigel weave a rather unsteady path towards the bar, then glanced at Christine's flushed face. As if reading her thoughts, Christine said: 'We polished off the best part of a bottle of Daddy's whisky before we came out, but I prefer gin, it makes me feel amorous.' The fur coat slid from her shoulders and, reaching over, Lee hung it round the back of her chair. 'Sally,' she said, 'you look wonderful.' She raised her eyebrows at the glass of beer. 'Maybe beer does for you what gin does for me? Oh, my God, what a dump round here.' She smiled brilliantly. 'Made any good tanks lately, Sally?'

Leaning forward she moved a finger round the wing above Lee's breast pocket. 'Why don't you marry her, Yank? Marry her and turn her into a camp follower like me?' She fluttered her eyelashes. 'Honestly, love, it's a great life if you don't weaken.' She turned to Nigel as he set the drinks down on the table. 'We can recommend it, can't we, darling?'

'A great life if you don't weaken,' Nigel said promptly and everyone laughed.

After another round of drinks fetched by Lee, Sally felt her head begin to spin a little. Lee had been right. There'd been no call to get embarrassed. He was enjoying himself hugely, she could see that, and that was how she had wanted it to be for him. Just for this one weekend she had wanted him to forget about the war, and here he was throwing his head back and laughing as if he was coming apart at the seams, swapping jokes with Nigel, flirting mildly with Christine, and oh, dear God, how beautiful he was. Sally allowed herself a little private giggle.

Beautiful wasn't an adjective applied to men, especially in the north, but her American was a beautiful beautiful man. He was like a young god with his bright gold hair and chiselled features. And if the truth were told she felt a bit immortal herself, all floaty, as if being deaf and unable to follow most of the conversation bandied about round the glass table was of no consequence whatsoever. If she missed what was said she merely nodded as if following every word. If the others laughed, then she laughed with them.

Nigel brought her a gin and lime and she drank it down feeling foolishly and wonderfully happy, as if her head was up in spinning clouds. Underneath the round glass table her feet did a little dance. Her grey eyes shone, and the colour in her cheeks deepened to a wild rose. The drabness of her days spent at the factory bench was replaced by a feeling of marvellous euphoria, and she leaned against Lee, giggling happily.

'Surely you'll be joining your own lot now we're all fighting beneath the same banner?' Christine asked Lee. 'Surely for lots of reasons you'll be doing that? Won't it be obligatory?' She struggled with the last word.

'Nope.' Lee shook his head. 'There's no law against me flying with the British and Commonwealth boys as yet. Besides it might put me back a bit.' He spread his hands wide. 'So no dice.'

Christine raised her glass. 'Here's to you then, Yank. One of the death and glory boys, is that the score?'

'Yes, ma'am.' Lee grinned. 'Wizard show. You bet.'

They all laughed again, then Christine touched Lee's cheek. Sally noticed that her finger-nails were varnished the exact shade of her copper-tinted lipstick, and that the diamond solitaire engagement ring flashed fire as it caught the light from the table lamp.

'Where did you get that tan?' Christine was asking. 'How, when the rest of us look like mushrooms grown in the dark?'

'From the same place I get these high cheekbones, ma'am,' Lee drawled. 'My hair and my eyes I get from my pa, but the

173

rest of me comes from my maternal grandma, honey.' His eyes twinkled. 'She was a *genuine* Indian squaw, ma'am. So it's not a tan, it's for real. Okay?'

Sally felt the gin rippling about inside her, and with an effort controlled an undignified snort of laughter.

Christine's eyes stretched wide. 'Oh, my God! You mean a real Red Indian?'

Lee nodded with exaggerated gravity. 'Yes, ma'am. The kind who fight with the cowboys at the movies. My ole grandpaw had more scalps to his credit than you've had . . .' He frowned, trying to think of the correct phrase. 'Than you've had hot dinners,' he finished on a note of triumph.

'You're kidding?' Christine turned to Nigel as he set a fresh round of drinks down on the table. 'Did you hear that, darling? Lee here has Indian blood in his veins. *Red* Indian. You know, feathers and totem poles, not Khyber Pass Indian.'

'Is that so, old man?' Nigel sat down in his seat next to Sally. 'How spot on. How absolutely spiffing.'

Nigel was nice, Sally decided. Very very drunk, but nice. Overcome by a feeling of unbounded affection, she smiled blearily at him. In a strange way Nigel reminded her of David Turner, so correct and polite, so much a product of his old-school-tie syndrome. Like David he wore good manners like a second skin. Her smile became even more sentimental. He wasn't even slightly pompous. Sally's eyes watered as she decided Nigel Myerscough had too much self-doubt for that. Enclosed in her familiar silent world of observation, Sally embraced Christine in her smile.

'You have to *look* at Sally when you speak to her,' Christine said suddenly. 'Otherwise she can't tell what you say, Nigel. She's deaf,' she mimed, pointing to her ears in an exaggerated way.

There was a startled silence. Sally saw the way Lee's hand tightened on his glass and the way his eyes hardened. She felt Nigel's hand on her arm and saw his face colour with embarrassment.

'I'm frightfully sorry.' His bush moustache quivered as he spoke. 'How ghastly for you. You must be very good at . . . I didn't realize.' He stared at Sally with awe. 'Then you must be the daughter of the woman who . . . Oh, good Lord!'

Lifting his glass he drained it quickly. 'I really think we must go, Christine. I'm due back at 21.00 hours tomorrow and that means an early start.' He hiccoughed, covering his mouth politely. 'I'm a teeny bit tight, I'm afraid. I hope I haven't made too much of an ass of myself? Last night of leave and all that.' Holding onto the table for support he stood up, holding out a wavering hand to Lee. 'Nice to have met you, old man.'

'Oh, sit down, Nigel!' Christine knocked his extended hand away. 'The war isn't going to come to a sudden stop just because you arrive back an hour or so later than your bloody 21.00 hours.' She smiled a glittering smile at Lee. 'I keep wondering who it is you remind me of.'

'Errol Flynn,' Lee said promptly. 'Same again all round?'

'I'll come with you, old man.' Weaving his way single-file behind Lee, Nigel stopped to turn round and wiggle a finger in his mouth at the girls.

'The Indian war cry,' Christine explained unnecessarily. 'Why do grown men behave like schoolboys when they're tiddly?' She lit a cigarette and waved it around. 'I wish you could hear this lot in here. One would think they were celebrating the end of the war.' She squinted at Sally through the upcurling smoke. 'I suppose being deaf has its advantages? My head's thumping as if someone was using it for a bloody tom-tom.'

Now they were alone Christine would ask about the baby, Sally told herself. She would want to know how he was and how much he weighed, and how he was taking his feeds. With a determined effort Sally tried to still her rising panic. It had been agreed that it might be better all round if Christine did not see him again, but now, fuddled with drink she might – she might even decide she had changed her mind! Sally sent up a fervent prayer.

'Oh, my God!' Christine swivelled round in her chair. 'Look at Nigel! He's just kissed that little Wren in passing and spilled his drink down her uniform! He's making a good job of mopping her up, I must say, and that great hairy sailor she's with isn't exactly seeing the joke. Oh, my God, Nigel! Don't make a meal of it!'

'Cheers!' they said when the drinks came.

'That Wren had a pair of nice titties,' Nigel said, and they all laughed again.

'Jolly good show,' Lee said. 'Piece of cake! Whack-o!'

Sally put her glass down and stared in astonishment to find it mysteriously empty. Suddenly the danger had passed. Christine had never had any intention of mentioning the baby. In fact, she had probably forgotten she had ever had one. This seemed to be such a hilarious state of affairs to Sally that she shook her head to and fro in quiet amusement. Now she could enjoy herself again.

When Nigel kissed her, brushing her mouth with his moustache, she smiled and said thank you very much.

'Don't mention it, darling.' Nigel slid a hand underneath the table and squeezed her knee. 'You have gorgeous eyes,' he whispered. 'Real come-to-bed eyes. I like you a lot.'

'I quite like you too,' Sally assured him sincerely and solemnly, 'but my heart belongs to this gentleman here.'

'Hard cheese,' Nigel said, and they leaned on each other, laughing till the tears ran down their cheeks.

When at last they decided to call it a day and went outside, Sally looked up at the ink-black sky, seeing a whirl of stars that didn't exist. For a while they stood together, the four of them, swearing they must meet again some day, saying good-bye all over again.

'We'll meet again,' Nigel sang in a throaty tenor. 'Don't know where, don't know when, but I know we'll meet again some sunny day.'

Finally Christine kissed everyone, the men full on the lips and Sally on both cheeks. 'I'll drive,' she told Nigel. 'You're pissed.'

'Sorry it's only a two-seater.' Nigel shook hands with Lee, then he turned back and took Sally by the shoulders, peering down into her face.

'Can you see what I'm saying, love?' he asked gravely.

Sally nodded. 'I can hear you, Nigel.'

The floppy moustache seemed to quiver with emotion. 'It was the only . . . the only decent way, love.' He jerked his head to where Christine and Lee stood by the little red car. 'As parents we'd be non-bloody-starters, whereas . . .' His eyes were dazed by drink, confusion and a sudden sense of his own inadequacy. 'You're a little corker,' he mumbled. 'And Hiawatha there, he's a lucky bloke.'

A bewildered expression came over his pleasant face. 'Turn me in the right direction, love,' he demanded. 'Maybe I am a weeny bit pissed after all.'

As the car roared away down the winding country road, Sally and Lee set off towards the bus stop, arms entwined. Bounded on one side by dry-stone walls and fringed by tall trees on the other, the road was a black ribbon, with only the newly painted white line down the middle shining dimly through the total darkness.

Suddenly, the drink inside him urging Lee to show off, his natural high spirits elevated to a careless height of optimism, Lee broke away from Sally to tread the white line, arms outstretched.

'Who says I've had too much to drink?' he shouted. 'Watch me, honey! Watch out! The Hun is coming at you out of the sun! Pull out, Skip! Whacko! Press the bloody knob, man!'

Swaying first one way then the other, he teetered along the white line, his greatcoat flying open and his cap over one eye, a child again, showing off to an indulgent parent.

'Lee!' Sally saw the oncoming car, a speeding black box, its headlamps heavily obscured according to war-time regulations, the beam almost totally masked.

The driver, a doctor on his way to an urgent case, had no chance at all. In his dark uniform Lee was invisible.

'Who?' the doctor was to ask over again in the weeks to come. 'Who would expect to meet a man doing a balancing act in the middle of a country lane in the black-out? But, dear God, I'll never forget that bump till my dying day.'

Sally was vaguely aware of being led gently away from the still figure lying there. She was even more vaguely aware of being taken into the little front room of a cottage, her hands closed round a mug of hot, sweet tea. She sat in a low winged chair imprisoned not in grief but in a tearing bitterness that precluded any attempt to comfort.

'He's dead, isn't he?'

The woman bending over her had appled cheeks and hair pulled back from her face with a childish slide. 'He wouldn't

177

feel anything, love. The doctor said it was instant.' She twisted her hands together and glanced quickly at her husband hovering behind her. 'Try again to remember your telephone number, love, or your address. I know thinking isn't easy just now, but try.'

Sally looked at her, totally without comprehension. 'That wasn't how he wanted to die.' Her little flat voice broke. 'Not mown down by a car. Not on the ground.' She lifted pain-dazed eyes. 'All he wanted was to fly.'

'Cry, love,' the woman said. 'Have a good cry.'

'Up in the clouds,' Sally said firmly. 'With flak coming at him. He thought he was immortal, but I knew different.' Her face rejected the sympathy coming at her from the kindly, decent, elderly man and woman standing helplessly by. Locked in a strait-jacket of anger, her grief was bloody-minded, her expression as hard and flinty as the dry-stone wall fronting the tiny cottage.

'I think I'm going to be sick,' she whispered pitifully.

Eleven

There was no way Sally could or would assuage her shock and grief in a healing flow of tears. Like a child she raged at the obscenity of Lee's sudden death. He had died, her beautiful American, in a way she could not accept. Fuddled with beer and gin, he had thrown his bright young life away, and her rejection of any attempt at sympathy was harsh and immediate.

Shutting herself away in her room she refused to eat, spending long hours staring at the wall, irritated to the point of hysteria when Josie or Stanley crept up the stairs offering crumbs of comfort and pleading with her to come downstairs.

'There's a box come for you, love.' Josie knelt down by the bed, forcing Sally to look at her. 'Do you want me to open it?'

'If you like.'

'Shall I bring it up here?'

'Oh, for God's sake, do what you like with it!'

Josie backed away from the harshness in her daughter's voice. When she stood up she was trembling.

'Look, love. I know how you feel.'

'Do you?' Sally's tone dripped sarcasm.

Josie stood her ground. 'You can ask me that, our Sally? After John?'

Sally glared at her mother, her hands balled into fists. For a moment Josie thought she was going to be attacked, then her chin went up. 'Awful things happen in a war, you know that, but we have to go on, love. Life has to go on.'

The look that Sally gave her mother could easily have been construed as hatred. There were two safety pins fastened to the bib of Josie's flowered apron; she smelled of talcum powder and cod-liver oil. And in that moment Sally could hardly bear to look at her.

'John was killed in the war!' she shouted violently. 'In this bloody senseless war'! At least God had the decency to have him killed like a man. Fighting, as they say, that we might live. Lee was killed walking in the middle of a country road, balancing on a white line down the middle like a naughty schoolboy.'

'He was a bit like a naughty schoolboy,' Josie said unwisely.

'You never liked him.'

'Now, love, that's not fair. I liked him a lot. He was good for you.'

'How good for me?'

'He made you laugh.'

'And I never laughed before?'

Josie gave a deep sigh. How could she tell this angry child – because in spite of her nineteen years that was all Sally was – that one of the things deafness had done for Sally was to shut her away from laughter? True, she was bright and bonny, but until Lee there had always been a wary sadness about her. A haunting stillness that the American had managed to break through.

'I'm going down for the box,' she said firmly. 'And if you don't want to see what's in it, then I'll open it, because it might be flowers, and if it is then they'll want putting in water.'

But when Josie laid the box on the bed beside an indifferent Sally, then lifted the lid and peeled away the top layer of tissue paper, her heart did a downward flip.

There, in folds of slippery oyster satin, was a wedding dress of such exquisite simplicity and beauty that Josie, familiar with discreetly expensive model clothes, could not fail to recognize it as a superb example of the finest workmanship.

As she lifted it out the skirt fell into folds intersected by lace godets. The neck-line was heart-shaped, and the sleeves long and tight, finishing at the cuffs with a row of tiny satin-covered buttons. Lying at the bottom of the box was a note scribbled in a large twirl-embellished handwriting:

'Wear this on the day you and Lee marry, Sally. It should only need a few inches chopping off the bottom. Oodles of love, Christine.'

Silently cursing herself for her terrible gaffe in bringing the box upstairs, Josie handed the note over.

As she read it Sally's pent-up anger and grief dissolved at last in a noisy storm. Held fast in her mother's arms, the tears flowed as if from the depths of a bottomless well. Unable to hear herself, her wails were those of a desolate child, and when the baby from his cot in the next room joined in, it seemed to Josie as if the whole house rang with the sound of weeping.

When Easter came the weather turned so suddenly warm that the cherry blossom came out in the trees planted at regular intervals down Sally's road. One Saturday afternoon she saw a young man walking along with a tennis racket swinging from his hand, and stared at him as if he had dropped in from another planet.

That spring was a gloomy period for the Western Allies. The Americans were in the process of digging in, and the King gave the besieged island of Malta the George Cross.

Stanley gloomed over his wireless, and Josie brooded over her little grandson, stopping his crying by sticking a dummy coated with condensed milk into his mouth, and occasionally drying his wet nappies by the fire without rinsing them out so that the house smelled of baby and became more untidy than ever. To test his bottle she sucked the teat. When the dummy fell to the floor she wiped it on her pinny and stuck it back in his mouth. He slept propped on a pillow, was fed when he was hungry and put to bed when it suited Josie.

And as the weeks went by he grew and thrived in a way that would have confounded the writers of baby manuals.

Sally went to work, sat at the long bench smoothing the rough ridge away from the rounded curve of the heels until the palm of her right hand grew a hardened callus from holding the heavy file. She was much thinner now, and to avoid having to roll up her hair each morning she cut it short with a pair of nail scissors so that it curled round her head, giving her an almost boyish charm. At the weekends she took long cycle rides alone, riding far out into the countryside, pedalling furiously up steep hills, freewheeling like the wind down them, arriving back home in the late dusk too tired to eat.

And as long fine weekend followed long fine weekend, it was this lonely pedalling along one country lane after another that helped Sally to begin to come to terms with her grief.

By the middle of April the daffodils were out, fringing lawns and clustering beneath spreading trees. One Sunday Sally came into the house carrying an armful of them, and seeing her rosy face above the blooms Josie closed her eyes briefly to thank the God she didn't believe in for giving her daughter back to her.

As Josie went through into the kitchen to fetch a vase, Stanley turned round from the wireless, his face set in lines of disgust.

'We'll have to teach those Germans a lesson they won't forget. They've been bombing our historic cities now, would you believe it? Canterbury, York and Bath. Not one of them of any military importance whatsover. Unmitigated swines!'

'It was cold out today. Lovely and fresh, but a cold wind.' Unwinding the scarf from round her neck, Sally spoke dreamily.

'And Norwich,' Stanley told her. 'The uncouth bastards.'

'There were some ducks on a lake. A mother, father and two babies.' Sally went from the room, trailing the scarf and carrying her short jacket over her arm.

'Did you hear that?' Stanley appealed to his wife as she came back into the room with the daffodils in a blue jug. 'She was reckoning on she couldn't hear me, but she heard me all right. She's pretending the war doesn't exist, going off on that bicycle every weekend and stopping out all day. She only uses this house for eating and sleeping now.'

'Not much for eating.' Josie frowned. 'I'm sure all that fresh air can't be good for her. Did you notice how chapped her cheeks are?' Bending down to the sideboard cupboard she took out a folded newspaper. 'I've a good mind to show her this when she comes downstairs. It was in the evening paper the week after Lee got killed, so I put it away.'

Stanley shrugged his shoulders. 'Show it to her if you like, lass. I can't see it making any difference.'

'She always had a soft spot for him, though.' Josie opened the paper and spread it wide on the table. 'And once he hears that she isn't going to marry the American . . .'

'For God's sake, woman!' Stanley looked up from the book he was reading. 'You're not expecting her to jump from the frying pan into the fire?' He sucked furiously at his pipe. 'Even if what you're hoping for happened, that lad is flying over Germany night after night. We bombed Lübeck and Rostock last week and I bet he had a hand in that. Do you want her heart broken all over again?'

'She's coming down.' Josie turned as Sally came into the room. 'See here, love. I meant to show this to you the other day, but I forgot. Look. There's his photograph.' She moved her finger over the column, reading aloud:

'Flight Lieutenant David Turner, awarded the DFC for conspicuous bravery. In spite of terrible damage to his plane, the Flight Lieutenant was mainly responsible for getting it and his crew safely back to base.'

'It's obviously a studio portrait,' Sally said, giving the picture a swift glance. 'He looks as if both him and his uniform have been pressed with a hot iron.' She touched the paper lightly with an outstretched finger. 'Not a hair of his moustache out of place, and look at his cap! David never did squash his cap like the others. He looks too handsome to be real, doesn't he?'

'Where is he stationed now, love?' Josie ignored her husband's warning glance. 'Do you know?'

'Somewhere in Yorkshire, I think,' Sally said in her new quiet way. She moved over to the fireplace, and bending down took her knitting from behind a cushion on the settee. 'If I don't get on with this matinée jacket the baby will have grown too big for it before it's finished.'

Josie went to sit beside her. Her blue eyes were surprisingly tender.

'Why don't you write to David, love? Just to congratulate him. You know. He struck me as looking very lonely last time he called.'

'You could hardly bear to speak to him last time he called.'

183

Some of the bitterness crept back into Sally's flat voice. 'Why don't *you* write to him?'

'What, me?' Josie laughed out loud. '*Me* write to David Turner? What would I have to tell him? How much the baby weighs, and the colour of his motions? I can see David finding that fascinating. No, you're his friend, not me.'

'I'll think about it,' Sally said, then lowering her head began to count stitches, moving her finger swiftly along the knitting needle. 'Damn it, there's one too many. No wonder the pattern came out wrong.'

Sister Irene Margerison found the letter in the pocket of the airman's flying jacket, placed it in the bedside locker along with his other belongings, and promptly forgot all about it.

A tall girl with piercing black eyes and no claims to beauty, she had done her training at a West London hospital before the war. Then when the entire hospital had been evacuated to a country mental hospital near Basingstoke, she had applied for and got a transfer to a hospital in Yorkshire, wanting to be near her mother who was slowly dying of a chest complaint that had turned her days into a constant fight for breath, and her nights into a tortuous agony.

Now, at the beginning of that summer in 1942, her mother had been dead for eighteen months, but Sister Margerison stayed on, bringing solace to her patients and daily terror to the nurses who had the misfortune to come within her jurisdiction.

When the men from the nearby airbase began to be admitted as patients, Sister Margerison came into her own. And that May morning the officer with the clipped moustache, swathed in bandages over most of his face and his neck, presented her with a challenge she took up gladly.

Flight Lieutenant David Turner was going to live. He might think otherwise, but the sister knew different. The surgeons had done their bit, removing the shrapnel from his gullet and treating the minor burns to his face and head, but now it was nursing care which would count.

Checking the saline drip and taking his pulse for the twentieth time, Sister Margerison motioned to the nurse sitting at the other side of the bed, the lift of a finger indicating that a non-stop vigil was to be kept until the patient showed signs of regaining consciousness. Then she tiptoed away down the ward, her back as straight as if her starched uniform was keeping it so.

When David opened his eyes briefly the first thing he saw was a pair of eyes regarding him steadily. Above them was a white cap perched on a fringe of bright red hair. David closed his eyes again.

He could equate the cap with a nurse, and along with the nurse, by inference, he could slowly grasp the fact that he was in hospital. His eyes were all right; he accepted this gratefully, but the upper part of his face felt stiff, and he felt as if his neck was being forced up, out of his body. Wiggling his toes, he accepted too that he still had feet, then the effort of trying to assess his injuries overwhelmed him with exhaustion so that he drifted off into unconsciousness again.

There was a tube going up his nose and down his parched throat. When he squinted at it, it seemed to be filled with a nauseous dark green liquid that smelled abominably. The smell pervaded all his senses, so that he lay half awake and half asleep drowning in the stinking horror of it.

At intervals – he never knew the exact frequency – Sister Margerison would drag the tube out and replace it. Taking it out was hell, but swallowing a fresh one was worse.

'Swallow!' she ordered. 'Come on, now. You can do it if you try. Gulp! That's right. Now again! It's nearly down. We can't have you being sick at the moment. A few more days of this and you'll be able to be rid of it and maybe swallow a little soup.' She patted his shoulder. 'Then we can take you off the drip. *If* you cooperate.'

Shutting his mind to the indignity of it, feeling his throat spasm as the tube inched its way down, David choked, blinked the tears from his eyes and swallowed again.

'Clever boy,' Sister Margerison said, and propped him slightly on his pillows. She marched away, hugging the covered bowl to her chest.

The nights were the worst, for his feverish mind fought the sleeping pills, and each agonizing memory was awash with the evil smell of his own dark green bile.

He remembered the flak coming at them, tossing the aircraft about the sky like a bucking bronco. One lot had burst so close that his skipper had been forced to jerk violently off course at the end of the bomb run.

'Give me a course for home, navigator.'

Bending over his instrument table as if he were alone in a tiny office, David had replied: 'Steer two-seven-eight.'

The burst of a shell beneath the belly of the aircraft had made it arch suddenly. The gunner yelled: 'Christ! I've been hit!'

'David, get back and have a look at Jock.' His skipper's voice had sounded quite calm.

So, leaving his table, David had moved as fast as he could to the turret at the back. Jock, a sturdy little Glaswegian, was obviously done for. Blood was spurting from his mouth, soaking his fur-lined collar and choking his moans. His eyes were glazed with pain.

'Get the morphia! For God's sake, get the morphia!'

David's head had jerked back as the shrapnel tore at his shoulder, tearing an agonizing strip through his neck. He remembered the flames, then his mind exploded into a screaming torture. And that was about it.

There was the silent sound of his own cries in his head. There was someone holding him down. A woman in a white cap was bending over him. She had eyes that picked holes in his pain, and yet her hands on him were surprisingly gentle.

'It's all right, laddie. You've been dreaming. You're quite safe. That's right. Hold on to me.'

'I can't speak!' David mouthed the words into the terrifying silence. 'My voice has gone!'

Tearing at the tube taped to his cheek, David's dark eyes were deep pools of terror. The smell of green slime was sickening his very soul. There was pain spilling inwards from his shoulder and neck, then as he felt a faint prick in his arm the face of Sister Margerison was blotted out, and the long ward obliterated in a descending welter of darkness.

On the anniversary of the last big raid on London it rained all day. With the tubes finally removed, David looked better, but the bandages swathing his neck and shoulder still forced his chin up, so that the shy way he had always held his head made him appear vulnerable and very, very young.

He ate a little, slept less, and existed from one painful dressing of his wounds to another. He had accepted the fact that he could not speak even if he had not begun to come to terms with it, but he used the pad and pencil placed at the ready by Sister Margerison only when absolutely necessary.

'Will my voice come back?' he wrote one day, then with his free hand scribbled fiercely over the words, not ready yet to face what might be the shattering truth.

She tried one day to bully him into writing a letter.

'Your mother?'

'Dead,' David wrote firmly.

'Father?'

'Ditto,' said the pencil, and David stared at the sister as if defying her to continue.

'Girl friend?' Sister Margerison was not one to give up easily. 'Come on now, Mr Turner. Don't come that attitude with me. You've had plenty of visits from your Air Force buddies, so you're no hermit. A visit from a pretty girl is just what you need.'

'I hate women,' David wrote, the merest semblance of a twinkle in his eyes, and seeing that for the first time Sister Margerison went away with the feeling that if nothing had been achieved at least her patient had taken a short step in the right direction.

David came out of his apparently self-imposed trance the day he was helped to the bathroom for the first time and saw himself in the mirror. The burns to his face had been classified as not bad enough for plastic surgery, but one cheek was the colour of a ripe tomato, and the front of his singed hair was growing back into little spikes.

With the bandaged collar round his neck he looked, he told himself, for all the world like a man-made creature in a horror film, but the wound in his shoulder was healing. He could flex the fingers of his left hand, and when they took this ruddy collar off he would be fit to fly again.

'Fly again?' Tim Brazier, the pilot of David's recent crew, smiled a smile that left one side of his face quite stiff. 'Don't be such a bloody fool, Turner. How many times do you think you can prang and get away with it? Christ, man, you're a bloody miracle! You've been at it ever since the balloon went up in thirty-nine. Once you've got your ticket you can be away.' He rubbed at the jumping tic in his right cheek, a legacy from a crash during his training days. 'I must say your mug wouldn't get you a job in Hollywood at the moment, but then you never were much of a pin-up, old man.'

David saw the way his old skip kept glancing away from the notepad and pencil placed on the turned-down sheet. Not once had Tim mentioned the loss of voice. He had sat there by the side of the bed and nattered on for all the world like a nannie talking to her charge who had merely fallen down and grazed a knee.

'We're on a milk run at the moment,' he said. 'A piece of cake.' He got up to go. 'A few minutes over the target, that's all. Then home. Whacko!'

As he walked down the ward, jamming his cap back onto his curly head, David felt his heart begin to thump. He turned his head sideways into his pillow.

Tim had known something David didn't know. Even discounting his twitch his old skip had been trying to tell him that his flying days were over.

The man in the next bed, a skull-cap of bandages on a head as round as a billiard ball, leaned sideways and said something, but David closed his eyes.

If they took flying away from him, what was left? Since before the war he had lived in his world of uniforms, camaraderie, uncouth humour bordering on the juvenile. It was his life! Damn it, it was all he knew!

As far as his actual job went, he was the tops. He could plot a course with unerring accuracy. The seasons came and went, each filled with the sound of planes rumbling, taxiing into position for take-off. Some came back and some didn't, and those that came back often limped home with an engine missing, or more frequently, most of the tail. He was well into his third tour, only eleven operations to go. He was geared to night flying; the whole aspect of the war was hotting up. Before long the 500 German bombers that had almost flattened Westminster a year ago would be chicken feed compared to the retaliation which would surely come.

And if he was not to be a part of that, then where would he

188

be? Where would he *go*? Shuffling into civvy street with his blood-red face, half his hair burned off, and his throat held together with strips of gauze.

'Time for your bath, Mr Turner.'

The copper-haired nurse, a towel over her arm, his soap-box and flannel in her hand, touched him gently on his good shoulder, then blinked as the nice Mr Turner glared at her, his lips pressed tightly together as if holding in his fury.

Snatching the notepad and pressing so hard that the pencil made little holes in the paper, David wrote:

'I can bath myself. Okay?'

'Okay then.' The copper head nodded twice before Sister Margerison's training took over. 'No more than five inches of water, mind, and don't splash. Arm extended and wash up to the chest only. When you're ready to come out you ring for me. We don't want you slipping and adding a bruised bottom to what you've got to put up with already. Right?'

With his good hand David sketched a salute. As he made his way down the long ward, wobbling on legs as steady as lettuce leaves, the nurse sighed. That left hand of his wasn't showing any signs of improvement. In spite of the exercises the fingers were as flabby as uncooked sausages, and the prognosis was that the hand might never recover its grip completely. She walked across to a bed in which a fighter pilot lay and tucked him in fiercely. The pilot, a mere boy, had been fished out of the sea at Lowestoft Bay with his spine broken. His days were numbered. The nurse tucked a strand of red hair beneath her white starched cap and sighed.

'What day is it, nurse?' the boy whispered.

'Tuesday,' she told him briskly, before walking soft-footed down the ward to spy on Mr Turner through a crack in the bathroom door. Her faint smile was of the humour-the-invalid variety, but her bright blue eyes were as watchful and caring as a mother indulging an adventurous toddler to find his independence.

Sitting in the shallow water and soaping his thin body with his good hand, David contemplated his future, facing it and then rejecting it almost at the same time. His future was an empty void, whereas his past was a series of incidents as clear in his mind as if each episode had been crowded into one long yesterday.

His insistence on leaving grammar school at eighteen with a good matriculation certificate, guaranteeing his entry into the Air Force as a potential officer. His mother wringing her hands and wailing that in doing so he was letting her down, and somehow even betraying his dead father's trust.

The beginning of the war almost three years ago, and his years of training being immediately channelled into positive action. Those early spells of leave when he saw Sally Barnes change from a round-faced schoolgirl into a young woman of startling beauty. His blasted shyness whenever he met her walking down the road; the sweetness of her as she stared up at him, her grey eyes searching his mouth as she lip-read his abortive attempts at conversation.

The night he took her to the cinema and blotted his copybook with a thoroughness that put an insurmountable wedge between them. His heartfelt shame, and her obvious disgust. David stared at the wall, an ugly wall, painted garden-fence green at the bottom and a sickly yellow at the top.

The water in the bath was cooling, but he noticed nothing. Alone for the first time since his admission into hospital, it seemed important that his thoughts were caught and pinned down into some kind of pattern, like dead butterflies arranged for exhibition on a sheet of blank paper.

His home turned into a heap of rubble and him standing there poking around with a stick in search of – what? David stared down at the bath-water, his eyes narrowed into slits of concentration. The grave in the cemetery with his mother's coffin being lowered into it by strangers. His lack of feeling as the sun warmed his back and Sally stood by his side in a flowered dress with short puffed sleeves. The loneliness eating at him as she ran away from him to catch the tram with her parents after her rejection of his awkward apology.

The crashing down through the trees in Belgium with Jack's body swinging from a tree. The hayloft and Francine of the pale yellow hair lying in his arms, as close to him in that moment as if they had made love.

Good days back on the squadron, laughter-filled days in spite of everything. Knowing you could be dead tomorrow but relishing the fact that you were alive today. Barging into

Sally's house in a state of euphoria after his escape back to England, so sure that he had only to ask her to marry him for her to fall into his arms.

The unknown American with his crew cut and his reckless smile. David's mouth twisted. He had never met him, but for God's sake, the Yanks *all* had crew cuts and reckless smiles. And in all probability Sally would be married to him now.

David tilted his chin, his scarlet face and singed hair rising from the neck support as he sat there, very still in the ugly utilitarian bathroom, an incongruous sight to anyone with a warped sense of humour.

Sally had sent him a letter, just five lines long, congratulating him on his blasted gong. Very kind, very proper. And that was that. That was definitely, decidedly it. Finish. QED. Out of his life. For ever.

David turned his head awkwardly as the red-haired nurse bustled into the bathroom, noticing her half-smile as he covered himself decently with his flannel when she held out the towel.

'Enjoy your bath, Mr Turner?' she asked. 'I knew you would,' she added, just as if he'd replied.

On the Sunday it rained again. Sister Margerison, on her afternoon off, listened to the wireless in her tiny room and heard that the Americans had sunk Jap ships, ostensibly to save the Australians from invasion. German planes had been spotted over Northern Ireland, and it was rumoured that Exeter Cathedral had been hit. Remembering a long-ago visit there, the sister sighed. It was difficult to focus her mind on wider issues when her own particular battle was being fought right here in the huge grey hospital, with the shattered bodies of young men taking too long to heal, and shattered minds improving even more slowly.

Switching off the wireless, she sat for a while in the darkening room. Heavy rain dashed against the window-pane, and outside the trees swayed into nebulous shapes against the cold east wind.

The boy with the broken spine had died. The boy with the damaged skull had gone berserk twice in as many days. Because of an immovable piece of shrapnel, he was destined to move through what was left of his life in the doubtful sanctuary of one mental hospital after another, his pretty young wife spending endless hours travelling to visit him, their two children growing older as their father deteriorated year by year.

'Waste!' Sister Margerison got up from her chair and went over to the mirror to pin on her pleated cap. 'Stupid, man-made waste! The war going on indefinitely without the end even remotely in sight. More broken bodies, more damaged minds.'

Securing the cap with kirby-grips, she stared at her reflection, her eyes as hard as flint, a woman coming up to middle age destined to walk her wards till she was pensioned off, anticipating that day occasionally with a dread that chilled her heart.

The first bed she approached as she went back on duty was Mr Turner's. He was sitting on top of the covers staring straight ahead, clenching and unclenching his left hand round the rubber ball provided as exercise therapy.

'You should be in the day room, Mr Turner.' Sister Margerison gave the end of David's bed an angry push, setting it into line with the others. 'There's nothing to stop you having a gentle little game of ping-pong now if you're careful not to move your head too much. I can see you being discharged in a month or so. They're sending someone to talk to you next week. About what you're going to do,' she went on firmly. 'And stop looking at me as if I've gone loco! You're a king to some of them in here. At least you're alive!'

Not used to flinching, the sister blinked as the nice polite Mr Turner shot her a look spiked with what could have been taken for hatred.

'You'll be *trained* for something,' she went on firmly. 'A trained civilian can be worth even more than a trained flyer. You boys are so damn dedicated you put yourselves in the same category as the flamin' Nazis! It's all very well giving up your life for your country but there's a damned sight more sense in living it in some less glamorous occupation.'

She was speaking so quietly that it was impossible for anyone but David to hear. Her plain face was suffused with colour as she tried to beat some reason into the quiet man staring at her in amazement.

'All you do is sit there and gloom about not being able to fly any more, instead of thanking God that for you the war is over! You've made your sacrifice! So pull yourself together, Mr Turner, and get off that bed and go into the rest room! And communicate!'

Thrusting the notepad and pencil at David, she stood straight-backed watching him as he shuffled slowly down the ward, the cord of his dressing-gown trailing down at one side, his feet in the hospital slippers making little smacking sounds on the brown oilcloth. His back looked defeated, his faltering steps were those of a man drained of initiative, and she was sure that if his head had not been held up by the supportive collar it would have drooped too like that of a man in despair.

Sister Margerison turned away, her anger evaporating. She had exceeded her brief in speaking so forcibly and she knew it. But somehow, somewhere, there had to be the means of giving back that gentle lovely man his reason for living. No human being could be or ought to be as alone as that.

Appalled at her own vehemence she turned to march back down the ward, then suddenly as if her memory had been jogged she remembered the letter taken from Mr Turner's pocket on the day he had been admitted more dead than alive. Against all the ethics of her profession, she knelt down and rummaged around in David's locker.

Not for the first time Sister Margerison was going to take matters into her own capable hands. She might be going to stick her neck out. She could be walking down a blind alley, but, by George, Mr Turner wasn't going to sink into a state of self-destructive apathy – not if she, Sister Irene Margerison, could help it.

Stuffing Sally's letter into the starched bib of her apron, she set off down the ward, frowning at a patient who was furtively smoking a cigarette behind a copy of the *Daily Mail*.

Twelve

David was staring unseeingly at the open pages of a paper-back book as Sally came through the swing doors into the ward.

The last time the boys had visited him they had let it drop discreetly that there was a big show coming up. It might be some time, they had said, hinting at an operation so vast and with so many aircraft taking part that the mind boggled at the thought of it.

'We'll blot the bloody sky out, the Yanks and us,' Tim had said, talking too quickly as usual, his mouth moving and his eyes flickering anywhere but on David's face.

'Good show,' David had mouthed.

'A piece of cake.' Tim had grinned his lop-sided smile. 'I'll be around.'

So on that rainy Sunday afternoon David kept his eyes fixed on his book, listening to the murmur of voices and the scrape of chairs as visitors settled themselves, depositing cakes made with dried eggs or a precious apple on the bed-side lockers.

He was so much inside himself, so detached from his surroundings that when Sally stopped by his bed and touched his arm he gawped at her in open-mouthed amaze-ment, the book dropping from his good hand and sliding to the floor.

Frantically Sally latched on to her self-control. It was David all right, but nothing the sister had told her in the corridor outside the ward had prepared her for this.

'Hello, David,' she said quietly.

The face, once so handsome her mother had referred to it

194

as better looking than Clark Gable's, turned to her, the fringe of singed hair a bright orange above the scarlet shiny stretched skin of the forehead. Only the eyes were the same, and as they looked at each other she saw a tear gather in the corners and begin to slide slowly down David's cheeks. For a long time they stayed like that, without moving, then Sally saw his right hand close convulsively over a pencil as he drew a notebook towards him.

'No need for that. Not with me.' Sally leaned forward and gently took the pencil from his hand. 'I came as soon as I heard.' She sat down on the bed, facing him, unbuttoned her coat and, with a gesture as familiar to him as his own breathing, ran her fingers through her curly fringe, lifting it away from her forehead.

'How?' The eyes were dark and questioning on her face. 'How, in God's name?'

'In Sister Margerison's name.' Sally smiled. 'She wrote me a letter, telling me that maybe I ought to know where you were as I'd been kind enough to write congratulating you when you . . .'

'Got my DFC.' David tightened his lips in a shy smile. 'Wait till I see her, the crazy woman.'

'But you're glad I came?'

David's right hand came out and covered her own. 'Just what the doctor ordered,' his lips said, and Sally blinked sudden tears from her own eyes. She glanced through the high windows to where a pale sun shone through the grey clouds.

'It's stopped raining, David.' She glanced at his blue trousers beneath his woollen dressing-gown. 'Sister told me you were a walking patient. Do you think we could go out on the terrace? It's quite warm.'

'For the time of the year,' David mouthed promptly, and they smiled at each other and went on smiling.

As they walked down the long corridor together, the copper-haired nurse burst into Sister Margerison's room without knocking.

'They were *talking*!' she said. 'Mr Turner and the girl visiting – I saw them. Talking! He wasn't writing a word down and yet they were – '

'Conversing,' the sister agreed. 'My guess is that Mr Turner's friend is totally deaf. I could tell by her voice, even without realizing she was lip-reading me. So I am not in the least surprised, Nurse.'

The round eyes beneath the unruly red hair took on a sentimental glow. 'Well! Would you believe it? It's like the films. Like a Joan Crawford film where she comes in and the hero gets out of his wheelchair and walks towards her, except of course that it's Mr Turner's voice and not his legs.' She clasped both her work-roughened hands together. 'Oh, Sister, it was like witnessing a miracle!'

'They do happen sometimes, Nurse.'

Sister's curt nod was one of dismissal, but her eyes as they followed her nurse's bustling little figure out of the room were kind.

'Let it work right,' she whispered to herself. 'For that poor laddie's sake, let it work right.'

Outside the air was warm with the promise of the spring sunshine yet to come. The sky was now a pure pearly white, and raindrops shimmered on the newly green grass. They walked together, David and Sally, along the paved terrace, stopping by a low brick wall, sheltered from the weather by the overhanging sloping roof of the east hospital wing. Before them stretched the lawns, ending in a fringe of trees, bordered by shrubs dropping pink and white blossoms to the dark brown earth beneath their branches.

There were no bluebells yet, but Sally imagined she could already sense their sweet bruised scent. Suddenly she turned to face David, looking up into his face above the high white bandage encircling his throat.

'Lee is dead,' she told him. 'I couldn't have come to see you at the time, but I'm better now. He was run down by a car in the black-out on a country road. It was his own fault really. That was what made it so hard to bear.'

She reached for David's hand and held it for a moment against her face. 'Don't look so stricken. *Please*. I was so filled with anger when it happened I couldn't see straight. In spite of it being a stupid accident, it was still because of the war. If it hadn't been for the war Lee would never have left his father's farm in Texas. And if it hadn't happened like it did, he would probably have been killed when he started flying on operations. What are the chances of coming out alive for you and your sort, David? One in three? Or is it less than that?' Her voice rose harshly. 'This awful war! How many must lose their lives before someone decides enough is enough? Will it go on for years, till there's nobody left to fly their stupid planes?'

Her unexpected bitterness shocked David so that he hardly recognized the hardness of the flower-like face staring up at him.

'I'm so very, very sorry,' his lips said. 'I wish there was something I could say.'

'You must sit down now.'

Abruptly the shadows left her expression as Sally guided him towards a bench set against the hospital wall. 'Is it my imagination, David, or can you smell the bluebells? They'll be out soon, down in that little wood.'

'You've got so thin.' Facing each other, he touched the curve of her cheek gently with a finger. 'Being thin shows your dimples up more. Before, they were hidden.'

'Fat-chops,' she said. 'That was what my father used to call me.'

'He's okay?'

'Lives from one news bulletin to another,' Sally said, then she told him about John's baby and her mother's obsession with it. 'I think I might find a room to rent somewhere near the factory. I think it's time I left home.' She stared away from him for a moment. 'Since Lee died I don't feel I belong at home somehow.'

'Why?'

'Not the person I am now.' She moved round on the bench again. 'And you, David? Where do you go from here? Your war is over, thank God. They can't hurt you any more.' She looked down at the flagstones, obviously searching for the right words, then saying them with difficulty: 'You won't always be like this, David. The sister told me you stand more than a good chance of getting your voice back, and your arm is getting stronger every day.'

Her flat little voice with the emphasis on the wrong vowels

tailed away as she saw the hopeless despair on his face. The scars of his terrible injuries were deep inside him, she knew that, and yet he was trying to smile at her, sitting there in the pale May sunshine, pretending that he was going to be okay. For a moment Sally closed her eyes, seeing him again striding down the road towards the tennis club, his racket under his arm, a tall, lanky boy in white flannels with a cravat tucked into the open neck of his white Fred Perry shirt.

'David?' she whispered suddenly. 'May I come and see you again? May I come and see you wherever you are?' She swallowed hard. 'I've always been your friend, so may I go on being just that? Maybe your *best* friend?'

'Because you pity me?'

He opened his dark eyes wide as she rounded on him.

'Pity you? You talk to me about pity, David Turner?' Sally's face flushed. 'Shall I tell you what I think about pity? I *hate* pity! I spit on pity! To pity someone you respect is to *insult* them!' Her voice cracked, out of control. 'All my life I've had to put up with pity, and I can tell you now you'll be getting none of it from me!'

'And you respect me?'

'I . . . oh, David, at this moment I respect you and like you, and I've got to say this now or never . . . at this moment I *love* you, and it has nothing at all to do with feeling sorry for you. So now you know.'

He sat there, unmoving, a quiet inarticulate young man who should have been at the peak of his manhood. His head, tilted upwards by the bandage, had a touching nobility about it. He sat there for a long time, then in a sudden rush of emotion put his good arm about her and pulled her to face him.

'Sally? I should have told you this a long time ago, but like a fool I kept silent. One day I'll tell you about the bravest girl I've ever known who told me in a Belgian hayloft what a fool I'd been not to speak out.'

He laid his lips against her cheek then drew away from her.

'I've always loved you, Sally. Since I saw you in that awful school cap, flattened like a bean-bag, I've always wanted and loved you.' His mouth trembled. 'When I'm better – not until I know I'm going to be better – would you . . . could you consider marrying me? In a long time, when you've got over . . . and I've come to terms with the way things are going to be . . . Could you, Sally?' He shivered, and at once she stood up, helping him to his feet.

'I'm not much cop,' he mouthed, looking down at her as the shyness she remembered so well clouded his eyes. 'Not at the moment, but I've come through before and I'll come through again.' He touched the bandage round his throat. 'Once this is off I'll look quite presentable, and they say my face will improve.' He grinned, stared down and shuffled his feet. 'At least old ladies won't faint when they see me in the street.'

'And you'll get your voice back.' Sally nodded with conviction. 'But in the meantime it makes, as my mother would say, not an 'aporth of difference.'

'Think about it, Sally. Write and tell me if you can't bear the thought. But I couldn't let you go without asking. I put up a black once, and I wasn't going to risk losing you again.'

There was a soothing silence inside her. In a strange way Sally knew that David asking her to marry him was merely an echo of what should have been said a long time ago.

'David,' she whispered. 'You have made me feel . . . it means a lot to me that you should want me. I was very silly that time when I ran away and left you outside our house. I was young and silly and treated you badly. I should have known, but the war hadn't touched me then, not really.' She took his arm. 'But a lot has happened since then. Lee helped me to grow up. He made me into the person I am now.'

'And the person you are now will think about marrying me?'

Standing on tiptoe Sally reached up and kissed him, letting her lips rest sweetly on his own, feeling him tremble before she drew away.

'Oh, God, I love you so much,' his mouth said.

'I'll come again. Next week,' she whispered. 'But I know now what my answer will be.'

She gave him her answer as they walked together back down the terrace and when they parted they kissed again. Her heart was full as she watched him go from her, tall and straight and with a little of his terrible suffering already eradicated from his young-old face.

*

Sally was walking from the tram down the long street to the factory the next morning when the line of trucks came towards her.

The Americans had been three weeks at sea; they were exhausted and unshaven, and their first glimpse of England did nothing to raise their flagging spirits.

'Even the sky looks smaller,' one of them grumbled, as his truck bumped along the winding street. 'And get that cop there. He's ninety if he's a day.'

Then he caught sight of Sally, hurrying along the pavement, her bright face glowing from the early morning wind, her dark hair curling over her red bobble cap.

'Hi, honey!' The American whistled and grinned, then shrugged his shoulders as she walked straight by without even turning her head.

'Oh, boy, that's sure one icy lady!' he yelled out. 'Do you figure they all come gift-wrapped like that? D'you reckon her momma's told her not to talk to Yanks?'

They all looked like Lee, Sally told herself as she walked along. All alive with the sheer joy of just being. Far from home, with photographs of their families in their packs, all eager to join in a war that was none of their doing.

Some day they would take part in the invasion of the Continent; her father said so. There would be a massive all-out effort and Hitler would be shown once and for all that his dreams of conquering this little island had been doomed to failure from the beginning.

But Lee's war was over. His war had ended before it had begun. Stopping suddenly and turning round, Sally saw the last of the trucks trundling away over the brow of the hill. Standing there with her scarf blowing out behind her and the wind stinging her eyes to tears, she remembered the habit Lee had of throwing his head back when he laughed, as if he were coming apart at the seams. His gaiety, his jaunty way of walking with his hands thrust deep into his pockets. The drawl in his voice that she could sense without hearing, and the kindness of him, the simple acceptance of her love, his exuberance, his wanting to be, to do, and the way he would fling out his arms as if he would embrace the whole world.

Finally the trucks were gone from sight. The convoy disappeared. Sally turned and hurried on her way.

The American had been hers for such a short time, but she would remember him for ever. David would understand. Maybe some day when they were married David would tell her about the Belgian girl who was the bravest girl he had ever known, and she would want him to remember her too.

The war had left deep shadows on both their lives, but together they would face whatever the future held in store.

'Oh, David,' she whispered, then began to run, the wooden soles of her utility shoes tapping the pavement with a clattering noise she did not hear.

THE CLOGGER'S CHILD

Clara Haydock had the voice of an angel – but she had the devil's own will to live . . .

Lancashire in the early 1900s was a place of poverty and hardship, where singing was for church and life was for getting on with. But Clara's unbreakable spirit and passion for music made her shine against the bleakness of that life.

For she knew where her destiny lay . . . and that destiny would lead her to love.

LISA LOGAN

Lisa Logan was still a girl when she learned that it was a man's world . . . A man's world and no place for the weak.

When her beloved father deserted them, she and her mother were left with nothing. Her mother could not cope with this new and harsh reality, but Lisa swore her revenge.

A WORLD APART

It is 1947. The war is over but life is still very harsh. Following the death of her husband Joshua, the indomitable Daisy Penny resolves to sell her boarding house in Blackpool and start a new life in the country. But her dream of roses round the door gives way to the reality of a damp, draughty cottage and little money coming in.

To complicate her life even further, she has a devoted admirer in young Dr Armitage, yet finds herself increasingly attracted to the outspoken, no-nonsense Bill Tattersall. Soon she must make a choice that will affect her life forever . . .

MARIE JOSEPH OMNIBUS

Here in a specially chosen edition are three of Marie Joseph's best-loved novels, *Gemini Girls, Footsteps In The Park* and *Maggie Craig*.

'Marie Joseph has the same rare magical gift as Catherine Cookson for turning everyday people with everyday lives into the stuff of fascination. She writes about strengths and weaknesses, hopes and fears, life and death with a compassion that never cloys into sentimentality'
– *Kent Evening Post*

EMMA SPARROW

She was a woman of unbreakable spirit and quiet pride, and nothing – neither the drabness of her life nor the boredom of her job – could stop her from reaching for the stars . . .

But Emma's happiness lay with Simon Martin, and Simon was the boss's son. Between them stood the differences of class and background – a huge gulf that threatened to destroy Emma's one chance for a true lasting love.

A BETTER WORLD THAN THIS

In a small Lancashire town in the 1930s, Daisy Bell dreams her life away. At twenty-six, still a spinster and heiress to her mother's potato pie shop, she's resigned to a lonely old age. But toiling over the bakehouse fire she dreams of a better world – a world of glamour and romance as seen on the silver screen.

Then she meets Sam a dashing Clark Gable look-alike and chauffeur to a wealthy London businessman – and suddenly her life is changed forever . . .

SINCE HE WENT AWAY

It is New Year's Eve 1936 when Wesley Battersby leaves his pretty wife Amy to go and live with Clara Marsden.

Ashamed and frightened, Amy struggles with loneliness and hardship while Wesley is spending his money on buying the love of the flighty Clara. But Amy's warmth and vitality win her friends who give her renewed courage and confidence. And when the frivolous Clara leaves Wesley in search of a wealthier replacement, he realises his foolish mistake and returns home, but to a woman changed almost beyond recognition . . .

WHEN LOVE WAS LIKE THAT

From the bestselling novelist Marie Joseph – a collection of heartwarming, life-enhancing stories that show her at her very best.

In them Marie Joseph explores the many aspects of love as it was in the sixties and seventies – its nostalgia, tenderness, pitfalls and moments of never-to-be-forgotten happiness.

ARROW BESTSELLERS

☐ A World Apart	Marie Joseph	£4.99
☐ A Better World Than This	Marie Joseph	£4.99
☐ Emma Sparrow	Marie Joseph	£3.99
☐ Since He Went Away	Marie Joseph	£4.99
☐ When Love Was Like That	Marie Joseph	£3.99
☐ Omnibus	Marie Joseph	£6.99
☐ A Leaf in the Wind	Marie Joseph	£3.99
☐ Lisa Logan	Marie Joseph	£3.99
☐ Maggie Craig	Marie Joseph	£3.99
☐ Lovers and Sinners	Linda Sole	£4.99
☐ The Last Summer of Innocence	Linda Sole	£4.99
☐ Cross Stitch	Diana Gabaldon	£5.99
☐ Great Possessions	Kate Alexander	£3.99
☐ The Dreambreakers	Louise Pennington	£3.99
☐ The Diplomat's Wife	Louise Pennington	£3.99
☐ Sandstorm	June Knox-Mawer	£4.99
☐ A Woman of Style	Colin McDowell	£4.99
☐ Folly's Child	Janet Tanner	£4.99

ARROW BOOKS, BOOKSERVICE BY POST, PO BOX 29, DOUGLAS, ISLE OF MAN, BRITISH ISLES

NAME _____

ADDRESS _____

_____

_____

Please enclose a cheque or postal order made out to Arrow Books Ltd. for the amount due and allow the following for postage and packing.

U.K. CUSTOMERS: Please allow 75p per book to a maximum of £7.50

B.F.P.O. & EIRE: Please allow 75p per book to a maximum of £7.50

OVERSEAS CUSTOMERS: Please allow £1.00 per book.

Whilst every effort is made to keep prices low it is sometimes necessary to increase cover prices at short notice. Arrow Books reserve the right to show new retail prices on covers which may differ from those previously advertised in the text or elsewhere.